ALSO BY ADAM SCHWARTZMAN

The Good Life/The Dirty Life/and Other Stories

Merrie Afrika!

The Book of Stones

Ten South African Poets

EDDIE
SIGNWRITER

EDDIE
SIGNWRITER

ADAM SCHWARTZMAN

PANTHEON BOOKS · NEW YORK

Copyright © 2010 by Adam Schwartzman

All rights reserved. Published in the United States by
Pantheon Books, a division of Random House, Inc., New York,
and in Canada by Random House of Canada Limited, Toronto.

Pantheon Books and colophon are registered trademarks of
Random House, Inc.

Library of Congress Cataloging-in-Publication Data
Schwartzman, Adam, [date]
Eddie signwriter / Adam Schwartzman.
p. cm.
ISBN 978-0-307-37873-6
1. Boys—Africa—Fiction.   2. Young men—Africa—Fiction.
3.Voyages and travels—Fiction.   4. Africa—Fiction.
I. Title.
PR9369.3.S32E33 2010
823'.914—dc22   2009019509

www.pantheonbooks.com

Printed in the United States of America

First Edition

9 8 7 6 5 4 3 2 1

FOR MBS AND LRS

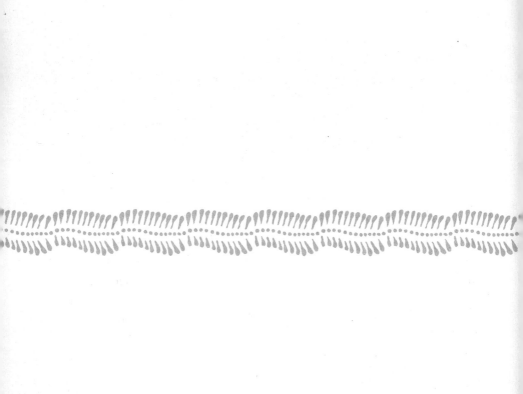

HOW NANA OFORIWAA DIED

WITHIN HALF AN HOUR of their laying out Nana Oforiwaa on the long table in the entrance hall of her rest house, people began to gather, the prominent in the hallway itself, the ordinary people on the verandah, where they crowded around the door and flowed back onto the lawn, many still damp from the evening's downpour.

Slowly word passed out to the search parties that at two o'clock in the morning were still scouring the valleys and ridges for the lost children. Wherever two or three people met confused words were exchanged: "Found? Who? *Dead?* Is it not her niece we are looking for?" So that later in the morning, after the sun had come up and the body had been taken away, when the children actually appeared on the main road, walking towards Aburi, nobody approached them; nobody said a word even as they arrived at the steps of the rest house.

All through the early hours of that Monday morning people had continued to gather: men who had been involved in the search parties, those woken from sleep, others who had seen lights on the road at that strange hour—whole families, the youngest holding on to their parents' legs, eyes open but still sleeping. At one point the police corporal came from Nsawam, then left. A blanket was placed across the body, but still it lay there, in plain sight, for three hours, not because the thought of moving it didn't occur to them, but because nobody dared.

At a little after five on Monday morning the schoolteacher arrived. Light had begun to gather beneath the horizon, and the sounds of the earth waking could be heard through the half-darkness, and through the restlessness which was growing among those gathered there. Irritated by the crowd, the teacher pushed his way through the steps up to the verandah and they realized then that he did not know (perhaps the message that reached him was confused), or that he did not want to know. "What the hell are you people doing here?" he was saying, but his words had an opposite effect to their intention because the people pushed in around him as soon as he passed, slowing his movement to the table that stood in the hallway. As he came towards it, those who were standing closest turned their heads to see who was coming through, but did not move, so that the force of the teacher's pushing propelled him through and he stumbled a few steps forward into the circle that stood around the body.

For more than half a minute he stood there. The room had gone still. The first birds had begun to wake. It was cool and quiet, and the air was gray with half-light.

Then the teacher spun about, his mouth working soundlessly. "Get out, all of you, get out!" he was shouting, until he realized he was making no sound at all, only a hard sucking noise as his tongue worked in the back of his throat. The people moved back, but they did not get out, as he stood before them, his face bunched, choking with anger, his limbs twitching in uncertain, incomplete movements.

And then it stopped. Understanding seemed to drain from his face, leaving an expression of exhaustion, but also of satisfaction because in his mind he had achieved his wish: he was alone. He had banished them all from the room and now there was only himself and Nana Oforiwaa.

Her lips were slightly parted, as if a fruit were about to be brought to her mouth, as if there were thoughts in her, and words waiting to take flight. Nobody stopped the schoolteacher, though later they wished they had, but nobody could have guessed what he was going to do, so that when he began to move, already it was too late. He stood by her head and bowed, and touched his ear to her parted lips— still they were a person's lips, solid, not yet sand, but cold. It lasted only seconds. Then there was a hand on his shoulder, softly pulling him away. But in those seconds his ear closed on her mouth and made a seal, so that nothing separated them. Everyone saw from the teacher's face that he was listening. Though listening for what, nobody could say—with Nana Oforiwaa's life already gone.

Then the seal was broken, and the air rushed between them. On her cheek there were drops of water—water from the stream where they found her, or from the rain when they carried her in. On her forehead there was grass like green stitches. Her eyelids were closed. Someone moved towards them, and there was a hand upon his shoulder, and voices talking, saying to come away. Then there were people between him and Nana Oforiwaa. Turning, the teacher looked at her for the last time.

A little while later, the Deputy Commissioner himself arrived from Nsawam with three uniformed men in the back of his car. The people stood back to let him pass, and though a few stayed to watch, the room was almost empty as the body was wrapped in a gray blanket and suspended, a man at each corner, and taken out through the back door.

Many of the onlookers left now, some to go back to their search for the children, who still were missing, but most stayed in the precincts of the rest house, not as before in a state of confusion, but aware now that the events of the night must have started somewhere. And that they would lead to other places still. That now there was something to be done: a story to be pieced together—of what happened that night—that not one of them could have told singly, though already it had begun to form, and was living, among them.

There were ten days more to run before the first parts of the story were heard out loud. They had to wait until the funeral was past and the newspapers had finished their work, but all the while, wherever people met the story was sifted and mulled and woven and connected, and always some old fact was remembered in a new way, and another was linked to a further still, and opinion was spun backwards and forwards between the twenty or so things that could be said definitively, until it made a platform so complete and strong as to constitute knowledge. Then one person was chosen to tell the story: Kwaku Wilkins-Adofo, town doctor and former unit head at Tetteh Quarshie Memorial in Mampong, now retired. A month after Nana Oforiwaa was discovered, a meeting was held of townspeople, which he was called on to address, not because he'd been witness to any of the events leading up to the death but because in the days that followed he was the only person who had had access to the teacher, and so, everyone believed although in fact it was not so, access to the last hours of Nana Oforiwaa's life.

The assembled people listened quietly as Kwaku Wilkins-Adofo stood up to speak that Wednesday evening in the largest of the town's church halls, although not even it could accommodate all the people who wanted to attend and chairs had to be set out behind the podium, and the doors opened onto the quadrangle between the hall and the church so that those outside could also hear.

The doctor stood at the front of the hall, seated behind him a row of dignitaries and other senior people. Next to him was a bare table on which he placed his hat and spectacle case. Though he spoke clearly and slowly the people outside had to strain to hear him, as his voice was soft. At first only those in the front heard his opening words, "Agoo," *I would like to talk,* so that the response rippled slowly back to him through the crowd like a wave, "Amee," *we are listening.*

He was methodical in his testimony, embellished nothing and missed nothing. "It is true that Nana Oforiwaa died alone" (a sound of indignation rose through his listeners that such a death should befall a woman of her stature—cold, drowned, covered in mud under a bridge), "but we are all alone at the moment of death. That is how death takes a person." It was quiet enough after that for them to hear the hollow thonk of glass on wood as he put down his cup. "It is true," he said, "but also, nothing happens invisibly among people."

And then he said how in being seen there is a kind of company. And how therefore, to his mind, while Nana Oforiwaa was alone, still she was in their company, right until the last moment. And he said how everything he was going to relate that evening had been seen or heard by one person or another. That these things were signs of the company they, Nana Oforiwaa's neighbors, had kept with her until the end, and that they had nothing to feel shameful for.

Here, for a little more than a moment, he paused, so that some thought he had lost his nerve, though those closer to the front saw the concentration in his face, as when a doctor listens to the pulse in a child's wrist, or the breathing of a chest.

And then he began.

"Everyone remembers the heat and then the rain."

Already, he said, the air had begun to condense on the skin by the time Nana Oforiwaa arrived at the school on the day that would be the last of her life. The gardener saw her car entering at the school gate. Almost half of the fifth form saw it pass on its way down the hill. A handful of children on detention, who were weeding the grass along the road, saw her car come to a halt outside the teacher's quarters, saw her open the back door before the driver could come round to open it for her, saw her step out onto the sand of the road and smooth her dress over her knees with sharp swipes of her hands and squint into the sun.

As it was Sunday, classes were out. The young boy sent to summon the teacher found him up a ladder in the school hall inspecting some recent repairs to the ceiling.

Returning directly to his quarters, the teacher met Nana Oforiwaa pacing up and down in front of the steps.

A group of children playing in the shade of a tree nearby heard some of their brief exchange, catching only Nana Oforiwaa's last words, "So, we go inside then."

Further up the road Nana Oforiwaa's driver was leaning over the open front door of the car. He too saw Nana Oforiwaa and the teacher enter the house.

Two hours later the sound of a bell brought the children from the upper fields. The light had deepened and a light breeze began to stir the leaves in the shadows as the children passed the parked car on their way to the dormitories. The drowsy undertow of insects and bird calls disappeared under the noise of voices and falling feet. It was six o'clock in the afternoon. Nana Oforiwaa's niece had now been missing over four hours. So had the boy.

Some time after that the teacher emerged from his house and spoke to the driver.

Nana Oforiwaa would stay where she was, he told the driver, until her niece and the boy were found.

But she did not stay where she was, because during the night she left the schoolteacher's house and went out into the rain.

"She wasn't hungry," said the old woman, who had served her evening meal and was the last person to see her alive.

"She didn't look like a person about to die" (though what such a person should look like she couldn't say), "only a little occupied with thinking." And she shuddered to recall how all that night she had gone about her business below in the kitchen as usual, while Nana Oforiwaa was pacing about above her, turning over in her head whatever it was that led her to that bridge in the night in the middle of a torrential downpour. But the old woman heard nothing, she said, not even when Nana Oforiwaa let herself out, which she must have done on account of the fact that the back door was swinging open on the breeze when the old woman came in the next morning.

She had told all this to the police, and later to the doctor, who now repeated it to the gathered people, so bringing to a close his account of the last hours of Nana Oforiwaa's life. He looked to the people seated behind him for a sign of whether they should stop for a rest, or whether he should continue with his story. They nodded to him to continue, since he had only begun and there was a long way to go. Somebody went to refill the doctor's water jug, and when that person returned the doctor began again, setting out the rest of the story, from the moment the children's absence was first noticed to the moment of their return, and further back still, to the events that preceded their disappearance.

All the while as he talked his eyes were fixed above the heads that

At weekends, people would see him waiting for her at the back of the Methodist hall, as the solemn hymns came rolling slowly down the hill, waiting to take her away, to couple like monkeys in the shade of the banana trees. Afterwards they'd come out into the church square, where people attending funerals congregated in their red and black robes, and walk together openly, her books crossed in his arms against his chest. Many times they were seen taking the shortcut back to the school, up the steep paths from the other side of the main road, down through the alleyways between the collapsing bungalows whose old steps were covered with moss, down the rocky paths on which washing was laid out to dry. And if they felt it was safe enough, and that they were not followed, they would do it again, stripping off their clothes in the tall grass, surrounded by the noise of women talking in their compounds, of carpentry and of sick children.

Now, in Nana Oforiwaa's anger, in her indignation and impotence, many felt their own anger and indignation and impotence, which they had endured for many weeks; and it swept them up in a rush of sympathy. Nana Oforiwaa had not seen it all clearly before, they said, but now she had, *now* she understood. And such was the strength of the resentment unleashed against the boy that he might just as well have murdered Nana Oforiwaa with his own hands, while the girl remained immune from their anger, on account of the fact that she was Nana Oforiwaa's niece, even if both she and the boy had run off that Sunday together.

And so, when on Monday morning the two of them had come walking up Aburi Main Road, passing Peduase Lodge, brazen as the day and ignorant still of what they had caused, two different receptions awaited them. As they reached the rest house they heard from inside the sound of a prayer meeting in full swing. They had not yet climbed the stairs when there emerged from the door a phalanx of churchwomen, bustling with the determination of martyrs, that pushed the boy aside (not violently, but as if they had not seen him) and swept up the girl into the bosom of holiness and propriety.

As for what had passed between Nana Oforiwaa and the teacher before the first search party set out to find the missing children, the listened, gazing out through the door, where the black outlines of the trees stood against the speckled sky. His soft, even voice moved fluidly, like water, and soon it was as if the words had a natural life of their own. They were not coming from him, it seemed, but rose around him, as if conjured, until the sound of the words saturated everything and nothing was possible outside of them. And when it was over the people assembled there knew that what they had heard was true, though they did not quite remember how it had become so.

The doctor told of how earlier that Sunday Nana Oforiwaa had taken her niece to the Botanical Gardens after church. The boy had been with them too, and Nana Oforiwaa had gone into one of the glasshouses, leaving the children outside. When she returned both children had gone.

She had summoned the groundsmen, who searched the gardens for them, but that took over an hour on account of the size of the gardens, and all through that time Nana Oforiwaa had stayed, alone, at a table under the trees in the café. There were plenty who would have sat with her, but none dared. She sat, her arms folded heavily across her breasts, her mouth tight as a hairpin, and her eyes full of righteous hostility.

Later, they discovered from the park guards that the children had not gone out through any of the gates. But that meant nothing. There were many places in the fence where they could have slipped through. That was when Nana Oforiwaa decided that the children had purposefully disappeared. "Look now what has happened," she said, voice raised, and the groundsmen stood quietly, heads lowered, as if they were responsible. But Nana Oforiwaa was more than angry: she had begun to panic, and the people said (her driver, the customers under the trees, the waitresses) that she feared now for her niece, she feared for what the boy had done with her, a girl she'd brought up as her own.

Everybody knew about Nana Oforiwaa's niece and the boy, the half-foreigner. It was a matter of silent outrage, their shameless public intimacy, touching each other like the whites did on the streets of Accra. It was spoken of by everyone (and not in lowered tones either).

doctor could add little. What he could tell them he had learned from remarks the teacher had made to his companions during the night's search: that Nana Oforiwaa had come directly from the Botanical Gardens to the school; that she was upset and anxious; that she'd wanted to search for the children herself, and immediately, but that the teacher had persuaded her to wait a little longer, arguing that the children might return on their own.

When later the doctor had tried to talk to the teacher himself, he told the crowd, he had met with no success. The teacher was, by this time, beyond rationality.

"He says things over and over again. Nonsense, unintelligible things . . ." the doctor said. "Otherwise he lies completely silent for hours, his whole body clenched . . ."

Then the doctor stopped talking. There was silence for a long time. Silence that was full of pity for the teacher. Though not only pity, but gratitude too for his carrying such grief. And as the doctor stood there, looking out over the quiet people, it occurred to him for the first time how much the grateful will forget.

And how much they will forgive.

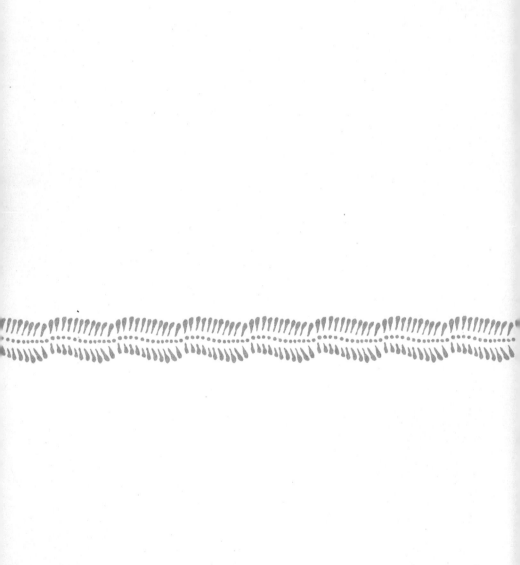

THE TEACHER'S BARGAIN

WHEN NANA OFORIWAA DIED, the teacher was not permitted to attend the funeral. Nor the hearings that followed. It was two months after her death that he was again seen in the town. For two months he was kept away, in a compound somewhere on the other side of Koforidua, on three occasions restrained, and never alone. In the first days he could make little sense of what was around him. The hands in the starched shirts that brought him food. Smell of naphthalene, rain, and urine (his own). The doctor (who only later he recognized as his friend of thirty years). The green walls, in the bathroom the blue barrels of rainwater for bathing and for the toilet that was flushed for him. The red balcony of the bungalow, set aside from the others, which were white, and by the low wire fence that separated it off.

At night, the movement of his body turning in sleep wrung the sheets around him. By day he sat in a deck chair on the balcony in his pajamas, the intention of his thoughts twitching in his fingers. And then after a week he could no longer keep his memory at bay, and the contents of it spilled out, jumbled up and unjoined, but all of it somewhere in there, and every bit as he had feared. It was like light streaming, blindingly white, leveling the world into a single dimension, still, like an unending plane of flooded water.

The doctor signaled that soon it would be time to bring the teacher home. Not long afterwards he was returned to the town, though it was a further two months before he resumed his duties. During his convalescence an informal routine regulated his waking hours—the visits of the doctor in the morning, a walk before lunch, his afternoon sleep, and then the evening visits, as the prominent people of the town took it in turns to call upon him. Although there was nothing to constrain him during the time of his recovery, he had no desire to disturb the new order into which he had been returned. His life grew back slowly. The gaps filled in.

There were times still that he asked after Nana Oforiwaa, that he asked after the children. It didn't matter that they were gone, it seemed; that Nana Oforiwaa was dead; that the boy had been sent away; and that the girl had been removed to Kumasi to complete her education, where she had distant family that would take her. Still he wanted them to visit, and did not understand why they could not. Were there recriminations, was there anger?—he could understand if there were, that he could. But surely nothing that couldn't be worked out by speaking it all through? Yes, they had all gone a little far in their different ways, even himself. Himself as much as any of them. But the truth was that nobody had meant any harm, none of them, even if they'd been forgetful of themselves, thoughtless, unwise—all those things perhaps, but not to do harm.

He tried to explain—to the old woman, to the doctor—but didn't seem to be able to make himself understood. And so for a period he stopped talking at all. He saw no point. He refused to answer questions. Refused even to communicate his own needs—food, water, medication, help in getting up—but instead would point or gesture, and when visitors came around he'd pretend to be asleep, and would listen to them whispering to each other at the foot of his bed.

A full week of silence gave him time to gather his thoughts, and one evening, as the doctor was showing visitors out of his room, he decided to try again. He waited for the latch to click shut, and then he opened his eyes and called to the doctor, whispering as loud as he could.

The doctor turned and looked at the patient. The doctor's hand was still flat on the face of the closed door. These were the first words he'd heard in a while from the teacher, and it made him smile—the teacher, wrapped up in his blankets, calling out to him like a guilty child.

"Hello," the teacher whispered.

"Hello," the doctor replied, and came to sit on the teacher's bed.

The teacher tried to sit up, but only managed to lift himself a little up the pillow.

"I thought you'd forgotten how to talk," the doctor said.

The teacher snorted.

He said, "Now I am ready to talk. Before I was not ready."

"What is it?" the doctor said, picking up a medicine bottle beside the teacher's bed and reading the label.

"Kwaku, we need to get the boy. You need to get him here. This is important. Listen—"

The doctor gave the bottle a small shake, then put it down. "John," he said, and then he began to explain, as he had many times before, and would many times again. How the boy was gone. How they had to send him away. That they did it on the exact day of Nana Ofori-waa's death. They didn't even call his parents, but came to find him in the afternoon, and they took him from the dining room of the school where meals were still being served, and they put him in a taxi and told it to take him back to wherever he came from, with a message to his mother to come pick up his belongings within a week.

The teacher would listen. He would nod gravely, and seem to understand, but the very next visit he would ask again after the boy. The doctor tried to be patient. He needed to keep the teacher settled, and isolated too until the teacher could better fend for himself. The questions that the teacher asked, with more and more lucidity, were dangerous. They told too much.

"John, enough," the doctor replied eventually, allowing his frustration to get the better of him, "For your own good. The boy is gone. Do you understand? I need you to understand."

"Kwaku—" the teacher began to plead, but the doctor would not let him continue.

"John," he said, and then he hesitated, since they had not talked directly before of what had happened on the day of the storm—"for the memory of Nana Oforiwaa."

As soon as the words were out he saw their effect in the expression on the teacher's face—of slight. As if the words had wronged him. Though a moment later it was gone. And whatever it was inside the teacher that had jumped up and grasped the knowledge fell back again, and all that remained on his face was a look of tiredness, and a few moments later the teacher closed his eyes, and his head went to the side of the pillow.

Perhaps it was to soften the shock of it, the doctor reflected on what he had seen. How much better it would be if the teacher could just realize one day that something had always been true, without having to encounter it for a first time. But the time was nearing that the doctor would have to start getting the knowledge through, in the way that the teacher now absorbed knowledge—through repetition.

And so, when he felt the time was right, the doctor raised the issue again, as the two of them sat together outside the teacher's house in the late afternoon. Cups of sweet tea were on the table between them, steaming, and a soft breeze moved through the canopy in the trees surrounding the plot. The teacher had lost a lot of weight, and the shirt in which he had been dressed was now too big for him. His neck was too thin for the stiff collar, and his hands, sticking out of the ends of his cuffs, sat dumbly on the tabletop, as if they didn't quite belong to him.

The doctor had enquired after the teacher's health, and the teacher had said how much better he felt, and that the humidity seemed to have departed in the last few days. He never liked the humidity, he said. Neither he, nor Nana Oforiwaa.

The doctor saw this as an opportunity. He turned towards his patient. "John," he said, "you know what has happened. You know Nana Oforiwaa is dead."

The teacher looked at the doctor. His neck was like a stalk in a pot.

"I know that," he said quietly.

"I'm so sorry," his friend replied, and put his hand on the teacher's arm.

"You don't have to treat me like a fool, Kwaku," the teacher said.

"I know," the doctor replied.

Then they fell into silence and the teacher looked away.

"Let me take you in," the doctor said at last, and he helped the teacher up. The teacher was leaning on his arm, and when they got to the door the doctor turned to the teacher, and saw that he was crying.

"But how, Kwaku?" he said.

"It was an accident," the doctor replied. He spoke firmly and clearly. "It was an accident—she went out into the rain looking for her niece and she slipped and hit her head and she drowned. That is what happened, John."

"And the children?"

"Celeste is fine. She is in Kumasi with family. One day we shall bring her to see you."

"Yes . . ." the teacher said, ". . . and Kwasi?"

"He has been sent away."

The teacher asked why.

"He's gone," the doctor said firmly, and the teacher stopped, and though he did not ask, his face asked, and the doctor felt he had to say.

"People feel that the boy is to blame."

"I thought you said it was an accident," the teacher said quietly.

"You yourself know what he has done."

"But that's not how it was," the teacher said, and was about to speak again when the doctor stopped him.

"John," the doctor said, "I don't want you to tell me anything."

"Kwaku, please."

The doctor shook his head.

"Why?"

The doctor's voice was lowered when he answered. He spoke quickly, his face close to the teacher's, and there was a firmness in his voice that he'd never used before, neither now nor in thirty years of friendship.

"All I want for you to do is know your own interest. Do you understand? Know your interest," he said, holding the teacher by the shoulder, and the two men looked each other in the eye until the teacher's eyes agreed.

And that, in the end, is what the teacher did. So much so that at times he himself even felt outrage at how the children had behaved and what their behavior had led to. And why not? Were they *not* responsible for what had in fact happened? Was the drowning of a woman not the outcome of the train of events that their running away had set off?

Of his own experience of those events, the teacher felt at first nothing, and then later only their shape, but not their immediacy. His nerves were lined with wool. Later, over the weeks and then months and years that followed, they would seep back through the cracks of dreaming, or burst through in a memory and leave him reeling. Still it could rage a war inside him. But now at least there was a territory he was defending, an existence that did not include grief. There was something to be won, if he chose, and was able.

Day by day he grew stronger. Slowly he learned the place of everything. In that, the place of himself. From the passing glance. From deference in those who could not now meet him as an equal. From the eyes downturned, the voice lowered in the street. From the visits, the long silent visits, in which neither courtesy nor human warmth was passed, as if what people sought was to bind the presence of his body among them, and no more.

At times he could sense and draw some satisfaction from the order his life had taken on, if he thought not much further than the bounds of his house, the fence that surrounded it, as far as the border of the school and the forest beyond. He taught. He administered. Though even as he began to feel his command return, he remained mindful of his weakness. Mindful that if he stayed whole it was still by the flimsiest of means, as if his life were held together with glue and cotton. But with time he grew steadier, more confident. He began again to trust in the shape of what he saw around him, that things would be tomorrow where he'd left them today.

In the evenings he would sit on the balcony of his house after dinner, above him the night sky, the stars (he'd think to himself) surrounded by the same darkness that surrounded him, joining everything seamlessly. *Nothing between me and infinity,* he'd think, though it was not his insignificance that moved him, but the fact of being able to survive it, to face it with calm. *Just a soft, small thing, nothing compared with the fire of stars, nothing compared with even a small rock thrown with a little force.* But none of that would interfere with him. Despite all the power around him, he would live out his life exactly. And at length he thought: *Who are the strong men, really?* And he knew it was not the men one is taught to love, nor the men one is taught to follow, nor even the rich, but the ones who keep what is theirs, however small. And that this was what he had to do: keep what was his.

It calmed him to sit out there in the undependable, fragile pool of light cast by his kerosene lamp, which he'd reach forward to cup his hands around. Not to steady the flame, but to feel the warmth in his palms. Then the light would spill through his fingers, shine red through the soft tissue between the bones, and he'd move his fingers to see the machinery in his hands, and notice their minute shaking, like the wings of insects. *People survive everything,* he told himself, *millions survive every day.* And there was no wonder in it anymore: how a person survives with the nerves so shot through and the flesh so riddled with living. How people cut out their own hearts, not to repent or be good, but simply for a little peace, and live twenty years still, or only ten or five, tending a garden, and being kind to dogs and children.

Except also he knew that the heart is never truly out. It regenerates. That somehow inside it starts beating again, growing itself from the ragged arteries, and beating, with all its wiliness and trickery, but also—surprisingly—with generosity, kindness, with a conscience. And if anything had really surprised him it was this: how compassion could still exist, even alongside the instinct for self-preservation. Compassion—that was hardwired so deeply that he would have said to the boy, if only he could have chosen the manner and the time, "I did not forget you. I did not leave you." That if he ever chose a thing, it was *not* to choose, with Nana Oforiwaa dead a few weeks, and the boy long since sent away from the ridge, the girl sent to the convent school in Kumasi, and nothing to confront the world with but his feeble body weakly beating. To obliterate the possibility of choice, like the faithful who believe without choice in their unknowable gods. That he too submitted, not as a man, but as a child submits to the only language it knows, who has no choice but to find the world self-evident and natural and knowable through words. *Bear this grief,* the people said, *show us it is true, make us believe, and we promise that will always be how it was.* Which is what he'd done, as he would have done whatever they said, and did.

KWASI EDWARD MICHAEL DANKWA

OF ALL HIS PARENTS' CHILDREN, Kwasi Edward Michael Dankwa was the only one delivered in a hospital. When he was born he came out of his mother's womb backwards. The doctors said that he would be the last.

Leah was born the next year, but already it was too late. "This will be the naughty one," his mother said as his father handed him to her in his blanket.

His father chose the name Edward, after the doctor who saved his mother's life. His mother chose Michael, after Saint Michael, protector of the holy church, the children of Israel, and patron saint of sick people, mariners, and grocers.

Born on a Sunday, he was Kwasi.

Kwasi Edward Michael Dankwa, the naughty one—every one of his mother's children had to be something. A mistimed somersault in utero sealed his fate.

His father, however, hardly distinguished among his five offspring. Without particularly knowing them his father looked on his children with benevolent, distant affection. They were his people.

Every Sunday morning, while his father read his newspaper on a chair in the sun, the children would line up before him, scrubbed, polished, and ready for church. "Ah, very good!" his father would exclaim, putting down his paper, and he'd look the lot of them over, like the cloth merchants inspecting bales in Makola, before clapping his hands together, raising himself from his chair and leading them, their mother at his side, the two blocks down the road to the King Jesus Is Our Saviour Church of the Pentecost.

He is, in the beginning, his first memories of home:

Four concrete walls, a red zinc roof, wood fence, cats in the front yard, chickens in the back.

A home porous to the world. Full of neighbours, siblings, an ever-extending family that appeared and disappeared with little warning.

Where in the afternoon the butterflies jumped through the leaves of the banana trees, and the adults drank tea, and later it grew less hot, and the flies began to settle and jump away, settle and jump away, while children were passed from adult to adult.

For a week each year his grandfather would visit from the village. Once he was a fisherman but now he was old. By day he slept, waking only in midafternoon, when he'd take his meal, and walk the yard in a string vest, ironed trousers and belt, his pectoral muscles parting either side of his rib cage like deflated balloons.

When his grandfather smiled, his head opened with happiness along the wide hinge of his mouth. His tongue was like a cross-section of cured pink ham. His laugh—hí–hí–hí–hí–hí—was a long stutter of happiness. And when he sneezed, his mother said, his grandfather's friends in the next village would send their sons to bless him.

At the bottom of the hill, at the end of his road, was an open field, embroidered with paths marked by the feet of people walking the same way over the dry season. As a child he played football there, with a ball made of rolled-up plastic bags. When the ball unraveled the game had to stop until they could bind it again.

Beyond the field, beyond the Fish Pond Drop, was the end of Nii Boi Town, from which suburbs he did not know stretched out to the sea, where the children of the fishermen caught fish on long lines threaded with baited hooks, attached at one end to a length of driftwood.

He remembers seeing it. How first the strongest boy would take the line beyond the breaking waves. Then the smaller children would reel it in, fish hanging from it like disks of tin which, left in the sun, would slap the sand softly until they died.

What place was that?

Nii Boi Town.

But not Nii Boi Town. Somewhere more complete, more capable of containing the world. A place without an outside, somewhere disallowing the existence of everything else.

Throw up a handful of stones and you catch only the largest stone.

Step outside and it becomes a mythology. Try to step back in and it disappears.

His father, born in 1942, was fifteen when the British left Ghana. His father's father was a gardener. His father's mother was a cook. His father, however, was the child of Independence.

Independence—that gave his father an education, a profession and a wife.

His parents met as trainee teachers in Cape Coast. His father, arriving with two pairs of long trousers in his suitcase, and two shirts, was not much more than a boy. Photographs show unassuming looks, an earnest smile, a pair of wire-framed glasses fastened to his skull.

He cannot remember a time he did not associate his mother with the smell of soap. His mother is both louder and larger than his father. She has hips strong and wide as a horse. As a young woman her girlish enthusiasm, touched already with officiousness, awoke in his father an attitude of wry indulgence that soon turned to tenderness.

His parents were married a week after graduation. A government loan helped them to buy a plot of land outside the city, beyond the furthest taxi drop in Nii Boi Town, which in those days was barely established.

Their road was marked by painted white stones laid out through the bush, the plot that they bought by numbered poles in the earth. But by the time he could remember, there were houses as far as the eye could see, and the water supply was already insufficient to reach the outermost houses.

His parents had been working barely two years when the world for which their education had prepared them changed suddenly. The first his father knew of it was when he came down for breakfast in the morning. Instead of the regular programmes Colonel Kotoka started speaking on the radio. It was six a.m. The president had been deposed while visiting Asia. Flagstaff House was besieged. Those who remained loyal to the president were overpowered, surrendered, or were killed.

Though the whole of Accra was rejoicing, his father felt the beginning of something inside him go cold. It was the end of the political kingdom.

It was also then that his mother began to turn to religion, and throughout his childhood Nkrumah and God were mysteriously but inextricably linked.

They continued to celebrate Independence Day, 6 March, with the family pilgrimage to Boti Falls. The seven of them wedged into a taxi as they made the journey up to Koforidua. Along the road the tall white trees grew straight and smooth as marble, and in amongst the groves of palm on the sides of the road the palm-wine tappers appeared, blowing coals in the scars carved from the tapped trunks.

The taxi driver would find a spot in the parking lot in the forest at the top of the falls among the other cars and buses. Slowly the family would make its way down. The children held on to the grasses and strained the roots of the small plants to steady themselves on the steep path. Then they would reach the bottom, and stand in the great hollow made by the mountains, to the applause of the water and the spray. His head would be filled with the thick, furtive smell of the wet ground.

His mother, directing activities, would stand with her sandals in her hands, her skirts rolled up, her toes in the wet sand, curled from the cold, surveying the appropriateness of everything. Her Bible would be tucked under her armpit, the bookmark sticking out like a snake's tongue.

He'd see her smiling, sun streaming in shafts over the falls behind her head—smiling at the world, smiling at him—her teeth, lovely and straight except at the very front, where they seemed to burst from her gums in chaotic astonishment like half-dressed students.

Then the family would sit down and eat, among all the other families, and his father would begin to tell the story he told every year. Of the petitioners shot down on the street in 1948, where now they've built Black Star Square. How Kwame Nkrumah went to prison. How even in jail Nkrumah won the elections, and one midnight in 1957 stood up, it was the moment of Independence, and he said how Ghana would be forever free, he was crying—Lord, how good it was, how proud he was, how full of dignity.

And then his mother would read from the Bible, always from the end of Exodus: "Then the Lord said unto Moses," she said, " 'Now shalt thou see what he will do to Pharaoh: for with a strong hand shall he let them go, and with a strong hand shall he drive them out of his land.' "

His parents worked hard at survival. His mother spent the greater part of the first years of her marriage making, and looking after, her children, and occasionally teaching other people's if a substitute teacher was required in any of the local schools. His father rose to the rank of head of department at the school to which he had first been assigned as a trainee. But the money that fed and clothed the family came from the private lessons his father gave to the children of the politicians and diplomats, to prepare them for their secondary schools in England or America.

Having put the children to sleep, his mother would wait for his father late into the evening. She would sit with his father as he ate and ask about the homes he had visited in the airport suburbs.

Shaking his head, his father would tell her, "If only they were as stupid as they are rich, but many of them are not."

Already his father was making his own plans to leave.

He tries to remember it, quick, before it's gone:

The women selling kenke at the last taxi drop, mounds of it in enamel dishes, like a tortoise's back.

The storm clouds blooming like carnations.

The sweet, clear milk of a green coconut after church, the northern boys selling it from brown wheelbarrows on the other side of the road, pangas balanced on their heads.

He remembers the insects floating in the field behind the house where he played with his friends and his siblings.

He tries to remember it all.

Throw up a handful of stones and you catch only the largest stone.

Step outside and it becomes a mythology. Try to step back in and it disappears.

After the coup of 1982 his father left to work in Botswana as a school inspector and designer of secondary-education mathematics syllabi.

Mathematics, said his father, is true, with or without him. Two and two are always four, no matter who is in power.

A year into his contract his father flew the family to visit him in Gaborone for the summer holidays. That was the last he would see of Ghana for the next nine years—the coastal plains dissolving in the humidity of an approaching evening storm.

One night, he lay asleep with his brothers and sisters on the mattresses laid out on the floor of the living room in his father's rented accommodation in Gaborone. Outside the insects were crackling like fat on a pan. In the next room, his father asked his mother how she was coping with five children, alone in Accra.

If his father could look after him, his mother said, she could handle the other four. He, she said, was the naughty one. But so that he wouldn't go lonely, it was decided that his junior sister would stay too.

This he learned only much later.

The new arrangements were revealed at the airport, on the day of the family's departure, when two bags too few emerged from the boot of the car. He saw his mother and three siblings off from behind the metal detectors. He and Leah wept in the back of the car as his father drove back to their new home.

Their tears disturbed his father. His father had never had to deal with the prospect of their unhappiness before.

In bed he would stay awake into the early hours of the morning, listening through the wall to the radio of the old woman next door, who forgot to turn it off when she went to sleep, or didn't hear it herself in her deafness.

Later he learned to sleep through it too, letting the deep frequencies of the male announcers' voices mix with the sound of the distant highway and become the sound of a sea breaking far away.

When finally the old lady died and her radio was taken away, he couldn't sleep for two weeks, the silence was so loud.

In his first months in Gaborone his father showered him and his sister with gifts. His father took them to the lion park at Saint Clair, and to see the vultures at Manyelanong. His father pampered them. He read to them, he bought them a great book from the nursing college, full of pictures of the inside of the human body.

He watched them playing together with puzzled concern.

One weekend they went to a safari park, where they sat at a trestle table in the sun, barely protected by the thorn trees, while his father read aloud from the guidebook about how to recognize different kinds of antelope. He and Leah listened quietly as their father's voice grew softer and softer, sapped by the heat and the sun and dust.

Then his father stopped and they all sat looking at the tall grass that could equally be hiding something camouflaged, as emptiness for miles. His father had forgotten to bring anything to drink. His father took a deep breath and that was all. He knew that his father was alone and felt sorry for his helplessness.

At night his father would come into the children's room after they'd put themselves to bed. His father would sit beside him and his sister on their bed, and touch their heads with his fingers, or their arms if they were outside the sheets, as they lay looking up at him. It was as if his father were assuring himself of their reality, touching the weight of his responsibility.

"How many degrees in a triangle?" his father would quiz them, or "What is the capital of Burkina Faso?"

His father's fingers smelled of his pipe, of sweet tobacco, and his clothes had a smell that was all of his own—smoke, the mothballs with which he protected his suits but which got into everything else, and something that smelled always of wool, and his own body, like salt and dry meat.

"But Daddy," Leah told him, "you already asked us that last night."

"Ha, but I'm asking you again," his father said.

"Ouagadougou," he and his sister answered the third time his father asked, the two of them exploding simultaneously with the answer, pronouncing it oo-ga-dou-gou—they'd gone to the encyclopedia at school and looked it up.

"Wa-ga-dou-gou," his father said, correcting them, and made them repeat it after him.

"Ah, very good," his father said, clapping his hands as once he had on Accra Sundays, making them laugh.

And so they forgave him.

He became happy for his father's sake, then forgot why he was happy. He went to a new school, began a new life.

Emotionally his father came closer only slowly, ultimately incompletely. There remained something of an abstractness in his father's love, an overconcern for his happiness that he sensed concealed a fear of really knowing him.

There was a great deal that they all felt was true, and beautiful, and always there when they were together, but for which there were no words—mutual recognition, different kinds of gratitude, gentleness, it seemed, on his father's part.

They were tied together by deep silences. After Nii Boi Town, Gaborone was a place of empty space and time, and it nurtured things that could not be said.

His father's job in Botswana changed the family fortunes. Savings, in pula and pounds, were enough for his father's own household and his mother's in Accra.

The house in Nii Boi Town was reroofed—he saw it years later on his first visit home. His mother had bought a cast-iron gate. She had painted above the verandah, in letters visible to all the neigbourhood, "My father's house has many rooms." Looking up at it he felt the first stirrings of his rebellion against religion.

Though half a continent away, his mother was not entirely absent. Nor was Ghana. So that none of them forgot their roots, she sent them parcels of dried fish and gari that would arrive regularly at the central post office. Although the parcels were intended as treats, he came to resent these rationed offerings from home, which his father shared among them on special occasions with great show and fanfare. He didn't want his food dry, smelling of envelopes and sealing wax and plastic. He wanted to walk down to the Nii Boi Drop and buy it himself from the ladies at the bottom of the hill beside the reeds, eat it still steaming in the hand.

But he had been the naughty one and somebody had had to stay behind.

Years later he'd dream of Gaborone.

Of opening the gate to the house, the gate turning in its hinge like bone grating in its socket.

In his dream he'd step into the house, cool as water, deep with shadows. Light would shine through the coloured square panes of the door set in the yellow pine, varnished like molasses.

His father would be standing in the hall. He'd sense that his father had been there a while. He'd greet his father and his father would nod in acknowledgement.

Often his father called him "my friend," but it was a reflection of goodwill between them, not intimacy.

"Why not bring Mama and the rest of the family to come to live with us here?" he asked his father a few weeks before his mother's last visit, attempting to intervene in the great silence that had befallen his home.

His father did not reply, looked straight through him.

His father, the creature of the house.

He'd think: *Would it have always been like that?*

Or was it Gaborone? And the sense that he had—for all of them—of not being anywhere?

Of there being just them and the land and the sky, the soil from which nothing of his had ever grown; the overwhelming presence of space, that sends you into the world knowing that even when you are most happy, even with the woman you love most in the world, even when you are *in* that woman, you are still alone?

In his dream he'd step out onto the stoep of his father's house.

The sound of the road would be like a river, flowing and flowing.

The moon would be so high up. Beneath it, a thin, angled plane of clouds would move across, tracing the roof of the sky, filling the world with a sense of its emptiness.

That great hollow place hypnotized him with its dimensions, drained the spirit, numbed the senses. It was something that could *not* possibly be owned, he thought—at least it had never been his, and it made him wonder what ever had.

He slept in Leah's room on the night before his mother's last return. They stayed up late, talking. What had their mother said to *her* in her last letter? Would their oldest brother have a beard? What would their mother bring?

They drew and coloured in a "Welcome Mama" banner that they hung across the entrance hall.

He doesn't know why he was afraid of that night, of what *real* thing. There was a wind, lifting the curtains up from the window—it was cold, especially early in the morning—and the bobble at the end of the curtain cord tapped against the windowpane.

(But he knew wind. He knew cold.)

It didn't matter that the windows were closed (in the early hours of the morning the two of them got up and fastened each one in the house)—the air was coming in somewhere. The stronger gusts he could hear in the rafters, like the sound of a sheet shaken out. Maybe that was what frightened him—not so much that the wind was there, but that he couldn't keep it out.

At different times during the night he knew that he was still awake.

Then asleep.

The crickets started and it was six a.m. He saw the light of the sun rising over the veld, thin and cold, and come like a knife sideways into the room. He could feel the cold of the morning in his nostrils.

He wanted his sister to be awake, to share it with her. He wound the knots of the blanket tighter around his feet, pulled it up to his ears, and watched from the envelope of warmth, the regular movement of her breathing, her shoulder rising and falling. She faced into the wall—that was how they both slept.

And then he fell asleep again and somehow nobody got him up in time. When he woke up the room was full of a strong yellow light from the thin curtain, which made a transparent screen and trapped the heat of the morning. He heard his sister and got up on his elbow, his body still moist with warmth in the stuffy room. He heard the hadeda's hard cry pitting the sky (he realized he'd been hearing it for some time in his sleep). Then the *blaf-blaf* of the city dogs. Then he lifted the curtain and saw Leah outside the window, running toward the house in thick woolen stockings under a summer cotton dress— "Papa, Papa, they're here!"—and shortly after that the door to the room opened, and there was his mother's shape in the doorway, and he got up and ran into her arms, and his father stood behind her, smiling as he had not for many months, saying, "Ah, very good!"

That night he sat with his siblings watching the snowy programmes on South African television. His father called him into the study, where his mother sat on the windowsill with her hands folded in her lap. His father went to sit next to her at his chair. Both of them wore the expression of people with news to deliver.

Then his parents told him that when his mother left he would be going back with the rest of the family to Ghana.

"Why, Papa?" he asked.

"To finish your schooling there," his mother said.

"And to teach you to become a Ghanaian," said his father.

HIS PARENTS SENT HIM to a boarding school not far from the village in which his father had been born. Accra was an hour away. Nii Boi Town an hour more.

On his last night in Gaborone his father said to him, "When you go home it will be for all of us. That is our place."

They were sitting on the bed in the room he shared with his sister. Then his father left the room to let him finish his packing.

He began to cry.

Partly he cried out of sadness, to be leaving the house, and his father and sister. Partly out of gratitude to his father, for giving him the thing his father wanted so much for himself but could not have— to go home, when his father could not.

"You will be so happy," his father told him as they said goodbye.

"I will, Papa," he'd replied.

But he wasn't.

His first few weeks in his mother's house, before school began, were an unexpected shock. He grew fat from the kenke at Fish Pond Drop. But most of his childhood friends had grown up and left. They'd built houses on the football pitch. His grandfather was dead. The electricity never lasted for more than a few hours. He was bored. He missed his sister and father, he missed the life they'd had, even out there in the desert where the emptiness never stops threatening and safety feels temporary even if you are with people.

When they sent him to school the water made him sick for a week. He did not speak the language well, he was used to his privacy, he was used to quiet, and a feeling soon came over him, of disaffection and despair that softened his will and made the world lose its shape, and as a consequence many things happened at that time that should not have happened, and would not have happened except for that.

This was in the town of Akwapakrom, on the Akwapim Ridge, in the mist and the thin, crisp air, and the weather that can hide behind mountains and appear from anywhere, and is always unpredictable and forever changing. The missionaries chose Akwapim when they came to Ghana because it was too cold for the mosquitoes that killed them down on the coast. And though they're now gone, the ridge is filled with churches and schools, and the old buildings they left behind, falling to ruin slowly.

What happened to him here, over the course of a few months, started one evening as he sat with the five hundred other students in the school hall where meals were taken. The rain was coming down, as it had been on and off for a few days. It hammered on the tin roof so hard that night that it drowned out the sound of the talking and shouting of the children gathered there, so that soon people stopped trying to speak at all, and they ate in silence, surrounded by the storm, while the smell of the wet ground began to rise up, rich and choking.

After the meal the rain still had not stopped. It was at least a five-minute walk to the closest dormitory, and so the children all gathered outside under the eaves of the dining room, pressed against the walls.

As he stood there somebody dashed out—a girl, running, laughing at her daring. He'd never talked to her before, though he'd noticed her a few times—the first, a few weeks before in one of the telecentres in town, from which his mother had made him phone to let her know he'd arrived safely. The girl had been there with a friend. They'd seen him staring, and laughed as they left.

Now, standing under the eaves, he watched the girl running out into the storm, as the rain wrapped her up in her clothes.

Something beautiful passing by, he reflected.

Then gone.

The sky was a little short of night. There was texture still in it, and he could make out the rise of the hill that separated the school from the town, and the half-presence of electric light behind it. There was a breeze—not cold, but damp—and he felt it in his shins and through his shoes, as if it were trying to flow into him. He stood for a few moments there. And then there seemed no point in standing there any longer, and he put his hands in his pockets and stooped his head into the evening and walked through the rain the distance back to his boarding house.

By morning he had a fever. He spent the next four days in bed. On the first night he was given an extra blanket. Meals were brought down to him, then taken away untouched. He lay in his bunk during the day while the other boys were in classes. He slept, and when he was tired of sleeping, stared at the ceiling and thought.

He thought about many things. He thought about what had happened. He thought about how his life was now, and how it had been before, and why his father had sent him back, and why he felt so alone, and how these things were connected.

And then he was so tired he could no longer think. He could hardly go to the other side of the room to get water. Noise came in through the windows all the time, but he was defenseless against it. The fan above him was catching, crinkling like plastic, throbbing in the ceiling, but he needed the breeze to keep his temperature down.

And as he lay in bed, sweating and distracted and wishing for things to be different, he suddenly felt a lightness—which at last was calming, and felt like sleep, so that he gave into it, and when he woke he no longer felt agitated at all, but rather disconnected from himself, as if he'd become an observer, a mere witness, removed from events that were happening in his own life.

While his body recovered, he continued to feel this strange feeling of absence. He continued to attend classes. He continued to speak to people. Complete distance was impossible. They slept ten to a room at that place, on double bunks, and woke, and washed and ate together, worked, then slept again, and the physical living of their lives was very closely bound. But he did not join in with other children. He had no friends. Friends did not interest him. And nor, after a while, was anyone interested in befriending him.

Though undisturbed, he did not go unnoticed. His aloofness attracted the attention of his teachers, and eventually the head teacher, who took an interest in him, saw him as a challenge, and so invited him to visit him in his quarters after class.

The head teacher's quarters were on the school property, near the water tanks on the hill. His house had two stories, and large empty rooms, and only him to fill them, except for the old woman who was his cook and stayed until the evening. Inside, the house had a wooden staircase and smelled of tobacco. On the walls there were original art-works—paintings and drawings done by artists from around the area—which he had not seen before in a house, and thought of at the time as being very beautiful.

The head teacher was a small man. But also he was very self-possessed and calm and thoughtful, and difficult to raise to anger. There was something impressive about that. He had a lot of authority and respect in the eyes of people because of it and the boy respected him too.

If other children visited the head teacher in his quarters, or he was the only one, he did not know, and he never asked. Maybe seeing the teacher became another of the routines he fell into. But also the teacher had known his father once. They'd attended training college together in Cape Coast, before the boy was born. The teacher liked asking about his father and he liked answering the teacher's questions. About how his father was. How it had been to live in Botswana.

In some ways his father and the teacher were alike—in their seriousness, in the way that it was often difficult to guess what they were thinking. Also, like his father, the teacher had traveled. He read and had interests, judging by the books that he took out from the library at Legon. About history and painting, and the biographies of generals and politicians. Napoleon. Churchill. Martin Luther King.

After a time he and the teacher established a friendship. He told the teacher about what he felt without it seeming like an effort. He told the teacher about the things that were important to him and the things that disappointed him. About returning to his mother's home, and finding everything so much smaller and different from what he remembered, and how his homecoming didn't feel like homecoming at all. The teacher listened to these things, and he offered advice. Although mostly the teacher just listened, which was all that the boy wanted.

Also the teacher was kind. The teacher took an interest in him, encouraged him. Sometimes with books, or with ideas, or through conversations in which the teacher tried to challenge him to think, to draw him out.

It was late one afternoon, as he was leaving the teacher's house to go back to classes, that the teacher first mentioned his idea of chance. He was standing on the step of the teacher's door, and outside the mists were beginning to draw in for the evening, and the lamps that had already been lit were surrounded by milky halos.

"Do you think you're lucky?" are the words the teacher used.

The teacher had a way of slimming his eyes when he asked a question and was already anticipating the answer, which was how the teacher looked at him then.

"Sometimes," he said.

"But what if there isn't such a thing as chance?" the teacher said. "What if chance is a choice. What if you choose to be lucky?"

The teacher was talking fast now. He was excited because of his idea and it was difficult not to be drawn into his excitement.

What the teacher said was that people believe too easily in chance. They believe that chance has power over them. That chance explains why things turn out or don't. But what if we choose not to believe in chance? What if we banish the idea of it? This, he said, is what great people in history have done, perhaps even without knowing it.

"What?" he asked. "They haven't been lucky?"

"No," the teacher said, "they have been lucky, but not by accident. Their wills are so strong that their own luck is a choice."

He thought he saw what the teacher was trying to say to him and it seemed all right to him then. Not that he knew too much about great people in history—about Napoleon and Churchill and Martin Luther King. Though he did know for sure that he wasn't going to be one of them. And so the fact that many things seemed to happen accidentally in his life was no argument against the teacher's. But it set him thinking, and the next time he was at the teacher's house he told the teacher about something that had happened when he was younger and living in Botswana. Not to him, but to a neighbour who was murdered by South African soldiers, who came across the border looking for somebody from the ANC but threw a grenade into the wrong person's yard, and killed a man's wife, and how afterwards they all came and saw the cotton dress flapping round the body like a chocolate wrapper, and the rest of the woman's flesh hanging in a thorn tree.

And he asked the teacher, "What kind of luck was that, to be the wife of the wrong person?" And was there something not great enough about her that this is what happened to her? And he told the teacher about something he often felt was true: that things didn't have to happen for a reason, that they happen for nothing, as that woman was dead for nothing.

The teacher was quiet for a while, and then he said, "Do you think about that a lot?"

He said, "Not until last week," although that was not true. He lied because he thought the teacher was sorry for him and he didn't want him to be.

"That's bad," the teacher said, and he thought that was the end of it. But then the teacher added, "especially for her." And he was surprised by that, because it seemed that the teacher was laughing and inviting him to laugh with him at what happened to this woman, as children laugh about cruelty, and he didn't know the teacher to be that way.

But he didn't laugh. He said: "It was very bad. I felt sorry for her."

The teacher said, "Not the destiny she would have preferred for herself."

"I don't know what she thought about herself," he said, and although he tried not to show it, he was confused, because he didn't know what the teacher meant when he said the word *destiny* like that, as if the whole idea were a joke that the teacher was contemptuous of himself.

And he thought the teacher noticed his confusion, because he turned his head away suddenly, as if struck by an unconnected thought. When the teacher turned back to him he was himself again.

"A person has to learn to live with their life," the teacher said, and that this was the advice he was giving him. The teacher said, "Try to own what happens. Try to have a view on things."

But maybe he didn't have any ideas about how things should be, he said. Or maybe he hadn't yet come across a view that made much sense to him, and didn't have one of his own, unless having no view itself constitutes a view.

He said, "Maybe it's easier to let things happen to you. That's what they're going to do anyway. It's easier than being worried all the time."

"Do you *feel* worried?" the teacher asked.

He told the teacher that he didn't, that in fact he felt nothing.

"You don't have goals?" the teacher asked, "Ambitions?" and there was that mocking tone again in his voice.

"Of what?"

"Of how you'd like your life to turn out," the teacher suggested.

He shrugged.

The teacher did not respond.

It seemed to him then that what he had said to the teacher had saddened and exhausted him. First the teacher looked at him and then he looked away again. The teacher was very still. He could see his breathing. He sensed at first that the teacher was making up his mind. That he had decided something important about him, or possibly himself, and so he waited for the teacher to finish thinking, and say something. But the teacher didn't say anything, and when he looked up again he saw that the teacher had not moved. And he'd remember very distinctly what it was he thought he was seeing in the teacher, and how surprised he was to see it. As if the teacher had found himself caught out, and wanted to hide himself in silence.

All of this was very long ago. Not much later he met Nana Ofori-waa, the aunt of the girl he saw running through the rain, and many things happened after that to dull his memory of the time before.

But he'd often come back in his mind to that conversation he had with the teacher about chance. He'd wonder what the thing was that the teacher gave away, then tried to hide. Were the things he said too much like what the teacher believed himself? Did his own weaknesses illuminate weaknesses that the teacher knew were also his own?

That, at least, was the opinion that he formed at first and held for a long time. Though later he began to wonder something different: that really the teacher had not been trying to teach him anything at all, as much as he'd been testing him. To see how far he might let things go in his life. How far he could be taken, before there'd be a story to pull him back.

THE FIRST TIME HE MET Nana Oforiwaa it was early in the evening at the rest house she owned near the Botanical Gardens. Some time before in the afternoon he'd received a message from the teacher to prepare himself for an outing. The teacher wanted him to meet her. Nana Oforiwaa was rich and a senior person on the ridge and a friend of his, from the way the teacher talked.

The journey by taxi from Akwapakrom took twenty minutes. It was the first time he'd driven on the ridge road since he arrived. He was dressed in a jacket, and long trousers which were tight in some places, and his shoes were polished. The teacher sat up front. At the back he drew the window down and let the air come in over him.

They drove through the fields and small towns. Nobody talked. In Mampong he saw the old men with their chairs out in the shop fronts. All along the road outside Obosomase wine tappers were heading into the hills with their jerry cans and machetes. He could feel the engine through the body of the car. He closed his eyes and felt all right.

Just short of Aburi they came to a road with a wire fence, beyond which he could see trees, sheds, and a water tower. The taxi turned right and after the fence ended there was a building. The entrance was a set of wide wooden doors that were shut. Closer to the fence there was a smaller door.

The taxi stopped and the teacher climbed down and knocked on the door. He stayed in the car as the engine idled. There was no answer. The teacher motioned for him to get out.

"We will have to go through the gardens," the teacher said. "She is in the front and cannot hear us."

The teacher paid the taxi driver, who watched them walk a few paces before driving off.

"Do you know this place?" the teacher asked.

He said he did not.

"This is Aburi," the teacher said. "We are at the Botanical Gardens. There is every kind of tree here. You will see it is very beautiful."

They walked the length of the fence. He looked in, at the trees and the palms and a solid wall of bamboo. Then the road and the fence separated, and there were buildings between them and the gardens. They turned into the town. They passed a taxi rank which he recognized as the staging post down to Accra, where the buses stopped. Women were selling pineapples under the telephone poles. It wasn't rush hour and there was little action. Music came from a parked tro-tro, its door open, its driver chewing a match.

They walked up a path beside a steep bank, and passed the Methodist boardinghouses. The last in the row was abandoned. Part had collapsed and rooms were open to the air. At the gates to the gardens the teacher had a word with the guard and they were let through.

Emperor palms, twenty feet high, lined the graded sand path up which they walked. Grass stretched to the side into the garden. There were hills, and trees, on their own and in groves. They stayed close to the boundary fence. The sound of a lawn mower buzzed somewhere.

They approached a series of sheds. One of the groundsmen saw the teacher and joined them. The groundsman and the teacher spoke. The groundsman led them to a gate in the fence. He opened a large padlock and let them pass through. The boy could see that the building separated from them by a stretch of grass was the same one they had tried to enter from the road.

They approached. It was a low structure, but with a tall pitched roof made of zinc. They walked up a set of red stairs and through a covered portico onto a restaurant floor, the other side of which was open through a series of large ceiling-high windows to a verandah out front with a view over the flank of a deep, long valley. A waiter was arranging glasses at a bar as they passed through the rest house. The waiter nodded at the teacher. He ignored the boy's nod.

The floor was made of polished gray concrete, and their shoes made a squeaking sound above the heavy fans in the ceiling, turning the slow cool air round. The verandah had chairs and tables arranged on it. All of them were empty except for one, at the front, where a woman was seated with her back to them. She was large, and the boubou flowing over her made her seem even larger. That's what he noticed first, and the elaborateness of her braids, which were woven in patterns in her hair.

The teacher approached. The boy followed a few paces behind. Before the teacher reached the table Nana Oforiwaa turned and saw the teacher, and she smiled and she said, "John." He had not ever heard anybody call the teacher by his name before, nor address him with the warmth that there was in her voice.

"Nana Oforiwaa," the teacher said, and there was a shuffling of his feet, and it looked for a moment like the teacher was bowing to her from the waist.

From behind the teacher he looked at Nana Oforiwaa. She had a high, wide forehead and large eyes that curved exceptionally.

"Oh, John," she said, laughing.

The teacher gave a small smile, and introduced the boy.

The woman continued to laugh. They were still standing. Then she put out her hand to him. It was warm and strong and she held his hand firmly, and there was a lot of power in this woman, he knew it immediately, in the strength of her hand, and in the strength of her presence.

"This is Nana Oforiwaa," the teacher said, "a very important woman."

He said, "Pleased to meet you, ma'am."

"Hoowh," she said, the end of her laughing coming out in a breath. Then they sat down.

He had no part in the rest of the visit. The teacher briefly said who the boy was, that his father had sent him here into the care of the community, and that this was why he had brought him to visit. Nana Oforiwaa asked the boy a few questions about himself, nodding as he answered, as if he were confirming what she already knew, but soon she and the teacher were talking of things that did not concern him.

When he understood that he would not be called on to say any-thing more, he grew more relaxed. He watched Nana Oforiwaa and the teacher talking. He drank a cold drink. He liked being in such a fancy place, with the view, and the tables, and all the fine things inside. He turned to his own thoughts as he looked around and observed for the first time things at the rest house that would later become very familiar.

It seemed, from the lip of the spur where the rest house stood, that they were poised on the crest of a wave. The rise of earth from which they'd been lifted trailed back beneath them in a shifting patchwork of greens crossed by olive shadow. The sound of insects around them seemed at once to rise from the valley and the earth itself and flow up into the small garden planted on the rise, up onto the verandah and into the rest house.

The good part of half an hour had already passed when his drifting thoughts were disturbed by a movement from behind him, of some-body passing by. He looked round. It took only a moment to recog-nize the figure of the person who had entered the restaurant as that of the girl from the telecentre, and later the rainstorm. He followed her progress as she walked, stopped self-consciously, then walked on again.

Then everything was over very quickly. The teacher looked back, pausing in midsentence, and saw her too, and smiled in her direction. The girl moved out of the room. The teacher turned back to Nana Oforiwaa and continued talking.

"Aha," Nana Oforiwaa was saying, though the boy could see that his reaction had not been lost on her.

He felt his face go hot and lowered his eyes, and sat still, looking into his lap. He wished they could leave.

They didn't stay much longer. It was growing dark and people were beginning to come to the restaurant. Candles appeared on the tables behind and soft music started to be played.

"I am sorry we did not get the opportunity to talk properly," Nana Oforiwaa said to him as he and the teacher were leaving. "I hope you will return. John will organize that."

"Of course, Nana," the teacher said.

"May God keep you," Nana Oforiwaa said, holding each of their hands in hers.

TWO DAYS LATER, out of the corner of his eye, he saw the girl again leaving the hall after lunch. She was at the other end of the room. There were many people between them. He almost didn't see her. But his eyes saw, despite himself, the image of the beautiful girl which, still vague and unfocused in his mind, would otherwise have dissipated into the shifting surfaces that were the background to his state of near constant dreaminess. Except his eye was too quick. The image of her sharpened. There she was. It was the background that began to dissolve. Suddenly there was something rather than nothing.

He got up from his table and followed her the short distance from the path to the trees as she returned to the dormitories. She did not hear him, so that when he touched her arm he startled her, though it had not been his intention.

He heard his own voice talking with its own volition.

He said, "It's me, from Aburi. I came with the teacher. I visited on Tuesday."

She was smaller than he'd remembered, somehow not the girl at all who'd laughed at him in the telecentre. She seemed fragile, younger than him, which she was.

"You're hurting me," she said.

He was gripping her hand, though he didn't know how it had happened. He let it go. The places where he'd been squeezing were a paler colour for a moment, before fading back into the brown of the rest of her arm.

And then his nerve was gone, or perhaps just his indifference to humiliation. He was suddenly afraid. He was afraid of having touched her and of leaving a mark, and afraid of wanting what he did.

Which was what?

Her? An idea? For the ache of loneliness to release?

"I'm sorry," he said, and he was, for what he'd done, but also for becoming overcome by her and himself and not being able to hide it, and he waited for the rebuke that would make him feel as powerless as he knew himself to be.

But she didn't say anything. She looked at him square in the face. He could tell she wanted to get away, that she was alarmed. Yet she didn't move, and it occurred to him suddenly that without her friend she was unsure of what to do, or how to do it.

He noticed her close the fingers of her other hand round her wrist, where he'd taken hold of her, and raising his eyes from her wrist to her face he thought suddenly of the woman the teacher had taken him to visit. Nana Oforiwaa.

He could see it now, very clearly. They were made from the same flesh, these women, except the the girl was more beautiful. She was unformed. She had youth, sweetness—but no power.

He said, "Miss, please, don't scream."

"I'm not going to," she said.

"I didn't mean for you to be frightened," he said.

She'd gathered herself.

"Of what?" she said.

He had no reply.

She started to walk.

"Miss, please," he said, "what is your name?" though already he knew it.

Her name was Celeste. She was the daughter of Nana Oforiwaa's brother, who had died. Nobody spoke of her mother, or of her mother's family. Celeste attended the school during the day, and would spend afternoons in one of the girls' dormitories until her aunt's driver would come to pick her up at around four p.m., and take her back to her aunt's rest house.

Many times over the following weeks he would make the trip to visit Celeste at the girls' dormitories. To get there unseen he had to pass through an overgrown garden beneath the administrative building, and down a steep embankment with a stream at the bottom. A path up the opposite embankment, through low weeds and bushes, would bring him to the regular path, lined by banana trees. From here he'd be able to see the first of the three girls' dormitories—all of them out of bounds to boys   spread out in a single clearing.

The dormitories were neat double-story buildings with balconies that kept the rooms shaded on both floors. Trees were planted at equal distance around them. Lines were strung between them, and girls' clothes would swell up with the shape of the wind, behind which he could hope to take some cover in his final approach.

Looking back, he'd realize that the fear of being caught with which he continued to approach the dormitories on each visit was ridiculous. His visits could never have been a secret from anyone. The wonder was why nobody ever stopped him.

He was, in fact, caught on his very first attempt, though never after that. Emerging that afternoon from behind the sixth form's billowing skirts, he walked straight into the head of house, waiting in the dormitory doorway. He could see she'd been watching him for some time. But he was prepared for this. Before she could inform him of the rules he'd broken, he stated his business.

"I have come to see Celeste," he said in the tone he'd heard his mother use with traders in the streets of Accra.

The girl considered, then relenting in the face of such plain fool-ishness, turned and led him through a corridor to a courtyard in the middle of the building, where Celeste stood taking sheets from a large red plastic basket and folding them into neat squares.

He had a couple of sentences ready about the reason for his visit, which he said more or less to plan. And then it was over and he was standing at her side. He was talking of ordinary things while she continued to work, and he watched her work, and the blood knocking in his head began to return to his heart.

It was a place he came to know well. The stone bench at which Celeste would be working, halfway along one of the inner walls of the quadrangle, in the shade of an old tree that had grown too large and wild for the square, and had already been cut away from some of the windows on the second floor.

They did not address each other by name in those first meetings, and he didn't think she even knew his until he was formally introduced by her aunt a number of weeks later. She was very plain about him being there. She did not make him justify himself and stopped him when he tried. For his part he tried not to come too often. Once or twice a week. But he would always come at the same time. She would always be in the courtyard and the conversation would carry on until the red plastic basket was empty and all the sheets were folded. And then she would take the sheets from the table and pile them back in the basket, and she would smile at him. A kind, friendly smile, though also distant, and uncommitted—a smile she would give to an old woman or a puppy. But it did not matter, since the smile was at him.

Time, during those visits, seemed to move very slowly. It was almost as if he could see the light moving through the branches and leaves, moving along the sand floor towards them. He would see it on the edge of the sheets. And then it would rise up onto them, over the surface of her hands and her face and her hair, and for the first time he would begin to collect in his head all the small details about her. Mostly she did not look at him while she worked and so he could look at her and feel unseen. Later it reminded him—although not at the time, since he had never seen such a thing—of how a young woman will turn her head away the first time she is naked in front of a man. Consenting to it, but still withholding her participation in the act of being seen.

Those drifting, lazy conversations, which seemed to promise so much just because they were happening, he would remember as the most intimate times of his knowing Celeste. When what they looked like was what they really were: a boy and a girl in a courtyard, talking under a tree. The girl sitting with her head bowed, the boy's hands at his side. Nothing else around them.

Though later he would question this vision of privacy, replacing it in his mind with a different image, in which they were not alone, but were surrounded by people, as in fact they must have been during those visits. By one, two, a hundred other girls. All of them like her, though none of them her precisely. And in the knowledge of that certainty, he would have to fight hard to keep Celeste there with him— sitting at the bench folding sheets. To stop her floating up to join the watchers. He would have to fight to justify there being her and not somebody else. To give her reality independent of himself, when he had left that place so long before and so many others had been at his side.

ALL THROUGH THE TIME he was visiting Celeste alone in the courtyard of the girls' dormitory he continued to see the teacher. Though they talked about many things, the boy did not mention her, nor her aunt, nor the visit they'd made together to Nana Oforiwaa's rest house. It was the teacher who first brought them up.

This was eight weeks or so since their first visit. They were sitting in the teacher's living room. The teacher had tea. The boy had a cup of orange juice.

"I was thinking we could visit the rest house again," the teacher said. "What do you say?"

"Why not," he said, watching the teacher.

"Tomorrow then. Friday," the teacher said. "I'll let you know."

And he did the next morning. A small boy brought a message to him to meet the teacher after classes. Later that day they took the taxi to Aburi as they had five weeks before.

It was all the same as the first time they'd gone there. The silent ride along the ridge road, the towns, the forest, the churches—except this time the rest house was open. They entered from the front, walking through to the verandah overlooking the valley. Immediately the boy could see that Nana Oforiwaa, seated at her table, was not alone. Her niece stood beside her.

As they approached, Celeste bent down to whisper in her aunt's ear, her hands held together in the small of her back, bent at her waist, her head tilted. She spoke a few words, and Nana Oforiwaa turned towards them. As Nana Oforiwaa stood up Celeste took a small step backwards, her eyes lowered. He did not see Celeste's face until they were all standing together, and the teacher greeted her, and she looked up to return his greeting.

"Edward," Nana Oforiwaa said, "do you know my child, Celeste? You are students together. In the same year."

"I do know her," he said.

Celeste had changed out of her school clothes and wore a loose patterned dress, a necklace of wooden beads, and nothing on her feet. It was the first time he'd seen her in anything but her regulation brown pinafore.

They exchanged greetings.

He wondered if Celeste had known he would be coming. It was the greeting of strangers, except that he could see her hands were shaking as they all sat down.

Nana Oforiwaa poured lemonade from a jug. They drank, and things were said that didn't mean a whole lot, and after a while Nana Oforiwaa suggested that her niece show him the gardens, which was a thing she was sure he had not seen before, so that she and the teacher could attend to issues that didn't concern them.

Nana Oforiwaa was right. He had never seen such a place before. Big and quiet, with its hills, filled with trees from around the world—

so many that when the wind blew it sounded like a storm. Most were identified on small plaques, with names in Latin and English, and a brief description: fan palms from Guinea and Kenya, fishtail palms from Burma, spine palms from South America, with their toothpick fronds, cane palms from India, a Malagasy traveler's tree.

In the middle of the gardens was the rusting shell of a military helicopter, placed on a mound in a clearing, and used by the visiting children as a jungle gym. Its nose was split open like a pod, and birds and lizards the size of a person's hand scurried round its carcass. Its shell was broken and peeling away, and its rotors were sagging, and its frozen hydraulics were cracked by the rust.

Many of these things he saw for the first time that day, walking round the grounds with Celeste, over the hills, into the groves, past the destroyed helicopter. The garden was her backyard. It was where she'd grown up, and as they walked she talked of the time she'd spent here, and the memories it was filled with. A childhood fall near the southern gate that cut her chin. The grass where she'd played in the shade of the Japanese cypress as her aunt would sit reading. The carcass of the helicopter she knew better than her own closets. The silk cotton tree, where she'd read to herself, hidden in the tresses of its giant roots.

It was, he realized, a childhood spent on her own. She mentioned no playmates. The only company she spoke of was her aunt's. But she never was lonely, she said. She needed nothing else.

"You must be close," he said.

"Yes," she told him, "we have been."

He thought she was going to say something more, but when she spoke again it was to tell him the properties of the medicinal plants where he was standing, as the groundsmen had taught her many years before.

So the afternoon passed. The light began to fade and though he was conscious of the time he sensed she was not. He said nothing, letting her take him on through the grounds, further and further from the rest house. The longer his walk, the more she'd say, and the more, he thought, she'd make herself his.

And then, unexpectedly, they came round through a grove of trees and he realized they'd been returning all the while. A few paces off was the gate through the garden fence, exactly where they'd started a few hours before. Celeste moved to unfix the lock, which she'd left half-closed.

"Well done," he said.

She opened the gate, and as he passed through, smiled.

By the time they were back in the rest house night had already settled in. The lights in the restaurant hung down from the ceiling on wires, casting shadows round the verandah. Nana Oforiwaa was waiting for them. His untouched glass still stood on the uncleared table where they'd sat.

"You two must have had a lot to say," Nana Oforiwaa said. She had her reading glasses on.

"Yes, Nana," Celeste replied softly.

The teacher had already gone, Nana Oforiwaa told them. "My driver will take you home," she said to the boy.

And then Celeste realized she'd forgotten the long-sleeve shirt she'd taken with her, and he remembered her draping it over the back of the bench close to the gate where they'd sat at some point in the afternoon. He offered to go get it back, and Nana Oforiwaa thanked him, and so he retraced his steps to the gate.

Though closed, Celeste had left it unlocked, and he went through alone into the garden, which the night had turned into a series of dark shapes retreating into the distance. It was cooler and only the sound of insect wings and wind in the leaves remained. He found his way to the bench and returned as quickly as he could.

When he came up the stairs ten minutes later, relieved to be back, the two of them were standing, waiting for him. He was happy, he could feel himself smiling as the two women watched him climbing the stairs. The expressions on their faces, he hardly noticed—whether they were smiling, or one was smiling and the other wasn't, or whether something completely different was happening.

Only when he got to the top of the step did they begin to move: Celeste turned and walked into the house without looking at him or saying a word. Nana Oforiwaa stepped forward. And though it was only her hand that touched him—guiding him at his elbow as she turned him towards the driveway, and the waiting car—he felt her presence close round him like an embrace.

SOON HE BEGAN to receive regular invitations to join the teacher on his trips to the rest house. No reasons were given and he had no intention of questioning his good luck. At first there were messages from the teacher, which were brought to him wherever he was by a younger boy. Later Nana Oforiwaa started inviting him herself, always to join them for the afternoon, though inevitably the visits would extend into the evenings, or the whole day on a weekend.

As time passed he grew used to the routines of the rest house. The long slow afternoons when he usually arrived, when the tablecloths had just been laid out on the grass to dry—it was something to see, if you passed by from the main road, with the purple and green batiks covering the slopes of the garden leading to the forest.

Then, in the late afternoons, preparations would begin for the meals. Ingredients would be delivered, and the chopping would start, the tables were laid, and the smells of the spices and the sound of pounding and frying, and the gossiping and laughter of the cooks would drift over the empty balcony.

Guests started coming at six p.m. Often there were tourists. They came in busloads, with their foreign currency and their taste for soft drinks and local beer, which Nana Oforiwaa overpriced scandalously and became relatively rich by.

But most of the clientele were from the towns around, in which there were many prominent people with interests, and retired teachers, and civil servants with pensions. Or else—especially on the weekends—from Accra: the pleasure seekers escaping the heat, who came to visit the garden, stay in the hotels, drink the palm wine, and see the waterfalls and streams that were all around the region, and often would stay at the restaurant until after closing time, when Nana Oforiwaa had them pile up their dishes in the sinks out back as they left, leaving the rest for the lizards and birds.

And so the visits to the rest house were not for Celeste alone, but also for the world that she came from. The gardens. The verandah. The rest house, with its low eaves, and its polished concrete floors, the vines on the pillars and the cool afternoon breezes flowing down into the valley. The restaurant in the evening—watching from the pantry as the cooks prepared the meals, the clientele from Accra in their finery, the prominent citizens of the town, quiet and elegant, speaking in hushed tones, and the private table on the side where the four of them—Nana Oforiwaa, the teacher, he and Celeste—took their meals.

And also—he'd admit it freely—for the infectiousness of Nana Oforiwaa's humour and confidence and her unashamed selfishness— the way she charged into the world and ordered it about, how she hustled it and cajoled until it did exactly as she pleased. It gave him confidence to stand behind such a person, to pass through the world in her wake.

Later, as the months drew on, he would begin to travel to Aburi on his own, without the teacher. Nana Oforiwaa had mentioned that he had only to arrange the time with her driver. Any time would be fine with her and Celeste, she said, he was to come over whenever he wanted. And that is what he increasingly did, letting Celeste know in advance, and planning an hour or so in which they could be together, before they'd join Nana Oforiwaa.

Celeste never said no. Whatever he proposed they'd always do. Walking through the gardens. Doing homework together in the back of the rest house. And even in those days, traveling a little further afield—to another village by taxi, or by paths that she knew through the bush.

Sometimes he thought she was afraid. Not of him exactly, but of the mechanics of closeness. Of the claim that being wanted made on her. Not that he did anything wrong. *Him* she liked well enough.

That he cared for her. That he made her laugh. That he was kind and respectful and listened to her and let her know the things she thought and said were important. And the fact of having a boy—that she liked too, in a childish, vain sort of way, which he didn't mind. It only made him laugh and want her more. But being willful, desiring, wanting—these were not things that came easily out of her. Nor were they things he could easily draw out himself.

They were in Aburi town once, out and about walking on a Saturday afternoon. It was hot and the taxi ranks were crowded and the stalls were selling fast, and they came to a table where a man was trading in food—pineapples, bananas still on the branch, bush meat, dried fish, a sack of grain, and such things. The trader was young and shirtless, and he hated the trader immediately for his loud, commanding voice, and his obvious, brilliant strength. He wished Celeste would want to pass straight by. But she stopped at one corner of the trader's table where oranges were piled up, and she turned to the boy and asked if he had money.

"Why don't you just take it?" he said.

She rolled her eyes at him girlishly.

"Do you have money?" she repeated.

He didn't have to look, since he knew he had nothing.

"Take it," he replied.

She did what he said and slipped the orange into the pocket of her dress.

Afterwards they went back to the gardens and they ate that orange together at the back near the workers' cottages, where the land slopes down into the forest, not saying a word, as the tall grass blew around them and protected them from view.

They were there a while, though he finished his half almost immediately. But she ate slowly, separating each segment, and stripping off the threads of rind. He knew there were thoughts working through her head, and so he sat quietly and let her be. When she finished her orange she put the rind by her side and folded her hands over her lap. He was sitting a little ahead of her, looking down on the forest.

Nana Oforiwaa had been talking about him, she said.

"What does she say?" he asked.

"That she likes you," Celeste said, and that she thought he was smart and well-behaved.

He was glad, he told her, he liked her aunt too, even if, without his knowing why, it made him uneasy to say it.

Yes, Celeste said again, her aunt liked him, she would ask about him, and she laughed—so many things—not so many things, but—again she laughed and had to stop momentarily because she was talking out of nervousness really and needed to stop for air—but some things.

"Oh," he said.

"Yes," Celeste said. And then she starting telling him how she'd come back from the school—this was not long after the first time he'd visited with the head teacher—and Nana Oforiwaa was sitting in her chair on the verandah, even though it was still hot. Which was unusual, Celeste said, because normally Nana Oforiwaa would be sleeping at that time, and would only get up as the evening cooled and it was time for the guests to come to the restaurant. But there she was sitting in the sun, dressed up, shooing gnats away from her with the newspaper, which was how Celeste knew something was wrong.

So she asked Nana Oforiwaa why she was there, Celeste told him, and what the matter was. But Nana Oforiwaa said that nothing was the matter, and that she was fine, except that Celeste could get her some lemonade if she wanted to, which Celeste did get for her aunt.

Then Celeste settled down at a table in the back to do her homework, while Nana Oforiwaa continued to sit there in the sun, the dampness creeping up the back of her dress, the empty glass at her feet in the grass.

Celeste called out to her aunt a few times. "Did Nana not want to come in to the shade?" she asked. But Nana Oforiwaa said no, and the second time that Celeste asked, Nana Oforiwaa got cross, and said that she did not need to be told if she was hot, and so Celeste didn't ask her again.

None of this seemed like anything to the boy; it seemed like talk.

Still, to be in any conversation with Celeste was pleasure, and so he asked her if these things with her aunt were normal.

He needed to know her aunt, Celeste said. He would see himself.

Later that evening, Celeste continued, after the customers had gone, the two of them were sorting the knives and forks. That was when Nana Oforiwaa started asking about him. About what he was like, and such questions as that.

He was surprised to hear this. Celeste saw it in his reaction and she retreated. She said she probably ought not to be telling him this. That it was all strange and she didn't want to talk about it.

He pushed her. Not that he really wanted to know, or really suspected that she might say anything interesting, but rather to make something of there being a secret. For the drama of withholding and asking.

But now Celeste did not want to talk anymore of this, and tried to change the subject. Halfheartedly he continued asking, until he realized that his persistence was upsetting her. When he saw this, that she was not far from crying, he stopped. He said, "Celeste, it's fine," and that she needn't say anything. That it didn't matter. That all that mattered was her—kind words, comforting words, words knocking up against the limits of what was possible then between them.

But a little later he could see again that still she wanted to tell him, from the way she kept glancing at him, then looking down, and falling silent, only waiting for him to ask. And so he did. He asked her, "What?" he said gently, but also laughing.

And then she said that her aunt had asked her questions that didn't feel right. She asked if she and he were doing anything private, the two of them alone, and that she thought it was all right if they were.

"Ah," he said—a breath escaping him before he could stop it.

"I know," she said, and she too was embarrassed, for him and for the situation, and for seeing him so much at a loss, and she said she was sorry.

"But I didn't say anything," he started to explain, his throat dry. "I didn't say I wanted that."

"Yes," Celeste said, "I know," laughing, and he laughed too, though still neither of them could look at the other.

"But do you?" Celeste asked.

And then he did look at her.

Celeste was sixteen then, and didn't properly know what it was her aunt was expecting of her, what she'd be required to want, though for that moment all that was required was a kiss, and that—for then—was what there was.

ONE SUNDAY MORNING a few weeks later, when the rest of the school was gathered in the hall for prayer, he slipped away. He wanted to be alone. He climbed down the embankment behind the administrative buildings. A blossom tree was leaning over the path shedding purple flowers across the gravel. He made his way through a grove of ceiba trees with their branches spilling into the air like river deltas. Across the path ants flowed in streams thick as overhead power cables.

Then he came through the cover of the vegetation and was standing on the road.

Why, he wondered, when he had most in the world to feel happy about, did he feel so alone? And why, when he was most alone, did he most want to be apart from people?

For some minutes the sound of the bells of the valley churches had been coming through the mist.

A bead of condensation trickled down his forehead, gathered pace in the concavity between eye socket and cheekbone, then curled around the jaw.

He closed his eyes, breathed deeply. There was the smell of the grass, the smell of the soil.

He buried his hands in his pockets and walked toward the town.

The first structures, hugging the outskirts, were derelict, set away from the road, but still they were inhabited, the owners moved down-stairs, leaving the top floors to unfasten themselves, the roofs to thin like blankets, the bricks to melt like mud.

Further on, neat, new houses were set out down the hills, with flat concrete roofs and green mesh window frames.

The town itself was almost empty, the shops and houses closed for church. Only an old woman sweeping a doorway with twigs to observe him.

No people, he thought, but the buildings themselves, the buildings were alive—the paint on the old bungalows decomposing on the walls, breaking into elements, the pale olive and blue and yellow of oxidation. Damp grew through the plaster, that blistered as if with bacteria.

Above some of the better-kept shopfronts, second stories had been built of wood, which resembled barns raised into the air. Their walls were packed tight with thin planks and their shutters, made of irreg-ular slats, were fastened inwards or outwards or hung in the gentle breeze. He read the dates in plaster above the doorways. He read the names. "Hawkins Chambers," "Methodist House."

Has anything here ever been painted more than once? he wondered. Or was it the weather that turned everything into history instantly?

There was nowhere to get food. A single taxi stood at the taxi rank. Its driver eyed him suspiciously, but made no attempt to tout for business.

He passed through the other side of the town, heard music through the mist and singing. There were more people now on the road, fam-ilies dressed in Sunday clothes, walking quietly against him back toward the town.

The music brought him to a stone church set on the hill below the road. Its walls were made of rocks the shape and size of loaves of bread. Passersby had stopped on the road, some children in torn clothes, a man with a floral shirt and a Bible.

He stood to one side and looked through the window.

Inside there was a wedding. Closest to the window was a band and choir, the material of the cassocks catching with silver in the lights from the bulbs strung across the roof. A surface of light glossed the walls. It covered the people and spilled out of the church into the somber morning.

The people continued to pass him on the road. Families, groups of middle-aged women in hats, teachers leading rows of children, scrubbed and quiet, hand in hand.

Inside the church there was hardly room to move. The tom-tom player, tucked between the organ and the wall, peered casually over his dark glasses as he set the rhythm, that started out in his jumping hands and spilled into the matter of everything. The choir and band swayed and jumped in small movements from side to side as they led the wedding song.

The bridal couple danced in the middle of the room, pressed tightly by the congregation that flowed around them right to the back of the church. The congregation hopped and skipped, but the couple danced in half-time, one beat to every two, swaying together, hand to elbow.

Observing the scene, he put his head against the window frame.

He sensed the presence beside him before he heard the voice.

"I'm sure you're not where you should be," Nana Oforiwaa said. She had a look on her face of mock reproach. Or possibly just reproach.

He was momentarily surprised, but not alarmed, though he might have been. Something told him she would not turn him in for sneaking out of the school.

He said, "Good morning, Nana Oforiwaa," and that he expected he was not.

She didn't say anything.

He asked her what brought her there.

"Me? I'm free to come and go as I please. No morning church unless I want, no ten a.m. homework, for instance."

"That is true," he said. "I should go back," turning and looking toward the town.

"Not because of me," she said.

He said, "All the same."

"I can take you in my car," she said. "My driver is parked at the Methodist church."

"All right. Thank you," he told her.

"It is my pleasure, Edward," she said as they started to walk up the hill to the church. "Tell me where you want to go."

TO GET CELESTE took patience.

Just like Nana Oforiwaa said it would.

"Anyone can learn to wait," she said. "The courage you must find yourself." This was her idea. The story that protected him and Nana Oforiwaa—that she would teach him how to wait; everything else he'd do himself.

"You have to be brave," she said.

He knew, he said, and that he'd try.

She said, "Right now in your life you only have to want things badly enough to get them."

These were snatched conversations, exchanges that happened in between—between other conversations, between other people coming and leaving, in brief moments of privacy—at least at first.

She told him, "The things you want are easy. Everyone gets them in the end, even if it doesn't seem that way to you."

"You'll see," she said, and that probably he needed to get some of the things in life that were easy before he learned to want the things he couldn't have.

"Maybe," he said, "maybe that's right," because he felt she wanted him to agree with her, that she had a need for that. But really he wondered what she meant by this, because it seemed to him that Nana Oforiwaa generally did get what she wanted, and if she wanted that he'd have Celeste, then that is what he'd have.

Which in the end is how it was.

As well as for what Nana Oforiwaa wanted on her own account. The time she asked he spend with her. Keeping her informed, she said. That was how it started. As a condition for her help. Not the details at first. Although later, the details too. About where he went with her niece, and what he was doing, and what it was like, and where he might be at such and such a time.

And later other things, for which he didn't readily have proper words, and felt less easy sharing. But Nana Oforiwaa said she could always ask her niece. Which in fact was what she ought to do, she said, that she had a responsibility. Women spoke together of such things. And he knew that would mean telling—about what she already knew, and how; and about what he gave Nana Oforiwaa—and not unwillingly, Nana Oforiwaa reminded him, he was not unwilling in these things, and he had to agree.

No, it wouldn't be necessary to tell Celeste, he said to her, it wasn't necessary that Celeste know anything. In addition to which Nana Oforiwaa had a way of putting him at ease. Through her approval of him, through her affection. She inspired trust, confidence. And he was grateful to her.

As Nana Oforiwaa was grateful for him too. He was her consolation, she would say.

For what?

She wouldn't elaborate, would just repeat herself and smile sadly.

Some things Nana Oforiwaa hinted at, the least important things.

"She is so much like her mother," Nana Oforiwaa would say bitterly of her niece in unguarded moments.

"How?" he tried to discover.

But it was not a topic she would broach.

"No, Edward," she said, "we do not talk about that. We do not."

Celeste herself knew nothing of her mother that was not from Nana Oforiwaa. Her mother had died in childbirth.

And Celeste's father, Nana Oforiwaa once told him, confidingly, but in a way that forbade the prospect of any further discussion, "her father died afterwards of grief."

From what Nana Oforiwaa said, he could see that she felt she'd lost a lot in her life. In the first place, because of her brother. But more recently, because of Celeste.

This she never said aloud. But he knew. He'd observed Nana Oforiwaa long enough to understand.

She, Nana Oforiwaa—a woman of such power, who could make the world do anything—was consenting to no longer being young when other people still were. Lord, it wasn't easy—to give everything up for a child, a weak-willed child—but she was doing it.

"How old are you, Edward?" she asked him once.

He was out back at the rest house, stacking empty beer bottles, when Nana Oforiwaa asked him this question.

Seventeen, he told her, which he was at the time.

"That's a good age, Edward," she said, "don't you think?"

It felt all right to him, he told her.

"I'd like to be seventeen again," she replied. "I'd like to be seventeen and not know who I am."

He didn't understand what she meant by that and told her so.

And she replied, how could he, when he couldn't imagine anything different.

Then she stopped and thought, and sighed, and said how she just had a need right then to say these things. And she asked whether a person wasn't allowed to have a need every now and again, and whether he thought that was a crime.

No, he told her, he didn't think it was a crime.

She seemed to be pleased by that, and she smiled, and he smiled back, though he didn't know how much she believed him. Nor how much he believed himself.

ONE AFTERNOON he took a taxi to the rest house on his own. He'd done it a few times before, when he hadn't remembered to organize a lift with Nana Oforiwaa's driver in advance. When he arrived that day Nana Oforiwaa and Celeste were not there. They were at home, Nana Oforiwaa's head waiter thought, and gave him directions.

The house was a few minutes down the road. It had wood walls and a tin roof and a thirty-foot pylon in the driveway, which made it easy to recognize. When he got there he saw Nana Oforiwaa's car parked outside. Her driver was asleep on the back seat, with a newspaper over his face and his feet hanging onto the ground. As he approached the house Nana Oforiwaa opened the door and stood watching him, then embraced him on the stair. She smelled of fresh soap, and the edges of her dress were wet, and he thought that she must have just bathed. Then she turned into the house and he followed her.

"Nana?" he said.

"I was feeling tired today," she began to say, as if she hadn't really heard him, "—don't know. I had a sore head."

"I was wondering," he said.

She seemed pleased at the idea of his concern.

Then she let him go. "Celeste isn't here," she said. "You can see her later."

She walked a few paces to the other side of the room, then turned around and clasped her hands together.

"Sit," she said.

He sat on one of the chairs that lined the walls of the room. In the corner there was a table with a plastic cloth, and there were windows facing a shady patch of trees.

"I sent her out," she said, picking up the train of her thought, "to get some banku." And then she waved her hand, as if dismissing the thought. "She'll be back. Do you want anything to drink?"

She got him a mineral, taking nothing for herself, and they talked for a short while, about how things were, and about what he was doing. But after a while Nana Oforiwaa excused herself to get ready for the evening. He could drive with her later, back to the rest house, she said, and she went to her room, closing the door behind her, and left him to wait.

The kitchen was behind him. There was a small area for eating and the space where he was sitting. To his right was a short corridor, leading to the door through which Nana Oforiwaa had gone to her own room, and a last door that was closed and that he guessed must lead to Celeste's.

He got up and walked around. He could hear the pressure of Nana Oforiwaa's feet moving around on the wood floor. He looked at the closed door of Celeste's room. How unwise would it be for him to go in there, he wondered, with Nana Oforiwaa next door. But even before the thought was fully formed he had opened the door and was standing inside.

It was a small room and did not contain many things. The bed was neatly made. It had a knitted bear on it, and on the walls there were a few magazine cutouts, cards and photos, and a lizard made of wire with deep blue marble eyes. There was a desk with boxes and childhood toys, and in place of a cupboard there were open shelves on which shirts, trousers, socks, and underwear were folded, and a metal bar in an alcove on which Celeste's dresses were hung. He walked over and ran his fingers over them. The hangers made a tinkling sound.

He took a step backwards and there was the bed, just behind him, and so he sat down on it. It was hard. It had a foam mattress, its base made from an old door panel. He ran his hands over the sheets.

Celeste's body lay here at night, he thought. He felt the graininess of the material beneath his fingers.

"Well," Nana Oforiwaa said.

She was standing at the door.

He started to get up, but then had to stop, afraid that his thoughts would show. He was half crouching, still. He looked at Nana Oforiwaa. His throat was clenched. He wanted to cry with anger, and also humiliation, and humiliation again at wanting to cry.

Nana Oforiwaa smiled, sadly it seemed to him.

"You should sit," she said.

He did.

"Move over," she said.

He moved up towards the pillows. He could smell the sheets were recently washed.

She sat a small distance away from him.

Instinctively he moved backwards.

She said, "Why are you so unkind, Edward?"

"I am not," he said.

"Yes. You accuse me," she said.

He told her he did not.

"You do," she said, "but it's fine. You are young. I am not."

He did not know how to respond and didn't and so she began talking of other things. Mostly what she said he had heard many times before, these stories of her past. About coming to Aburi, moving into this house, and never thinking she would carry on after her brother died. About how much Celeste had been like her father, though now she was more like her mother, and how much it meant to Nana Oforiwaa that now there was him.

He listened, as he always listened, though he never liked it. He never liked it when she talked like this. When she was weak. When she needed him. Though more than this, he wanted to get out. He wanted not to be having *this* conversation, here in Celeste's room. To separate, where he could, the aunt from her niece.

But Nana Oforiwaa seemed unaware now of his discomfort even as he heard the sound of the front door opening. He couldn't imagine she didn't hear it too. Shame he knew she did not have. Did she also have no fear? Though somehow in the back of his mind he thought that if she didn't move, it was because she had good reason not to. Still he trusted her, even as Celeste came down the corridor, then stopped in the doorway to her room.

Celeste was smiling, she was about to speak, and then when she saw him beside her aunt, she stopped smiling.

There was a moment of silence for which even Nana Oforiwaa appeared unprepared.

"I don't . . ." Celeste began, then stopped.

Nana Oforiwaa cut her off before the thought could articulate itself.

"What on earth are you thinking?" she said sharply, as she rose from the bed. The boy rose slowly, but once he was up Nana Oforiwaa grabbed his arm and pushed him out of the room, instructing her niece over her shoulder to get ready so that they could all return to the rest house for the evening sitting.

Nobody talked in the car the short distance back to Aburi. Celeste would not look at him. Nor would she have anything to do with him once they arrived.

The teacher appeared a little after eight p.m. He'd eaten at home, and thought he'd come to the rest house to take a mineral, and pass the evening there much as he always did—at a table outside on the balcony, sitting with an oil lamp at the edge of the night, reading the paper, talking—while the boy and Celeste and Nana Oforiwaa came and went, as everyone pleased, or as things had to be done.

Instead the teacher left—he and the boy left together—no more than a few minutes later.

"What happened?" the teacher asked in the car.

There was no response.

The teacher said nothing for a while, and then he said very softly, "My boy."

He tried to put his hand on the boy's arm, but the boy shook it off.

HE DIDN'T SLEEP that night. He looked for Celeste during lunch and afterwards at the dormitory, but couldn't find her. The whole day passed before he discovered she'd been absent. The next day he saw her walking among her class, but she didn't stop. Again she wasn't in her dormitory when he went to ask for her.

On the third day he went up to the road where Nana Oforiwaa's car usually waited. The driver would always come early and sometimes they'd talk, but that day there were only the passing cars.

He waited long enough to know he was wasting his time. Then he turned back to the school. Just as he was getting down the slope he saw above him the car driving past with Celeste buckled in the passenger seat. She must have arranged the pickup further down the road to avoid him.

He did finally stop her the next day. There was only one other path she could take to the road to meet the car. He waited in the shade of some trees and called after her as she passed.

She let him approach.

"I didn't mean for that to happen," he said.

He was careful with his words, unsure of what she knew.

"It doesn't matter why," she said.

"Yes it does," he said.

She said nothing.

"What are you feeling?" he asked, taking a step towards her.

"I don't feel anything," she said.

"Can you try?" he asked, trying to get a smile from her.

She seemed to think for a moment.

"No," she said.

But still she let him put his hands on her shoulders, and then pull her towards him, so that her head was on his chest, and the palms of her hands were on his collarbones.

They only stood like that for a moment. For a moment he thought that this was how it would all turn out. Except then, from within his embrace, she hit his chest with the fist of her hand. Once, hard. It made the sound of a football being kicked.

He let her go, and she turned around and went away up the hill to the car. Though he could have followed her, he didn't.

His next visit to the rest house was excruciating. None of the cooks, nor the head waiter, cared to exchange much more than a cool greeting with him. But Nana Oforiwaa welcomed him warmly. She seemed pleased that he'd come—or maybe more relieved than pleased, he sensed. For the first time it seemed that she was at a loss.

They talked, but he couldn't find the words to say what he wanted to say. The sight of Nana Oforiwaa—with the life and vivaciousness all out of her now—filled him with shame. Neither of them mentioned Celeste during that conversation, though he thought of little else. When Celeste did come into the rest house, and saw him sitting with her aunt, she turned on her heel and left. Both of them watched her go, saying nothing.

He left shortly after that. Nana Oforiwaa saw him out at the door. He watched her in the side mirror of the car, through the dust in between, still standing there at the door as he departed.

What else was there to do?

Two more days passed. The teacher sent one of his messengers to the boy. The messenger returned with the back of his head stinging.

The next day the boy found one of Celeste's classmates during lunch and handed her a note.

"Give this to Celeste," he said to her, and he closed her hand around the paper and held it shut. "She can decide herself to throw it if she wants."

He ate alone, and waited at his table after lunch, hoping she would come, as the people cleared out to go to their next classes.

She did. He heard a chair scraping backwards and then she was walking briskly towards him. When she got close enough for nobody else to hear, she said, "You think she is a lady, but I think she is dirty. I think that what she is doing is disgusting."

"What? Do you think I come to drink tea with *her*?" he said.

"I don't care why you come," she said sharply, and threw the unopened note on the table in front of him, and left him sitting where he was.

"I think you do," he shouted after her.

People turned and looked.

But he did think that, and it gave him the courage to return to the rest house one more time, as awful as it felt. To drive along the road to Aburi, reach the turnoff, see the water towers appearing over the trees, covered in their vines, and get off at the door, and step down, and go through into the restaurant where so many happy things had happened, with nobody to welcome him except the one person whose welcome meant nothing to him.

He sat down with Nana Oforiwaa at the table. She looked a little better than she had the last time. She had done herself up. She was wearing perfume, a necklace, and a bright boubou, though also she was coughing.

"You don't look so well," he told her.

She rubbed her temples. The dry season was almost over and the pressure was changing.

"It's the rain," she said. "The rain is coming."

"I'm sorry," he told her, lying. Really, he didn't care.

The conversation between them started moving slowly. Mostly Nana Oforiwaa talked about herself, which made her seem old. He wasn't concentrating. He was listening for the sound of Celeste's presence in the rest house and so he heard her entering the verandah before she reached the table.

She stopped slightly behind Nana Oforiwaa, who wasn't aware, and so continued talking. Then Nana Oforiwaa saw him looking, and craned her head back and also saw Celeste.

"Come," Celeste said to him.

He got up. Celeste started walking, and he followed her.

They walked down towards the fence in silence. For a moment he turned back and saw Nana Oforiwaa watching them go, but then his thoughts were free.

Celeste was walking fast. He could hear their feet in the grass and leaves. They walked through the gardens. He remembered the first time she'd brought him there. Insects buzzed and clicked in the canopies of the rain trees. Brambles grew between their trunks and orchids flowed over their branches like streams. The birds called. They squeaked and whistled, plumbed, ratcheted, whispered, whined, and purred, and on the grass under the camphor trees and the nutmeg trees, rose into the air with the sound of sheets shaken out.

"Celeste," he called after her, but she didn't respond.

He could see her legs moving under her dress, which was made of cotton and had thin straps, like two pieces of string, that came down from her shoulders and held it around her body just over her shoulder blades.

He knew where he was. He knew the garden well by now. The familiar sites passed by, but where she was headed he couldn't tell.

Still a few paces ahead, she stopped at the helicopter on the mound, right in the centre of the garden. He stopped, too. She turned around and looked him in the eye.

Then she lifted the straps of her dress from her shoulders and let it fall to the ground.

"Is this what you want?" she said.

He looked at her standing. She was naked. Beautiful. There was nobody around, but he could hear the voices of people nearby. Children laughing. A man calling.

"No," he started, then changed his mind; "Yes, it is."

"Fine," she said, "then have it."

And that's what happened, in the carcass of a military helicopter left to rot in a grove of candle trees, as the evening approached and another day came to an end in the hills of the Akwapim Ridge.

AFTER THAT, everything people said about him and Celeste was true. How they shook away discipline and became uncontrollable, and were shameless and wild, and lacked modesty. And how on the day that Nana Oforiwaa died, they stole away from the garden after church, and took a car, and went down the ridge to Accra, and spent the day at the beach, at Labadi, while Nana Oforiwaa grew frantic, and later went out to join the search parties looking for them, and eventually lost her life.

That was the day the rains came.

The sea at Labadi was like a warm bath. It was the colour of a grove of cocoa—brown and green at the same time. The sky was full of heat and wetness. Groups of fishermen's children from the Jamestown and Ushertown slums were roaming around measuring each other. The city people sat out in chairs under the trees, and the children hustled to sell fried squid and prawns and oily damp cassava stained red with pepe.

They put down the tablecloth they'd taken from the restaurant at the back of the beach, where the shade of the trees could cover their heads and nobody was behind them to watch. He stretched out, the sun warming his feet. Celeste lay on her side, facing into him. They talked and watched the people, and later, while he was reading, she touched the side of his face with her fingers and the cup of her palm. And though he felt a rush of happiness, he also felt overwhelmed by sadness and shame for the things he could not say to her, and could not take back, and his eyes filled and his throat grew tight. She looked at him as he tried to keep his face still, but still the tears were coming out silently, giving him away.

Celeste got up to swim. He watched her walk towards the sea. Still she moved like a girl, long-limbed, gangly, her body keeping inside its new knowledge, of herself, and him.

And then the sky tore apart.

She was only a few feet away and she turned and began running towards him.

The rain came in like waves of stone, slapping the sand, whipping everyone's bodies. It was deafening. Lightning was catching like webs all over the sky. They both raced for safety, and found cover with other people under the roof of a kiosk.

Earlier in the afternoon a troupe of drummers had been playing there, who also found cover under the roofs, and soon they started beating their drums again—one setting the rhythm and the others taking turns to weave around it.

People began to dance. It wasn't clear who started first—perhaps it was a drunk. Perhaps it was a madman. But many years later he'd still remember the small sharp movements of that dancing, like a shock jumping through the dancer, a small series of convulsions in his legs, in his back and his arse. The dancer's face was ticking like electricity. And then a circle formed round him. Then there were many circles, with pairs of people taking turns in the centre.

And he'd remember when the turn came for the young hustlers—the gangs who had been roaming the beaches—how they began to chant the old Ga fisherman chants. Not only them, but the ordinary townspeople too. Even those who lived abroad, in Germany and

America. The songs leaked out of them all from across the kiosks along the length of the beach.

And then it ended.

The squall passed over and the people drifted away silently. There was no acknowledgement of what had happened, or what they had shared. People who'd been touching and shaking and contorting around each other walked away as strangers.

The air was now dry and clean and cool, and the storm moved inland, heading for the ridge, where it would arrive that night. But now the evening light shone through the braided clouds. The sea was cool, flat as a piece of stretched cloth, and it all felt as if it could last forever—this moment of reprieve—as for the rest of that day it did.

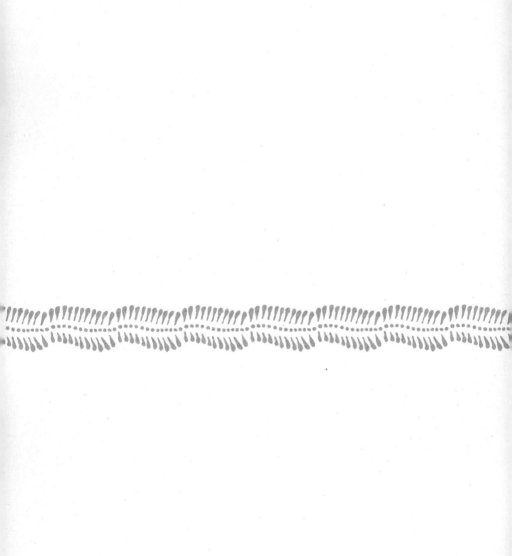

BIG HENRY

After Nana Oforiwaa's death the boy returned to Nii Boi Town, where he stayed for a short time in his mother's house. There was talk of his finishing his studies elsewhere that came to nothing. Shortly afterwards he moved to the city to live with his uncle.

His uncle's name was Festus Ankrah. He had a large property on Castle Street in the centre of town. He ran a fleet of taxis, which he'd funded out of cash saved over five years of wandering across the world—during which he traveled from Ghana to Jordan, through Arabia, to the Far East, and had ended up as a construction worker building cinemas in Manila for Ferdinand and Imelda Marcos.

His uncle's taxi fleet had done well. He employed six drivers, and no longer needed to work himself for his livelihood, though the thought of leisure had never occurred to him. Although he'd never married it is well known that he's fathered two sons since his return to Accra—one in the old colonial slum of Jamestown, one in the new post-Independence slum of Nima.

His uncle had been living on Castle Street for a little more than eight years when he brought him to the house. Though many people assumed as much, his uncle did not take him in out of duty, nor in observance of any rights to the care of his sister's sons—his uncle despised tradition. Nor was it out of affection—his uncle knew him even less than he did his own two sons (which was not very well either).

His uncle brought him to the house out of a sense of kinship, but not one based on family. Rather, his uncle sensed in the boy a younger version of himself. He identified with his nephew's disgrace—his expulsion from school and return to Accra—which, in his uncle's eyes made his nephew as much an outsider as his uncle felt himself to be an outsider.

That, and the opportunity to thwart his sister, mother of his nephew, who—in her self-assurance, her narrow-mindedness, her cultivated respectability—stood for everything his uncle hated most about the world he'd fled when he set out on his travels and had then returned to.

And so, after the boy had returned from the school, and had spent two months already under the discipline of his mother's household (doing nothing more than the chores of an eleven-year-old, and otherwise keeping to himself and his only interest, painting), it was his uncle who first suggested what his nephew had been secretly contemplating for a long time, but didn't dare, in his disaffection, propose.

"If the child cannot think of anything better than to lose his time through painting," his uncle said (repeating the words of his sister, who had been complaining for weeks about her son's disinterest in anything else), "then let him paint and make his living."

His mother was opposed from the start to the idea of a child of hers becoming a signwriter, and condemning himself to a life among artisans, hustlers, and small traders. But a week to the day after his uncle first made his suggestion, he arrived by car at his sister's house, unannounced, to take his nephew away.

"Mary, I want a word with you," he said in his soft, firm voice that had the authority of a man used to having his way.

"Come in," his sister said, swinging the half-door open. "I thought you'd be back," and that afternoon the arrangements were made.

To spare his sister the sight of her child's descent into the artisan classes, his uncle suggested he stay with him in his large house in Adabraka. And to spare him the prospect of undeserved failure, his uncle offered to get him an apprenticeship to learn the rudiments of the trade, a shed in which to paint when the time came, and the benefits of his contacts with traders and businessmen, who always needed signs and billboards.

And so he moved from Nii Boi Town into the city and what would be his home for the next three years.

The house on Castle Road had been built before Independence. It had front and back balconies, thick palm trees grown knobbly as a crocodile's back in the tall grass in what was left of the garden, a dirt-brown zinc roof, and a driveway parked with taxis in various states of repair, the most dilapidated still on bricks.

Inside it was a shell of wood and lime-washed walls, kept tidy by a woman employed twice a week. It was entirely bare, but for four rooms at the back inhabited by the boy's uncle, away from people and the road, and those in the front, where the boy established his quarters.

Given the whole house on Castle Road from which to select, the boy chose two rooms that opened up onto the front balcony, their entry on the upstairs landing. The original function of the rooms was indiscernible. They were relatively small and connected to each other by arches that had never known doors. In the room furthest from the landing he put a mattress. This became his bedroom. A chair and table turned the landing into his living room, from which he could look down between the railings into the empty entrance hall, where shafts of sunlight—that in the morning carpeted his bedroom—caught the dust as it crept through the holes in the roof.

He and his uncle got along well. He admired his uncle, who had traveled the world and lived as he pleased. An easy affection developed between them, as between people who are alike. Although they were alone together in the house, their lives revolved only loosely around one another's. They ate when they were hungry, together when they felt like company. His uncle said that his nephew did not need nurturing—something, in any event, that he could not have provided him. He said that his nephew needed to be left alone, to do as he pleased.

His uncle wasted no time in fulfilling his side of the deal with his mother. Shortly after his nephew's arrival at Castle Road, the promised apprenticeship was organized. The signwriter with whom his uncle arranged for his nephew to work had cut his teeth in the trade thirty years before, when competition was fierce and the formal economy ruled. Somewhere his real name must have been recorded, but everyone knew him by his moniker—Big Henry.

To look at, he was five-foot square of a man, wide almost as he was short, black as a seal, his whole skin sparkling with humidity. He was full of life. His flesh buckled under it. His heart was full as a wardrobe.

Though there was a suppleness about him too. He was *lithe.* In his manner, but also in his movements—the way he sprung up the stairs to his studio, agile as a goat, though the heavy stairs shook and the plates rattled in the kitchen below.

There was a kind of magnetism in that sort of bulk. People weren't laughing at him. They were sharing in something good about the world that his existence made possible. But also there was something more serious about him, something less about joy. A solidity to his presence, that was more than simply his physical bulk. This man exuded dignity. He was graceful, generous, had the balance of things.

In his own boyhood Big Henry had painted with love. But many years had passed and now he painted not so much with love as with honesty. He took a casual interest in the beauty of the world, drew simple pleasure from the fact that a surface made of paint could represent known things, and saw as much value in the intention to suggest something beautiful with his art as to succeed in it.

Though in his time Big Henry had been successful. He had made a name for himself—not only through commissions for the large European and later Ghanaian firms, but also for the piecework he'd continued to do around the neighbourhood for next to nothing. And it was this that became the mainstay of his business three decades later, when the formal sector had turned to photography, and many

younger men, more hungry than himself, and more mobile, were ply-
ing his trade.

Still, the signwriter painted with as much skill and enjoyment as
ever. Only now, for the first time in his life, he'd begun to suffer problems with his health. Even into his fifties he'd been able to drink as long
and late as any man, then sing as loud the next morning in church
as anyone on a full night's sleep and a proper breakfast. He could still
travel fair distances for even small commissions, happy to sleep on a
shop floor with his rolled-up trousers as a pillow if an extra day was
required.

But this had now come to an end. He had always been a large
man—as full of guts as he was of life, his friends said. Now sixty years
of carrying those guts around had made walking painful. He tired
easily. Often he was out of breath, especially on hot afternoons.

Many of those same friends who had shared with him his youth had
now retired—returned to their villages or their children's compounds. But he had married late, a woman much younger than himself, and had two small girls in school. Times were hard for everyone
these days, except for the rich perhaps, and he had never been rich.
And so when Festus Ankrah approached him on the matter of taking
on his nephew as an apprentice, Big Henry was glad of the opportunity to have somebody in the studio to help.

A day was set. Uncle and nephew arrived at Big Henry's house.
The signwriter was summoned by his wife from his studio on the second floor. He came down the stairs slowly, smiling, talking through
his breathlessness, as his wife went off to get water and food for Festus
Ankrah and his nephew. The signwriter's whole body gathered with a
small jerk in preparation for each step, then straightened out as he
arranged his weight delicately on the pads of his soft feet.

"Yes, yes, yes, hello," he was saying as he descended, while Festus
Ankrah and the boy stood formally at the door. "Good morning to
you."

The signwriter invited his visitors to sit. Festus Ankrah hesitated,
explaining that he would have to leave, but sat then nonetheless. The
boy remained standing.

"As for myself, I must have some relief," the signwriter said, lowering himself into a beaten-up old leather chair.

Then the boy's uncle and the signwriter talked. The boy stood quietly at his uncle's side.

Only when his uncle took his leave—"You will forgive me for not getting up," the signwriter said to him, shrugging a self-deprecating shrug—did Big Henry address the boy.

"*O-yeees,*" Big Henry sighed with gratification, then edged off his shoes and shifted in his seat exaggeratedly, as if shaking off the formality of the last five minutes. The two flat clubs of his feet began spinning slowly, like little fins propelling him lazily through the air.

It was a gesture of complicity with which he hoped to start his relationship with the boy.

The boy smiled, an uncertain smile, but did not say anything.

"Very well," the old man said, and introduced himself.

At first the signwriter thought the boy was merely shy. Although he made many attempts to put the boy at ease in those first few days, it seemed to make little difference. The boy was quiet, spoke haltingly, uncertainly, when he had to, and in a mixture of English and Twi, since he was not fluent.

"Something is wrong with him," Big Henry's wife said to her husband.

"As for me, I think he is only sad," the signwriter replied.

"What is it that he has to be sad about?" the woman asked.

The old man didn't know.

Though there was more to it than just sadness. There was mistrust too. Not of him. Of everyone. Or everything. Somewhere along the line, the old man guessed, damage had been done. And in his way of seeing the best in people, he looked on the boy's silence as something apart from the boy, an affliction; and so the apprenticeship continued, when others might have broken it off after a few weeks.

In the beginning Big Henry would start the morning with the boy at Amaamo timber market, where he'd give instruction in the selection of wood. As they made their way together through the winding alleys of the market, barrow boys would maneuver through with boards stacked on their heads. The air was filled with the sound of bargaining and shouting and the animal howl of wood being torn by metal, and as they walked, and the signwriter talked, sawdust would fall like snow from the board saws, and gather in piles like river sand at their feet.

The merchant from whom they bought their boards had his shop at the back of the market. He was a small man with little brown teeth and a scrubby head—an immigrant from Niger in a political suit that was cut from a piece of purple cloth so thin that the collars and lapels hung as loose and flimsily as a shirttail.

There they would find him standing outside his shed, in a row of identical sheds with tall frontages opening to a passage. All around his merchandise was piled up in stacks, like folded tablecloths, on which the night-shift machinist and porters lay asleep. From a distance the merchant would watch the signwriter and the boy approach, and the boy too would watch the merchant, clearing his ears with the head of a two-inch nail, from which he collected the yellow crust with his teeth and spat into the sand.

To the doorframe of the wood merchant's shed a monkey was tied by a rope attached round its waist. It was a pale gray creature with dangling limbs and sky-blue testicles that bounced between its legs like berries. It would take a banana with both hands gently, but it would also bare its teeth and shriek soundlessly at the porters and assistants who harassed it, hopping around the frame of the shack looking for a door in the plank wall where there was none.

After the lessons of the timber market, the signwriter taught the boy to sand and prime. Later they went through the mixing of colour. The composition of a board. The disciplines of the different fonts, varnishing finishes, and installation.

The boy followed instructions well. He seemed to take pleasure in his work. The signwriter noticed that having a task to do, with its specific requirements set and understood, gave the boy contentment. Perhaps a lack of structure had been part of his problem, the old man thought. That before there'd been nothing that necessitated the world being one way or another.

But at the studio there were always things that needed doing. And as time passed Big Henry found the boy a very useful assistant. He treated the boy kindly. The boy's presence became part of the sign-writer's daily routine. And because the signwriter loved his life—his wife, his girls, his house, his job—the boy became part of his general-ized sense of rightness and contentment.

He began to feel a fondness for the boy, as he noticed in his girls a fondness for anything that was familiar. "Hello sky, hello birds, hello sandy yard," the younger one, who was six, would say as their mother took them out to school.

It was something like that for him too—*Hello boy*.

The signwriter knew that to try to coax the boy into conversation would only make him withdraw further. But it did not stop him from speaking himself through the long days they spent together. He did not think the boy minded. Having somebody around to whom he could pass on his experience brought out of Big Henry all kinds of reminiscences and half-articulated philosophies.

He talked of the kindness of strangers, and the coincidences that had brought him into the trade, and why he had stuck with it.

"Long ago," he told the boy, "when I was young I started reading books about people that have died.

"The way they started, what they were performing.

"And one day in a little magazine I read that the former world box-ing champion Cassius Clay, the father was a signwriter—

"Now I say if the father was a signwriter, a prominent man like that, why can you not also follow in his footsteps.

"Ahaaaaa?

"Ah!

"And so what I had to do was to make a small box and put my lit-tle paints inside, and then get my brushes and put them into my hair.

"And moreover the clothes that I wore had to be full of paint so that the people see that you belong to paint.

"Now when I started I was walking in the street, and somebody would see me and say, 'O let me call this man.'

"Then he'd say, 'Are you a painter or are you an artist?'

"And I say, 'I'm an artist.'

"And then he asks me can I write on his shop for him?

"Then I have to put my paints down and we talk of price, and if the price is good then I start doing something."

It was late one afternoon that the signwriter told the boy this story. The boy had finished for the day, had washed up and had come to the old man in the room above the house where the old man had been continuing with the day's work. Naked to his waist, the signwriter stood painting at his easel, filling in certificates for the African Bible College for Christian Resurrection.

The old man's face was crumpled in concentration. Seams of sweat formed in the creases of his skin. Sweat rolled round the socket of the eye, gathered in the hollow between cheek and ear where the flesh folded inwards like rubber, then back under the pressure of its own weight. His flesh hung from his arms in solid blocks, like hot-water bottles. His forearms were large and thick, growing over the wrists. His chest hair curled like burnt spiders. The meat of his back fell away from the spine like the folds of gathered curtains.

All around there were planks of wood piled against the walls, some salvaged, some primed and washed, others half completed. There was an old clothes cupboard against the wall, two rusted trunks, tins full of paint—coffee and milk tins, brands just distinguishable beneath the paint drippings—bottles, rags, string, brushes, sandpaper, a lathe held to a nail against the wall.

Listening, the boy stood against the back wall, playing with his toe at the peeling linoleum, beneath which he could see through the rough wood planks into the room below, where one of the old man's girls moved about. The sound of her singing filtered up, a refrain beginning to catch in his head—*something, something, tra-la-la.*

For a few moments, as Big Henry completed a particularly difficult piece of lettering, he paused. Then he stood back and shook the beads of ink gathered on the tip of his nib, streaking the floorboards like squashed mosquitoes.

"And so one day," he said, "I met one man in town and he said to me:

" 'Are you a signwriter?'

"And I said 'Yes.'

"So he asked me where do I stay.

"So I showed him my house.

"About two, three weeks later he called me to a shop he owned where they sold Nashua radios, and the managing director asked me to write Nashua Radio on their main gate on the glass—

"In fact it's a very difficult thing for most of the signwriters to write on the glass, some of them have to write it on the paper and then paste it on the window.

"But I never did that—

"I only took chalk and ruled my base line and ruled my caps line and wrote it *freeee*hand, which was very beautiful.

"Then my friend the man advised me.

"He said, 'Henry, stop moving around, get a small apartment like a kiosk and put it at a good position, so that people will come to you and confront you.

" 'Since when you walk around town people will think you are cheap and you won't have a good price.

" 'But when people come to you, you can consult them and they can give you a good price.'

"So then one evening time, say around five thirty to six, I went to some people around the bottom of town where they sell some packing case, some plywood and some iron roofing sheets, and I started buying those things now to enable me to put up the kiosk . . .

"In fact anybody you meet on your way is your angel.

"I took the man's advice and put up the kiosk and people come to me now and tell me what they want.

"Me, I never reject price.

"Whatever little something somebody wants to pay I take it.

"Because a job is hard to come by.

"And since I can't manufacture money I have to work.

"And since you want to win *soooo* many customers you must be more religious, more patient, very kind, and you should know how to talk to people.

"And also, since you are serving the public, you have no business with anybody in the cemetery.

"No business in the cemetery—the cemetery is always quiet.

"People with whom you can do business are people who are living.

"In fact the money comes into your hand for something. You must know how to reward that money."

Later he talked of other things. Of his youth in Accra. Of the glory days of the 1960s, until politics stole it all. Though even that he remembered with humour.

"Our house," the signwriter said, "in Acheampong's time, they rationed the zinc for fixing roofs.

"In the rainy season we moved downstairs. Mosquitoes lived in the bedrooms.

"That man—he died on the beach from a bullet in his head.

"Blessed are the dead, but I was not sad.

"So always enjoy today," he said, "because tomorrow there may be no roof on your house."

And then he laughed—first his eyes would widen, his top lip rise, his face would open and the deep, rolling sound would come out of him, his whole body on fire with laughter.

As the weeks went by, and turned into months, the old man's family grew used to the boy's presence. They absorbed him into the life of the house. From time to time, when urgent work needed to be finished, the boy would sleep the night on the floor of the old man's studio and continue early in the morning, and the signwriter's girls would bring him breakfast as he painted in his vest and shorts.

It was they who turned the boy from a stranger into a member of the household. The boy's silence didn't frighten them. It didn't make them wary.

"It isn't good if people never talk," the younger girl said to the boy one day—he was painting in the yard, and her father was upstairs, and she and her sister had been playing nearby. While they played they had slowly approached, and were now sitting a little way off, watching him.

The older girl laughed behind her hands.

The boy thought they were alone, but the door to the house opened and the signwriter's wife came out and admonished the child.

The older girl apologized. The younger girl said nothing, tracing a crack in the concrete step with her finger.

"Leave Kwasi alone," the signwriter's wife said, "he's busy," and she turned and went back into the house.

"You know . . ." the younger one started, the beginning of a question mark at the end of her wondering.

"Maybe . . ."

She looked at the boy for encouragement.

He gave her none.

Though she didn't need it—"Did you do something . . . *bad?*" she whispered conspiratorially, glancing towards the door, then back at him.

The boy left off his painting. She was squatting on the concrete, her hands around her ankles. Her little knees were scraped from playing and her dress was streaked with dirt and grass stains.

"What's the worst thing you ever did?" she said encouragingly.

The boy could not keep from smiling. He wondered what the worst thing could be that she'd ever done. What she thought the world was capable of, what she was capable of herself.

He put down his brush.

"I cooked a child and ate her for breakfast," he said, and lunged towards them both, and they jumped up screaming, with pleasure at being chased, and ran towards the road, glancing over their shoulders, stopping on the path, as the excitement ebbed, like an intake of breath, then lifted them up, and they turned and ran up the path, screaming again.

The door of the house swung open, and the old man's wife came out once more, ready to raise hell. She watched the girls disappear, then turned toward the boy.

"It's fine," the boy said.

The signwriter put his head out from the upstairs window. "My children," he said, laughing, and then his head returned and he went back to his work, and the boy did too.

"People don't eat each other," the younger girl said to the boy a few days later. The boy was painting again in the yard, as he often did when the afternoons were too hot.

"Why not?" he said. Now that they were friends, he liked to tease the girls.

"They do all the time," he said. "Big people get hungry."

She looked at him uncertainly. She didn't like the possibility. She never knew when to take him seriously.

"You're funny," she said.

"You're funny, too," he said.

She smiled and went off to think and left him to work.

She knew her father didn't like the boy to be disturbed. As time had passed the signwriter had been giving the boy more and more responsibility. The boy was taking over much of his work. It had not taken long for the old man to notice the boy's talent. The boy could copy his work so closely that not even he could tell the difference. And the boy's own paintings were so skillfully drafted, and so clever and imaginative, that the signwriter wondered if the repetitive themes of their usual commissions would not hold back his talent.

Though it was the old man's wife, not the old man, who ever said anything about it.

It was past midnight, and the boy was staying over to finish a number of boards that needed delivery the next day, and she'd come to the door, and watched him as he painted.

"You draw like an angel," she said.

The boy hadn't realized she was there. Everyone else had gone to bed, he thought. He'd been working alone with a kerosene lamp and the radio.

"I paint like Big Henry taught," he said.

"In some ways," she said.

He stopped what he was doing and wiped his hands with a rag.

"My husband wonders if really he has anything to teach you anymore," she said.

The boy thought about this.

"Does he want me to leave?" he asked.

"No," she said. "We want you to stay. We like you here."

"You are kind," the boy said.

She shrugged.

"My husband wonders if people have not been very kind to you in the past," she said.

"As for myself, I have also not been kind," the boy replied, and she looked at him, and she smiled—a thin crease of acknowledgement—and wished him a good night.

The signwriter had nothing to worry about. The boy enjoyed the mercantile themes. He enjoyed making things for the real world. And when Big Henry started proposing exercises unrelated to the staples of the business—telecentres, hair salons, beauty salons, chop bars, church functions, general dealers—the boy soon lost interest.

That suited Big Henry well. While he knew that the days in which he could claim to be teaching the boy any new skills would soon pass, he was glad of the boy's presence. He liked having the boy in the house. Increasingly he passed on to him the major responsibility for new work and was glad of the extra time it made available to him. To concentrate on the business side of things, but more and more, to let the world pass by, and enjoy what was most important to him—being in the house that he himself had made through his labour, being with his thoughts, and his wife and girls.

This is how things went for six months.

It was now September and the city was waiting for the rains. The sky was the colour of gunmetal. The air was still, and the fronds of the trees hung down in the torpor of the sticky afternoon. It had turned out to be a busy period. Eight boards were set out in different stages of completion, some in the studio, some in the yard downstairs.

The boy was already in the house by the time the signwriter woke. The old man lay in bed and let the sun come in through the window onto him, or did not stop it, once he knew he was awake, and it spilled across his chest and his face, through the leaves of the tree that grew in the yard.

It was past nine probably, but the old man did not feel the need to rise. His wife had already gone to work and his girls were at school and he knew that when he got downstairs the boy would be in the yard, and his breakfast would be set on the low table in the sitting room.

The old man closed his eyes again and felt unhurried. He concentrated on everything that was happening at that moment—the light, and the breeze over the sheets, and the sound of the boy's humming in the yard as he worked, and it all felt good.

For the rest of the morning, he had the boy run various errands—buying materials, delivering messages to his clients and suppliers—while he stayed at the house to work on the signs.

The boy arrived back from his errands a little before noon. He saw that the old man was not in the yard, though the rags and paper were out on the sand, two tins of paint and various bottles on the verandah ledge, and three boards standing against the step in the shade of the mango tree.

The heat has driven him out today, the boy thought to himself. He went to look at the boards: a hairdressing salon (one of the sign-writer's specialties), a pawnshop and a spare-parts dealer. The sign for the pawnshop was fairly close to completion, while the other two were still rudimentary—a caps and base line for the lettering, sketches of the composition penciled in over the primed wood.

We will work outside this afternoon, the boy thought, and was glad. He preferred to be outside. He liked the smell of city mixing with the paint and the turpentine and sweat. Upstairs it was too stuffy.

He put down the white plastic bags, filled with supplies, beside the boards and went round the side of the house, where he expected to find the old man rinsing a brush at the tap.

But the old man was not there.

He came round again and into the house. The kitchen was empty, and so the boy came outside, took off his shoes, and entered by the front door.

Big Henry was in the front room with his back to the door. He was holding on to the banister that led up to the office, his weight slumped forward onto his left foot. He was shirtless, but the sweat had already dried, and the pattern of sand on his back showed where he'd fallen backwards in the yard. His ribs moved heavily under the flesh of his back. Slow wheezing noises came out of him.

The boy came forward and put his hand questioningly on the old man's back, while he stooped to see his face. Big Henry folded at his touch. The boy put his hands round Big Henry's trunk to stop him falling forward and managed to wrest him round so that they fell together against the wall, the boy half on the first step, with the man on his side on the floor.

There was a moment of silence until anything happened.

"So now you are here," Big Henry said, wincing. "What was taking you?"

"I was getting the paint and the other things, as you asked," the boy replied into the old man's shoulder. Big Henry was heavier than he'd thought, which was saying something.

"Of course," Big Henry said, and paused to get his breath.

The old man shifted his weight and turned his head to look at the boy. The boy's face was frozen in an expression of shock, and it made Big Henry want to laugh, though he knew if he did it would hurt.

"So was there any change?" he asked, smiling painfully.

The boy looked at him for a moment, as if he had not understood, then tried to move to get his hand into his pocket.

"No, no," Big Henry said, "I am joking."

The boy stopped trying to get to his pocket.

"Do you think you could manage?" the old man asked.

"We must go to the clinic?"

"Good boy," the old man said and then he passed out.

Five neighbours helped him carry Big Henry to a taxi. The boy went himself to the post office on Lutterodt Circle where the old man's wife worked. A relative picked the girls up from school and brought them to their mother at the hospital of Korle Bu.

At two in the morning the woman returned to the house with the children. In the yard she found the boy working from the light of the kerosene lamps. Seven signboards were set out in the sand to dry, the eighth nearing completion. She was not an expert in these things, but they looked like her husband's best work.

"Have you eaten?" she asked.

The boy had not.

"I have not eaten also," she said. "I will try to find some food." And then she asked whether it would it be possible for the boy to stay over that evening. That what she really wanted was to let things be for just a while longer, and would that be all right?

And so the girls were put to bed, and the boy and the signwriter's wife ate dinner together at the dining room table, as the boy had many times with the family. They were both hungry and ate well. After the dishes had been taken away the boy went out into the yard and finished the remaining sign. He slept briefly in Big Henry's studio, and left soon after sunrise to deliver the signs to their owners, while Big Henry's wife watched from her bedroom window, since she had not slept.

By the time the boy returned in the afternoon there was little left for him to do. News of the signwriter's death had spread around the neighbourhood. The house was full of women. There were plenty of hands to take care of the signwriter's daughters.

And so the boy left the house. He walked into Adjaben Road, then turned into Nkrumah Avenue. He walked and walked, without a destination in mind, with his pencils and his notebooks, which over the next months and years he would fill with sketches and drawings, covering the empty space of every page, because unless he could see himself feeling—unless he could see the colour and the shape of things, their susceptibility to light and shadow, unless in some form he made them again—he couldn't believe they were there.

He wasn't going to be cheated. He wanted the world on his own terms.

For what?

To redeem it. To forgive it. To hold it to him. To laugh at it. Kick it in the teeth. Cry with it. Tell its story.

The path he took brought him down to Jamestown, past the old department stores, broken down to their grand steel frames, cracked bricks and boarding, with their backs to the cliff edge. He walked onto the beach down the rotting cliffs, to which the houses clung. Past the fishermen's boats, over the sand strewn with muck.

Then he returned up Kojo Thompson Avenue, past the Grand

Market and the bus terminus, through the crowds fighting and fight-ing, with each other, with the world, to sell their batteries and fruit and caps, their plastic bags, their secondhand clothes, their electrical parts, their children's toys.

As he walked an old beggar, a bundle of rags covering a man, pass-ing in the same direction, began talking to him. In his broken mouth the words slid around like mud and stones.

"I cannot understand you," he said to the beggar in Ga. The beggar began to speak in broken English. The boy could not tell whether it was an insult or a mistake.

The boy tried Twi, the local dialect. But the man insisted on reply-ing in English.

The boy felt hatred well inside himself. Hatred of the man. Of his own inability to understand the man in his own language. Of the squalour and struggle and meanness of life around him.

He wanted to be out of it, he wanted the quietness and the empty space and the slow light air that he'd known from before, from another time of his life.

"Which country are you from?" the beggar asked in English, his voice curling with scorn.

The boy noticed that all the beggar's teeth were missing on one side, from incisor to molars. His tongue flapped over the gum.

The boy had to get away.

He ran, breaking left to escape the man, down the road he had just passed, before the beggar could make even the smallest grunt of departure. He ran towards Castle Street, along the side of the road, risking traffic all the way down Tudu Street, and almost knocking down a bystander at the corner of the vegetable market.

EDDIE SIGNWRITER

THE YOUNG SIGNWRITER stands in the door of his shop, surrounded by his paints and his boards, looking out over the yard.

It is 1996. He is twenty years old.

In the shack to his left, the locksmith is grinding keys. His eyes are pinched as he works, and there are fine specks of copper in the sweat of his face.

To his right, the shop of the stamp maker is empty, though the shutters are tied back, and pages flip over in an open receipt ledger.

The prostitutes are still asleep in the wooden lean-tos opposite, their boots on top of their zinc roof. The washerwomen have left some time before, and the passageway is wet with soap and water from the clothes they have pounded on the concrete.

From the street, which is joined to the yard by an L-shaped corridor, come the sounds of the neighbourhood. In the pavement market outside girls are selling banku and rice from pots on their heads. The barbers sit in the shade of the trees playing checkers as they wait for clients. Further on there is a school, painted yellow and gray, from which the children's distant voices drift like birds, and next to that are the stalls of the petrol bootleggers and mechanical-parts merchants.

All the while the locksmith has not stopped working, although he knows he is being observed. He lets a few moments pass, then lifts his eyes towards the young signwriter's shed. He can see nothing in the darkness of the doorway, though he can hear the signwriter in the creaking wood, shifting on the balls of his feet.

"It's a fine afternoon to be doing God's work," the locksmith says aloud.

There is no response.

It does not surprise him. They are all used to the signwriter's ways.

The locksmith's grinding wheel begins to slow. He removes his key from the vise, passes a steel brush over its new edge, and holds it up to the light for inspection. Then he slips it into a small brown envelope, on which he carefully writes some words, sits down and begins to hum.

More than a minute has passed before the signwriter's voice comes from inside the shed: "A fine day," it says.

The locksmith raises his eyebrows—this is more than the sign-writer has said to any of them in a while—and he smiles.

Though the signwriter is part of their small corner of the district, his neighbours rarely see him and speak with him even less. What they know about him can be summed up in a short conversation. The length of time he's been there: around eighteen months. The trade name by which he goes, painted above the lintel of his door in simple block letters: Eddie Signwriter. That his business is brisk. That he always pays his rent on time. That he grew up outside the country. That his Twi is not altogether fluent. That he lives with his uncle. That he has no friends. That some people say a young woman has been living with the two of them—him and his uncle—for at least a year, though nobody can remember seeing her.

Most of his time, when the signwriter is not away painting, he spends inside his shed, with the door closed and the windows hinged, sometimes into the late evening, well after the prostitutes have woken up and gone off for the night's business, and the stamp maker, the locksmith, and the washerwomen have gone back to their homes.

Though often he will come out for a few minutes just before closing time. He'll sit on the bench outside his shed and mix paint in a tin with a stick, or write in one of his notebooks, or sometimes simply sit there with no clear reason other than to say by his presence that he is the signwriter and this is his shed, and to share with his neighbours, in the way he is capable, their company.

It is a gesture they appreciate. And because of it, they have grown protective of his awkwardness. They speak kindly of him. They do him favours in his absence, often taking messages from clients, slipping small pieces of paper under his door to let him know who has come by.

And so he is largely invisible in the life of the district. When he walks through the streets, he does so unnoticed. He is not distinctive in his looks. When he changes out of his painting clothes, and moves about with his distracted shuffling stride, he looks like any labourer, tired after a day of lifting heavy things for little money.

His signs, however, are famous across the town.

Sometimes his lettering is crisp and precise; other times loose and flowing, as if twisting itself from the paint. His figures, especially the women, are full and fleshy, like ripe fruit. In his painting he is playful. He hides jokes in his backgrounds, or tells stories across multiple commissions, with the same characters advertising hair braids here, or a telecentre there. And because he can paint excellent likenesses, his clients often find images of themselves, or of local personages, featured in their signs.

Though he never signs his paintings, everyone knows when a new one has been commissioned.

His mural of the child under a sofa.

The man in the mirror shop, torn in two by his own reflection.

The preacher woman, welcoming people to church, robes flowing down her body, rich and purple like the colour of a ripe bruise, her arms thrown back, a great generous smile, as if all her teeth are for sale, her eyes two joyful asterisks.

A giant mattress for a bedding shop, floating out on the sea, two figures seated on the fully made bed, their feet distorted in the still water, each looking away.

People will walk across a suburb to see such murals and signs. Children will stand on the pavement in groups. Old ladies will pause on their rounds. And dogs will be beaten if they try to piss against the walls where his latest work has gone up.

Some think he must have grown rich from his signwriting. If it's true, he doesn't show it.

"The money comes into your hand for something," he says. "You must know how to reward that money," and he continues to work hard, and live his modest life, without anyone knowing much more about him than what they see.

IN THE FIRST LETTER he received she wrote that she hoped he had not forgotten her so soon, and that he still thought of her from time to time, and that he didn't mind her contacting him again.

In his letter back he apologized for not responding immediately. He said that he was sorry for the trouble he must have caused her. He was sorry about what had happened to her aunt. He hoped she could forgive him, and that she was with people who cared for her and that she was happy.

In her response to his letter she said that she did not blame him, and that she never had. She said that it was a great sorrow to lose her aunt, but the sorrow in fact was for a loss that she'd suffered before Nana Oforiwaa died. She said that she lived with elderly cousins in Kumasi. That the conditions were quite poor. She said that she'd lost a year of her schooling, but had started her final year again at St. Margaret's Convent School for Girls and that she had graduated. She said that she was working as a seamstress for a woman in the church.

Again he apologized for the delay in his response. He wrote that he was not surprised that she had finished school, and that she was very smart, and that he hoped she would continue to study. He himself had never been one much for learning, but it did not stop him from admiring those who were. He told her that he lived in Accra with an uncle and that he still saw his mother and his brothers and sisters, but the things that had happened had brought shame upon the family, and it was difficult for them to accept him now, and that it was fairer to them to stay away. He said that he had a job, that he enjoyed it, that it paid well enough, and that it meant a lot to him to be able to make for himself and depend on nobody.

She sent a photograph in the next letter. She'd cut out the image of herself from a larger photo, from which he could make out that she was sitting at a table with a group of people. She was looking beyond the camera, a little to the left of the photographer, a pensive smile on her face. Her long delicate hands were folded calmly, the one over the other. She explained that the picture was taken at her workplace. She said a few words about the people she worked with, who were connected to the church in various ways. She said they were kind, but that they were all much older than her. She said that most evenings she returned to her cousins' house, and that after dinner and prayer they went to bed early, and how boring this must sound to him, who was living in the capital, and did he like it, and did he go out a lot?

In his response he said that his job allowed him to move all around the city, which gave him the opportunity to know it very well, and that in fact he loved it. He said that from a distance the city all looks the same, but that every area was different, and because of his job nobody bothered him much and he saw a great deal, and that, in fact, was what he really wanted to do—to see the world, to see what was in it. He thanked her for the photo. He told her that seeing her photo reminded him of the crazy things they had done together. He said that he hoped it was not wrong to look back on those times with some fondness, which he could not help doing when he saw her face again. He wished her well. He told her he hoped that she too could take with her something good from the past.

In her letter back to him she thanked him for his kind words. She hoped that he did not mind her speaking openly with him, that her instinct told her not to, but she could not stop herself. Yes, she too thought about the past. Sometimes with happiness, and other times with sadness because it felt to her as if she had been cheated. If he'd loved her then, why had he not tried to contact her, or at least send her word, or in any way enquire about how she was? She knew that the time they had been together before probably did not seem significant to him now—now that he had a fancy office job and was a man about the town, but it had been significant to her. How could it not? She apologized if she sounded angry, and assured him that she was not, that she didn't want anything from him. Only it was important for her to know that what meant so much to her meant as much to him, or *had* meant as much to him. "Your dear friend," she wrote, "Celeste."

His letter dated 13 June, which he sent after three months of silence, read in full, "Dear Celeste, are you well I hope you *ARE* well. I am wishing you a very happy birthday for 3 July. I never say the right thing, I don't do the right thing either, to you or anyone but my intentions are good. Edward."

The letter contained a photograph of the side of an office building, on which there was a one-story-high mural. The lettering at the top read: "Selma Flowers, party decoration, travel agent. Best Deal." The image of the woman in the mural, holding a large bunch of red flowers, and dressed in an orange boubou, was unmistakably that of Celeste that she'd sent him in the mail, down to the last detail—the uncertain smile, the upturned chin, the same faraway look.

In her letter back to him she thanked him for the most beautiful present anyone had ever given to her. She said she kept it with her always. That during breaks at work she took it out and looked at it. That she looked at it before she went to sleep. She said he did not need to answer her question. She understood. She too had been overwhelmed. Had done as she was told. Did they try to make him feel ashamed? Well, he shouldn't feel ashamed. She had wanted it. She had wanted everything. She was telling him, and she still did. Did he?

A month later he sent a single business card inside an envelope. The card read: *Eddie Signwriter, painter of sign, purveyor of art.* Underneath was his address, and a telephone number. On the back of the card he'd written, "You choose."

THE DAY SHE ARRIVED was a Tuesday. It was the afternoon, warm and humid as a wash rag, just another day in a string of other days, and then there she was as he came down the street, sitting on her bag on the pavement on the corner.

He dropped his box with his paints. They fell on the curbstone, where some of the colour spilled out, so that every time they walked past that spot they remembered—how he'd run, bounded towards her, so fast that she took a step back, and the force of him swept her up, and momentarily she felt, in the closeness of his embrace, herself disappearing.

He held her a long time, her head tucked beneath his neck. He smelled her hair. Felt his collar grow wet from her tears.

He put his hand over the side of her face, her eyelid, and ear. He felt the warmth of her head in his hands, the warmth of her tears over his fingers, and suddenly all his past uncertainties and anxieties and regrets dissipated, that he'd felt even to the minute he'd seen her as he rounded the corner.

What were these things compared with the immediacy of a human body? What was more real than the physical sensation of holding Celeste in his arms? And in that moment he heard his own voice saying to him in his head: *This body will redeem me*—because that's what love can do if you only do it well enough. Love can make amends for anything.

Then, smiling, he held her out to get a good look at her.

She sniffed, lifted her chin, letting him take in the features of her newly adult face.

The curving eyes.
The cheekbones of her aunt.

SHE MOVES into the house. For a week he doesn't work. They lie in bed all day, smoking and talking, and having sex. To leave her for half an hour to go round the corner to the shops is unbearable. What if she's not there when he gets back? But she is. She's gotten up and is walking around naked—not a sheet about her, not a piece of under-wear, not a hint of shyness. She turns and looks at him. Her tummy curves outwards gently like the back of a spoon. She has a pout on her lips. "What?" she says, laughing. "Stop eating flies." His mouth must be open. He goes to her. Lifts her up from the ground, one arm under her knee. Her body opens up like a pod.

CELESTE, in a maroon dress, comes out of the door of the house in Adabraka and moves towards the gate in the low fence. She walks briskly. Full figure beneath the loose dress. A fold of flesh already between back and upper forearm.

He stands in the second-floor window—shirtless, square-faced, with closely cut hair, skinny, sharp-shouldered, ribs showing through his chest.

Celeste holds a straw bag, which she is swinging, causing the large wooden bangles on her right hand to slip down over her wrist.

Upstairs, cup in one hand, toothbrush in the other, he shifts his weight from his left to his right hip.

At the gate Celeste raises her arm so that the bangles slide back down her forearm. She puts the empty straw bag under her arm and begins to unfasten the gate.

Still at the window, he turns his head into the room. Somebody is calling him from another part of the house. He shouts over his shoulder—a vein in his neck strains—then turns back.

Celeste, standing at the gate, is looking down the street.

A foot back from the window, invisible, he follows the direction of her regard as he brushes his teeth.

Celeste turns towards the house and waves.

He spits into the glass and wipes his mouth with the back of his wrist, puts the brush in the glass, and the glass on the window sill.

Celeste begins to walk to the main road. She stops to speak to a street seller on the pavement. She buys two loose sweets, unwraps and eats one, and puts the second, together with the wrapper, into the bag.

He steps forward towards the window, palms on the sill, leaning, his forehead against the window pane.

Celeste gets to the end of the street, turns into the main road, then is gone.

He watches the empty street, for a moment rubs with the palm of his hand at the smudge on the pane left by his forehead against the glass.

He draws the curtains, locks the door. Waits to hear his uncle leave.

The things you want are easy, Nana Otoriwaa said.

He undresses.

Sits on the bed.

SHE LIES across a chair, reading a newspaper. He watches her. He looks at the way her jaw fits into her neck, how smoothly the bone flows into its soft curve.

She, the bare room with their few scattered things—what more can a human being expect of the world?

But by the afternoon an uneasiness comes over him. They have not talked of anything all day. Has she nothing to say?

Restlessly he watches her as she lies on their bed on her stomach, reading, kicking her ankles. He goes to the window, pulls aside the curtain. It's still there, the street, the houses. Little girls in their best dresses stand with their mothers, waiting against a wall facing the road. Older children, nearing an open shopfront blasting music into the street, turn a few steps of their lazy walk into a dance. A woman is asleep on her bench beside her table of oranges.

He turns back and looks at her. The clam of her. Where is she when she's so silent?

"Knock knock," he says.

"Who's there," she replies absently.

His uncle, on his way to Farrar Street, comes by.

"Aren't you kids going to go out to do something?" he asks.

"Hello, Mr. Ankrah," Celeste says, turning round from her stomach, then sitting up on the bed, smoothing her skirt over her knees.

"What do you want to do?" he asks her hopefully.

"Nothing," she says. "This is just fine."

She smiles.

He smiles back.

But *nothing* is not enough for him anymore.

In the evening he gets her to come out.

They make their way uptown. The electricity is out. People move about with candles sheltered in the palms of their hands. The weak flames trace their slow, careful journeys through the side streets, along the pavements through the dark.

When they reach the main road the cars are driving slowly, their headlights pushing shafts of blunt light through the dust.

"It's nice walking with you for no reason," he says.

She squeezes his arm—they are intertwined at the elbow and his hand is in his pocket as they walk.

He wants to believe that the gesture means a deep, silent understanding. But he knows that it doesn't. All that it means is that she loves him.

"You make me very happy," he says to her. "I love you very, very much."

He means every word he's just said. But at the same time he feels sick with unhappiness. Something has happened. How, why, he cannot tell; only he knows he cannot forgive her the distance he feels between them. Her absence. Her insubstantiality.

Sometimes when they sit together he feels a need to touch her, to assure himself that she is there, assuage the sense of loneliness that he often feels in her presence.

It isn't always like this. But as soon as he senses it might be, he finds a way to force the moment. Why? To prove it again to the part of himself that doesn't want to believe it; that tries to convince him that nothing is wrong.

And to show it to her.

Look, he is saying, *you see.*

He doesn't want to be alone in his misery. He wants sympathy.

"I love being outside at this time of night," he says with a gentleness he is trying hard to feel, "I love the people coming out to sell things, and the pavement becoming a completely different place. Going along is like being caught in the sea. And I love the smell of the smoke, in the cool air. It's like pieces of smell floating."

She squeezes his arm again. But it's not what he wants. He wants her to say something.

"Don't you think it's lovely?" he asks.

"Yes," she says quietly.

"What do you find lovely?" he asks, looking straight ahead as they walk.

They go on in silence, the two of them winding their way along the pavement, like people going somewhere.

Her hand drops away from him as they approach a telephone pole in the middle of the pavement, to walk on either side. When he reaches again for her as they pass the pole she refuses to take his hand and bursts into tears. She turns into a side street that will take them home another way—an empty alley pervaded by the smell of food and shit. He runs after her, gets alongside her, and walks with her in silence.

How dare she cry, he thinks to himself angrily.

As they approach the busy main road that runs parallel to the one they've just left, he grabs her by the shoulders, and he looks at her face that is covered with tears and he says, "Stop crying like this. Why are you crying?"

She says, "I am crying because I can't just walk with you enjoying myself. I have to think a thought for you. I can't bear it."

As he looks at her he is filled with tenderness and remorse. He hates himself for making her fail him, for letting her realize it. And he's struck by the reality of her, and the fact that she feels what's she's feeling so strongly, and he forgets about his own despair.

"O love," he says, "I'm so sorry. Let's do something nice. Let me buy some food to eat and go stand by the bridge."

And he feels that there is no more uplifting a feeling in the world than the strength of the love he has for this woman, as her sadness disappears, and they laugh and have long conversations of gentle teasing and private words and jokes—intimate and meaningless, though now he doesn't want meaning anymore, he wants love.

On a wall near Amaamo he paints a bed, floating out on a great flat gray sea.

He is lost. But not in the way he expected.

He did not wake up one day and find that things were different. What happened is that he woke up one day and found that things had always been different.

The past was gone. Their stories had fled.

His, of a boy falling out of love with the world, who loved a girl instead, and how that would save him, except it didn't.

Of Celeste's he has no idea—and worse than that, doesn't believe he ever did.

And yet the thought of being without her fills him with terror.

How is that possible? To be empty, yet full of love at the same time?

〽

Late at night, after painting, he comes home. She is lying in bed, her eyes closed. He can tell she is not asleep.

"Will you wake up?" he says, gently shaking her shoulder. He wants to talk.

About what?

His day. A story. An idea he had.

She tells him she wants to sleep. They can talk tomorrow.

He tells her he hasn't eaten, leaves the house to buy food at one of the kiosks on the pavement outside, and as he walks in the street again works himself into a quiet rage.

When he returns she is sitting up in bed.

He begins to feel ashamed of his impetuousness. He tells her he's sorry.

She tells him it's all right. She tells him she loves him. She makes an effort to ask him the questions he has wanted her to ask, to show the interest he has wanted her to show.

He kisses her on the forehead and turns out the light.

He comes to bed himself after she is asleep.

In the night he dreams of endless machine movements—not really dreams; more like flimsy images flashing on a screen. The next morning he realizes he is awake, and an image is clearing itself from his head, an image of his hand writing a letter (the words are written backwards, as if in a mirror—a secret message to himself), "Please let me go," and because the message is in his dream, he has to fall asleep again and then return to understand the story.

In his dream they are meeting, except both of them are different people meeting for the first time. Only he knows who they are. And while he is enjoying the prospect of falling in love with her all over again—as he saw her jumping over a puddle in the rain— he hears his own voice calling out to him, and it wakes him up, saying, "You cannot go back," and he hears his mind thinking, *Please let me go . . .*

He thinks to himself: *You know what I'd really like to do?*

To find a calm spot on the sea somewhere, even if he felt a bit lonely, and to look at the waves and read the book that she gave him on the first night they made love—the book he read the beginning of on the beach at Labadi, while she played woaley with a small child sitting next to them on the sand, and the storm clouds drew in, and he'd thought to himself, *If I try really hard will something of me stay here forever?*

Outside the morning starts. He is fully awake now. She continues to sleep. Lying beside her he reflects how unremarkable this feels. To have lost everything. To feel nothing.

The same twenty-four hours pass. The same breaths and exhalations. Nobody, to look at him, would know a thing.

Her waking disturbs his reflections. Instinctively he turns to hold her. She tells him she has not slept well. She does not want him to touch her. She is irritable. She looks for a long time at the ceiling, and then turns to look at him. He reaches out to her with his hand. He can feel the tear coming out of his left eye.

She says, "I know that look."

"What look?" he asks her.

"The look you get when you overhear a conversation that makes you reflect on something about your life. Something sad."

"Please let me hold you," he says.

"Why do you want to hold me?" she asks with irritation.

He looks down towards the foot of the bed, where their clothes are crumpled on the floor.

He tells her he doesn't want to hold her anymore.

She tells him not to be mean.

He says he's not being mean, he's just saying what he feels: that he wanted to hold her, but that now he doesn't want to hold her anymore.

She makes him tea. She's making an effort. They move around their rooms, the two of them, washing, eating, cleaning, as if the air were thick as water.

She smiles at him lovingly, thoughtfully, reflectively, as he smiles at her sitting at the table.

Love. Emptiness. Emptiness. Love. And so on and so forth.

||||||

Early one morning his uncle opens the front door of the house and finds him asleep on the step. A dried trail of spit has stuck to the side of his face, drained down into a puddle of light that's congealed around his head.

His uncle looks down at the body curled up at his feet. He prods his nephew with his foot. His nephew complains under his breath, then sinks down again into sleep.

His uncle steps back into the house and closes the door.

Inside a faucet is opened. The plumbing begins to rattle in the walls, then falls silent with a growl.

A kettle whistles.

When Festus Ankrah opens the front door again his nephew is awake, sitting up. He is rubbing his eyes.

"Take this," Festus Ankrah says, handing him a cup of tea.

"Thank you, uncle," he says. He takes the mug and puts it down on the stair beside him, and continues rubbing his eyes.

His uncle steps over him, avoiding the steaming mug, moves down the path, then stops. He stands in the sun, blocking the light, his hands in the small of his back, and stretches.

He watches his uncle.

"How did you sleep?" Festus Ankrah asks without turning around.

"Not well, uncle," he says softly.

"No," his uncle says, though he's already thinking of something else—of who he has to meet and what he has to say and what he has to do, and his nephew knows it.

Festus Ankrah begins to walk now down the path to the gate. He says, "The second time she won't forgive as easily as the first. Less so the third time."

"Oh, she'll forgive," he says from behind his uncle, with an unexpected vociferousness, so that Festus Ankrah thinks for a moment that his nephew may still be drunk, and pauses in his stride—though only for a moment.

"All right," Festus Ankrah says and closes the gate behind him.

He sits on the stairs drinking his tea. Between two sips he cranes his neck up to the window of the bedroom.

The things he says to her are sometimes terrible.

That people were right: that they killed her aunt. They were both of them murderers, and how did she feel?

It's all of it unforgivable, but he cannot stop it.

He leaves her crying.

Where does it come from, this anger? He does not know.

There are things he could tell her, he says.

"So tell me," she says, but he can't.

She calls him a stinking drunk, but he hasn't drunk a thing. It's anger that makes him slur his words.

She says, "What did I ever do to you?" and she's right.

"You? Nothing," he says, dismissing the fact of her rightness with a wave of his hand. "It's not your fault."

And then she does the worst thing she can: she forgives him.

It's her greatest strength, but to him it's the worst of her weaknesses.

Spineless, he thinks.

But then what then is he?

And it's true.

"Life is a series of choices," the teacher had once advised him in one of their talks.

Yes, he thinks, *though not always your own.*

He steps out of his shed. He should have gone home but he's lost track of time, and now he is hungry.

He puts his hands in his pockets and begins walking up Kojo Thompson Avenue towards Farrar Street.

The faint smell of the open sewers hugs the road.

It is evening and the boys from the villages who have not yet found a room in the city are lying out on cardboard, in the light spread by the neon glow of the Integrated Bookshop sign, a radio between them, or no radio, but just their conversation. By midnight the pavements will be dotted with bundles of people, wrapped neatly in thin cotton sheets, too thin even for curtains, and the children of the hawkers will be asleep on benches, or against a wall, as their parents ply the night for an extra sale.

But he can sleep later, he tells himself.

He takes a seat on a bench of one of the many improvised pavement food stalls that line the street.

As he eats his meal, absorbed in thoughts, a man sits down beside him. His shirt is silver and its sleeves are black and he wears a wide flat ring with diamonds buried in its gold band like the rows of a shark's teeth. His watch chain hangs from his wrist like a bracelet.

"How do you do," the man greets the signwriter.

"Fine," the signwriter says, and they exchange nods, and he thinks nothing more, until the two customers seated on the end of the bench insult the man.

"Now what black man go break his skin?" the one asks, and the two customers laugh as if they are sharing a joke with the stranger, inviting him to laugh with them.

The two customers are well-to-do themselves. They wear nice clothes. The neck of the one slopes back into his shoulders from his skull like an escarpment. They're finishing up their meals, putting back the bones from the table onto their empty plates.

"In Ghana de black man be black," the other laughs, running the length of the dark skin of his arm with his forefinger. The skin of the insulted man is light, and in places patchy—by chemicals, parentage or disease the signwriter cannot say.

"Let's forget it wit' a drink," the insulted man says. From his language it is now clear to the signwriter that he is Nigerian.

"No, you keep your drink, friend," the one customer laughs, and getting up wishes the Nigerian a good evening.

"Where you come from in Nigeria?" he asks the man after the others have left.

He can't tell whether the Nigerian is humiliated or disconcerted—he's keeping it all behind his face. But his gold looks as rich on him as it did when he sat down. Nothing has been stripped from his body.

The Nigerian's answer is short.

The two men drive by in their 4x4 with its tinted windows and chrome. "You have a good evening now," the one laughs, waving out the driver's window.

He leaves the Nigerian to his wounded silence, which eventually the Nigerian breaks by telling the small boy serving at the table to bring him water.

"I beg gimme dat ting," he says, pointing.

The small boy brings the cup and the plastic packet of water, jiggling like silicone.

"Put in da glass," he commands the boy with irritation.

The boy doesn't seem to understand. The Nigerian takes the bag in his teeth and tears the corner off, then hands it to the boy. The boy fills the cup with the water.

They sit in silence.

Behind them on two tables on the pavement the cooks prepare food. One cleaves chicken carcasses through their ribs. He cuts the leg in two, freeing meat from the joints. Embedded in the flesh the shards of bone shine like stones. The other cuts salad. A woman with a black shirt and an apron stirs the mixed vegetables on a gas-fed wok.

The Nigerian starts talking to her in tones he cannot quite make out. The flames hover under the pan.

The Nigerian turns to the boy and asks whether the woman is his mother. They talk a while. It is not clear what he is saying to the boy, but he can see the Nigerian is forming a confidence. The boy smiles.

The Nigerian makes parting words with the woman and leaves a tip.

"I de go now," the Nigerian makes a point of saying to the signwriter as he leaves.

He watches the Nigerian turn the corner into an unlit passage between the stalls.

He hears a voice, his own voice, talking to him: Anybody you meet on your way is your angel, it says.

‖‖‖‖

One afternoon he climbs up on a wall to paint an open, primed section. But the ladder is unbalanced, and begins to slide, and though he steadies himself the brush slips as he does, leaving a misshaped, panicked scrawl across the wall to where he got his balance back.

He climbs down and inspects the damage.

A scribble, a mess, though he can fix it simply.

He begins to work around the error, filling in space, adapting the shapes he's left, and as he does, the attempt at recovery begins to take on form. The possibility of a figure appears. An arm, a head turned sideways.

And he suddenly has a feeling, as he balances on a chair on the tin roof where the scaffolding won't reach, of being accompanied. That in all this madness, the swirl of survival, he is not alone.

That maybe the world is still with him.

The world talking back at him through his own shabby gift.

Nine in the evening. He's alone in his shop, the door open. A fresh breeze is up off from the sea, that clicks together the pods in the tree that overhangs the prostitutes' shed.

This week he has a big commission—a billboard for Makola Circle, so large he has to do it in pieces, spreading the panels over the yard and painting by night.

Lamps, their wicks cut long, stand all around, on stones, on the low wall beside the stamp maker's shop, thinly illuminating the panels spread out over the ground. Black smoke flutters upwards from the flames like string.

Everyone's gone, the daylight city folded up and put away for the night.

Inside his shed he's mixing paint, pouring turpentine into a tin to thin the pigments. Beside it his brushes soak in a jar.

The boards outside have the forms drawn on, ready to be filled in. He's painting a road safety advert. His brief is a car, driven recklessly, striking a pedestrian.

As he pours and stirs the mixture the fumes from the tin make his head feel light. The nerves in his brain throb behind his eyes.

He tries to calculate how many panels he can get done by four a.m. How many by five?

He wonders, *What time can I get home? Seven? Eight? Will Celeste be up? Will she fight me, or be kind?*

He brushes the thoughts from his mind, and without thinking rubs his eyes, which immediately begin to sting.

He runs to the tap, scoops the water onto his eyeballs.

The room starts to spin with the motion of his hands flapping against his cheeks. The bottles on the shelves want to lift into the air, the doors unhinge and shift to another wall.

Try to own what happens, he thinks in a familiar voice.

Thinks, or hears?

"Who said that?" he says aloud.

Nobody.

Nothing.

The paint.

"Are we not all responsible for our own actions?"

He sits down on the bench beside the wall.

"Isn't a person allowed to have a little need every now and then?"

He stumbles out into the yard. The cool air wraps around him.

Over the noise of the insects he hears the soundtrack of a film from the open-air Rex cinema, the people's laughter, the catcalling of the young boys, the women trying to hush them up.

He goes back into the shed and comes out with his tin and brush.

He gets down on his knees and begins to paint.

Faces first: the woman driving the car; the man and the girl in the back; the boy being hit.

He looks at his watch.

If the prostitutes come back around three or four, he thinks, then maybe he'll stop for a break to drink tea with them.

He smiles.

That will be good. They'll drink tea, share some food, laugh and chat—about neighbourhood gossip, local politics, the prices of meat and taxi fares, as each girl waits her turn for the bathroom inside, to wash off the city's muck from their legs and their mouths and their guts.

He starts eating more often on Farrar Street. He sees the Nigerian many times again before they next speak—arriving in a taxi, climbing out of other people's cars, always alone. The Nigerian's name is Ibrahim.

Ibrahim has grown familiar with the boy, who brings him a mug of mineral water with his chicken. He calls to the boy's mother and she comes to him, leaving her cooking. She wears a pair of gold earrings now with emerald-coloured teardrops.

The Nigerian never seems completely at ease despite the confidences he shares with the cooks. He eats as if he is alone. He never observes the faces of the other eaters, never shares in their conversations.

He always waits until a seat is vacant. If he arrives and finds the tables full he disappears down the road and returns once a customer has got up to pay. Or sometimes he will stand across the road and wait, taking a mineral as he cleans his teeth with a toothpick.

Only because the signwriter hears his own voice saying it does he know that the Nigerian has bought the place.

"Nigeria-man," he says one evening to the Nigerian, when the Nigerian takes his seat at a space at the table that has opened up; and he asks him to tell him what other shops he owns.

The Nigerian smiles. He tells the signwriter that he owns a shop called Awusi Unisex Beauty International in Asylum Down.

"I know it," the signwriter says.

He tells the Nigerian to come by his sign-painting shop in two weeks. He will have something for him, and he gives him directions to his shed.

The rest of the meal passes in silence.

It is all worked out—his escape. It's a simple plan.

He is to present the Nigerian with a sign for his shop, something very large and elaborate and expensive.

"What do I owe you?" the Nigerian will ask him.

"Nothing," he will tell the Nigerian, but that he needs his help.

And then the Nigerian will help him. He will put his ear to the ground. The signwriter will stop eating in Farrar Street. In a week the Nigerian will come back to him at his shed.

"There's a place for you," the Nigerian will say.

"Where to?" he will ask.

"Europe," the Nigerian will say.

"How?"

"Go to Dakar," the Nigerian will say, he has people there to take him onwards.

"And I must go to Dakar myself?"

That is easy. The Nigerian can get him the papers, connect him along the way. The way out is through Dakar.

No, stop . . .

He wakes himself in the middle of the night. His heart—is it his? This black, hard thing in the middle of him, cold and dark as a nugget of coal. What is he thinking? What is he doing? This is insanity. Is this just a dream?

This is a woman lying beside him, breathing. This is warm, loving flesh—this giving thing, this holding thing, this desiring thing, this woman whose face faces him, asleep on her pillow, her breath on his back—this is a human being.

But this was got dirtily and is therefore dirty.

No, he wants to say, *it is I who am dirty.*

He prays: *Celeste, whose name was taken down from the sky by men sailing the sea for money, be my guide. Wake up. Save me. Save me again and again and again.*

But what can she do?

He turns and puts his hand on her face.

"Hmm?" she asks in her sleep.

"Celeste," he says—he does not know what to say—"Celeste," he says. No more than her name.

When his uncle, returning home along Kojo Thompson, sees the smoke rising over the roofs towards the east, he thinks nothing of it.

He goes into the house and washes, and afterwards pours himself some milk and finds some cassava, which he's just begun to eat while listening to the radio, when he's disturbed by a knock on the door.

He looks at his watch. He is expecting nobody. On Tuesdays his friends come to pick him up for a night of cards at a chop bar they like in Nima. But today is Monday.

He gets up.

The person standing on the step is familiar, though he cannot remember from where.

Then he does—it's the locksmith from the shop next to his nephew's.

When Festus Ankrah and the locksmith get to the passageway off Tudu Street, a crowd has gathered. The concrete is covered in water. Some of the neighbours, the passersby, the local householders who all came to help, are wet from the water they helped carry and throw. One man whose shirt was once white is covered in soot.

The sharp, choking smell is unmistakable.

Festus Ankrah steps out of the car and goes up into the yard.

"It's a miracle only one shed was burnt," the locksmith says, trying to keep up with him.

"Yes."

"Praise be to God," the locksmith says.

"Yes, blessed be He," says Festus Ankrah dryly, under his breath.

The locksmith is right. The only shed to have burnt is the sign-writer's. The fire must have been very hot—probably from the paint and other chemicals—even if it was quick. The zinc from the roof is brittle as sand. It has caved in over the remains of a concrete wall at the back. The shack itself is a pile of charred beams, eviscerated tins, burst glass jars, nails and hinges. Smoke is still rising from it.

Festus Ankrah sees his nephew sitting on the steps of a shed on the other side of the yard, being fussed over by three women who look to be prostitutes.

He goes over to his nephew. The prostitutes step away deferentially, one about to smile though thinking better of it just in time.

"Are you hurt?" Festus Ankrah asks his nephew.

"No," he says.

"Is everything lost?"

"Yes," he replies.

His uncle puts his hand on his nephew's shoulder.

"I'm sorry," Festus Ankrah says. "Was it a lot of work?"

He shrugs.

Festus Ankrah, noticing that people are watching, withdraws his hand. He leaves his nephew and goes over to look again at the smouldering ruins. Already he's started to calculate in his mind the replacement cost, the lost hours of work—maximum, minimum, likely.

The locksmith comes to stand at Festus Ankrah's side.

"It was just after closing time. Many people were here. We got here fast," the locksmith explains.

"Where was my nephew?"

"He was here in the morning. And then he was away until . . . three or four. Where he went I don't know. I myself walked with him to the station. He was very upset when he came back."

"Thank you," Festus Ankrah says.

"Not a good way to end a bad day," the locksmith says.

"No," Festus Ankrah says, and looks back at his nephew, surrounded again by the prostitutes, with his head in his hands.

Late at night he lets himself into the room. The cloth is pulled across the window, but the light comes in in slants at the side. She has left the room closed for too long. It is full of the smell of blankets and dust. She's lying in the bed, beautiful and sleepy, and as he comes down to her he smells the scent of her body on her shoulder blades and neck. It is a very intuitive motion to sit beside her and stroke and touch her head.

Since the fire he has been strangely calm. Not a cross word has passed between them.

He asks her how she is.

"Fine," she says, *"now."*

He carries on stroking her head.

He says that things have been bad between them.

She says that she knows.

He says that it is because of him, and that he is sorry.

She says that she too is sorry.

He asks her whether she would be able to forgive him.

She sighs and turns over.

Smiling, she says that she might, and then, for just a moment, as he looks down at her, he believes that there is nothing more he needs in life than this beautiful girl. He believes he understands perfectly well what it is to be happy.

"Why don't you get into bed?" she asks him, and he slips beside her and she turns onto her front and he holds her with his arm under her stomach as they make love—she like shallow water that takes the weight of him gently like a boat.

"God, love," she says and falls asleep.

And as he lies there he calls on all his strength.

The next morning he is gone.

FESTUS ANKRAH

TWILIGHT. Tuesday.

The taxi turns off the main road just short of the town of Mamfi, onto a track through a field of grass. The single passenger steadies himself against the doorframe as the car rattles over the corrugations in the road, made by the rain, set by the sun.

A house, half-finished, emerges out of the mist, disappears.

Then they are there.

The sign on the wall says "Rolex Hotel."

The man gets out of the taxi uncomfortably. His shirt is damp with sweat. He isn't used to the ridge, the mist and heat together. Fifty kilometers from Accra, but it feels like another country.

The boy behind the desk asks him how long he'll stay.

"One night," he says. "I will leave tomorrow."

He signs his name in the register: Festus Ankrah.

From the window in his room there is nothing to see: the light is almost out now, the moon a dull stain, the mist covering everything.

Both single beds, with their loose slatless frames, are too uncomfortable to sleep on. He puts the thin foam mattress of the one on the floor.

He unpacks his clothes, undresses, and lies down on the floor between the frames of the beds. As soon as he closes his eyes he feels the sudden and strong urge to get up, pack his bags and flee the room, the hotel, the ridge.

Still he has time to catch the last bus from Aburi and be in his own house before morning. What is stopping him? The shame of running, as his nephew has run? The knowledge of what will be said if he does? Or fear of what awaits him in Accra, the accusation of his own empty house, where there is nothing to do but wait?

He lies on the mattress, turns towards the wall and waits for sleep to take him.

And then, as if on their own, his eyes snap open and he knows what is coming, this thing about to overtake him for the first time since his nephew's disappearance: anger—fierce and adult and raw.

His nephew has left. Pushed off. Why does he insist on imagining his nephew in his helplessness, as the victim of his own disappearance?

If I could only get my hands on him, if I could only grab him, hold him . . .

Hold what?

He stirs in his half-sleep.

"What have you done, you bastard?" he mutters under his breath, and sinks back.

Events of the last two weeks compete with each other for his attention like nagging children. Confused images shuffle over each other in his state of semi-wakefulness.

Since his nephew's disappearance his mind has been making a grotesque circus of itself. He is embarrassed by its need, its insistence, its unremitting self-accusations.

He closes his eyes.

This time it takes longer, but still it comes: the memory of standing in his nephew's room, before the empty shelves, Celeste, head bowed beside him, like a child confessing a sin. Again he turns away—he cannot help it: such deep pain disgusts him.

He opens his eyes, choosing consciousness over this.

To remember gives him some control. In his dreams he is at the mercy of himself.

Among the images to return, despite his vigilance, is the keening of his sister for the loss of a child she had lost so long before, of a child that was never hers. While all that he could do was to sit, as that sound came from her throat—beyond comfort, beyond rationality, an animal sound, until he couldn't sit anymore and went to stand in the garden while the neighbours came running past.

"I told you," she said, she gasped, "they shamed us all, and still you gave them a home."

Later, before his visits stopped, before he could no longer bear them, came the outrage. The mad, dangerous, uncontrollable outrage he saw in his sister's eyes.

"How was he to know?" he pleaded. How was he to know anything about his nephew's past? Though he knows that he did, even if nobody ever told him: about Celeste, the accident, the woman found upside down in a stream, and his nephew to blame because of his indiscipline and selfishness.

The family tried to hide the details, in particular the names; but the girl—he knew it the moment he saw her, when his nephew came to him; knew it the day she arrived at his house.

And now they are both gone. First the boy, and afterwards Celeste.

She could not stay. She knew it first, and saved him having to ask her to go. All through the evening on the day that his nephew left, Festus Ankrah sat on the lower verandah, smoking cigarettes, while above him, from the room she and his nephew had shared, he heard the sounds of her packing.

Then she came down and stood at the door. Her bag was at her feet.

"I'm going, Mr. Ankrah," she said.

"I know it," he replied, turning round, but he didn't get up.

She came over to the chair where he sat.

"I'm sorry," he said.

She stood there, the light breeze blowing her dress round her legs. Then she picked up her bag and went down the path and turned towards the main road.

Only once she was out of sight did it occur to Festus Ankrah that she hadn't told him where she was going, nor where to find her when his nephew returned.

Wednesday morning.

Festus Ankrah lies on his mattress, the last traces of his dreaming still vaguely in him—singing, the sound of singing, his nephew's singing . . . *Something, something*—some phrase, a few words of a song—and then it's gone.

Daylight is outside. Sounds and voices filter in, of workmen in the fields, a steel grinder, girls' voices, children coming from a school.

It looks like a sugar in a plum. Tra-la-la—that was it, what his nephew used to sing. Everyone knew the *tra-la-la* was stupid, old-fashioned, totally misplaced, but still he sang it, he liked that bit best, the voice inflected with irony.

The thought reminds Festus Ankrah how they used to sit, all three of them together at the beginning. Celeste and his nephew would talk, and it was talk of the small things, the words quick, overlapping sometimes, happy, he guessed. And when his nephew finished a point, or thought he'd got the better of Celeste, he would sing it, tapping the last refrain on the table with his fingers.

But his nephew had been at the house less and less, that was true. He and Celeste would eat together, mostly in silence, and the door would not open with the boy coming back from his work.

Though Festus Ankrah noticed it, he had not asked. His nephew was there, his nephew wasn't there. That was the deal.

It looks like a sugar in a plum . . .

Were there other signs? Probably there were—something that might have been caught early—not by him, that he knows, but by somebody else, more—he looks for the words . . . connected to the lives of other people.

In Adabraka, in the days after his nephew disappeared, people actually stopped outside Festus Ankrah's house—two or three a morning, standing outside the gate, looking; he saw them as he came and went.

They said, "That is the house."

They said, "It happened there, a boy who turned from his people lived there, and this is important, listen to this: It's a terrible thing to lose a child, nothing more terrible. And there he goes, coming and going—the one who lost his child."

And even the area boys stopped and stared, who drugged and swindled and stole, but still had cousins they sent through school, and old people they housed, and gave at the end of the month. No matter how tough, there was always some woman who'd brought them into the world who could beat them over the ear, and there was nothing to do but take it.

And he was the one who lost a child.

He wants to hate his nephew for it—for changing him into something defenseless and despised.

He tries but cannot.

And instead he hears the refrain in his head: *It looks like a sugar in a plum. Tra-la-la*—and what does that mean anyway, these words snatched away from somewhere into his living room? If he could only understand them, the little secrets to those passing, lost moments . . .

At half past six he sets out on the walk to his appointment, declining the waiting taxi parked outside. Still the mist is everywhere.

He walks for ten minutes through the field. The taxi passes him before he reaches the main road. Then he turns left toward the town. He crosses a bridge over a valley, the stream beneath hidden in deep vegetation. He passes a series of old bungalows on his left, weathered and bleached, doorways open, through which he can see right through to the open back doors, to a papaya plantation falling down the other side of the hill.

To his right a sign indicates the driveway to the school, though it's more like a road, which disappears through a gate, down a hill and into the mist.

A group of children approach from the other direction.

"Is this the way to the school?" he asks them.

The children take him on a shortcut through the bush, that crosses a stream, and passes up the side of a hill. They arrive through a plantation of bananas at the main administrative building.

He is taken to the teacher's office and is asked to wait. The window has a view of an expanse of grass, the open hall, and behind it the jungle climbing up the hill.

His trousers are wet up to the knees from the leaves brushing against him. His shirt has come up in patches of sweat. He puts down his briefcase, the handle of which has been digging uncomfortably into his hand, removes his jacket and goes to stand by the window so that the breeze will dry his shirt.

The teacher arrives at seven fifteen. He walks with the sharp, confident movement of small men, his arse like two ball-bearings at the top of his short legs.

They shake hands, exchange greetings, and sit.

The teacher says, "Although I am aware of what brings you here, as custom demands we must go over it again, to refresh our minds about those things that have already taken place."

Festus Ankrah smiles, but not with his eyes. He has related the story of his nephew so many times he no longer needs to think as the words form on his lips.

As he talks the teacher is struck for the first of many times by his solid features—the block of his jaw folded firmly into his head, the massive face, fortress of a face, the careful eyes. He thinks: *So this is how a face can carry such a thing*—though what had he expected? he asks himself. A brand upon the forehead?

"On the first day we had reports of him at Tema station," Festus Ankrah is saying now, "of taking a bus west. There is nothing more from there. I have been to Tokoradi myself, but there are so many cars on that route, and nobody remembers him there. He could have stopped anywhere on the way and changed direction. I do not know where my nephew has gone, or why. All I know is that he has gone."

"And the girl?" the teacher asks. "It's just that your nephew—he mentioned her, when he came to visit me. I thought . . ."

Festus Ankrah appears momentarily surprised. "They say she has gone to her family," he says. "She could not continue where she was."

"No," the teacher says reflectively, "so,"—he seems to be clearing his mind—"anyway, it is good you are here."

"Thank you for offering to help," Festus Ankrah says without the least trace of gratitude in his voice, just a weariness that flattens his sentences into monotones. "Thank you for letting me come here."

"No—it is not that I am letting you do anything. It is not up to me. When I heard your nephew had left—and then you called. There was too much to say for a telephone conversation, even a letter."

Festus Ankrah's eyes remain fixed, the expression of his face unreadable.

The teacher hesitates before he continues, is about to express his regret, to ask about the circumstances, but decides against it.

"It is thirteen days now since your nephew disappeared?" he asks.

"Yes," Festus Ankrah replies.

"Then it was two days more before his disappearance that he visited here. It was a Monday. He came to talk with me. He did not tell you before . . . ?"

"No," Festus Ankrah says, "I only learned from you, but now that I know I am not surprised. That Monday was not a good day for my nephew. After he came back his shop burnt down. All his work was lost, and his materials."

"Do you think there is a connection?"

"I don't know what to think."

The teacher does not speak, but nods his head, as if deep in thought, as if he has forgotten the conversation, and the man before him with whom he has shared it.

"Mr. Bediako, it has not been a long journey here," Festus Ankrah says eventually. "Still, it has been tiring."

"Yes, I'm sorry," the teacher says. "Well, it was brave of your nephew to come back here. I'll say that. After what happened. It was a very short meeting. In one car, out on the next. He must have been back by midday."

"What did he want?"

"To talk about the past, Mr. Ankrah. Except we didn't. He lost his nerve and left."

"Why did he lose his nerve?"

"I can only guess."

"Then guess."

The teacher smiles momentarily at Festus Ankrah's curtness, but it's not the right thing to have done. The face gives nothing back.

The teacher says, "I think he was ashamed."

"Why?"

"For getting caught up in regrettable circumstances. For losing his way."

Such talk angers Festus Ankrah.

"But I see you have your own views," the teacher says.

"I hope my nephew had more sense than to feel responsible for the death of that woman," Festus Ankrah replies, then moderating the harshness in his voice, "—Celeste's aunt."

"Celeste's aunt, yes. She and I were friends," the teacher says.

"I'm sorry for your loss," Festus Ankrah says, "it was a tragedy."

"It was," the teacher says.

"But it shouldn't be my nephew's tragedy."

"No," the teacher says.

"But people blame him. They blame him for his rebelliousness."

"People say that," the teacher responds softly, "but that wasn't what it was. Rebellion takes anger. Your nephew wasn't angry. Not then, at least. Maybe now he is."

"What was he then?"

"What was he then . . . ? Thoughtless. He was . . . without thought."

"And so you think he should feel ashamed," Festus Ankrah says scornfully.

The teacher says, "No. And so I think he *is* ashamed."

There is no response from Festus Ankrah.

"But your nephew was young," the teacher adds. "I should have told him that when he came. He wasn't in charge. But now he has left. So who knows, maybe now he is in charge."

It is moments before Festus Ankrah feels the first flush of anger. *I am being played with,* he thinks. Just as, deep down, he knew to expect. Because everything that ruined his nephew started here, in this place; because it cannot be anything else; and because after fifteen days of nothing there cannot be more nothing.

"I must find my nephew . . ." he manages to say.

"Your nephew did not come here to leave directions, Mr. Ankrah," the teacher says before Festus Ankrah speaks again. "If anything, he came here in order to be understood, if he knew it or not . . . That is how the young are, even today," he says gently now, "—wanting our approval even as they defy us . . . See, your nephew and I had a friendship. I knew him well—I mean I took an interest in him—how well can one know a person, after all . . ."

Still nothing.

"Maybe all I did was to be here, to be a witness. You see? And witnesses are storehouses. *I* am a storehouse—for your nephew. A place to leave things. And people always must come back for the things that they've left—this is what I have thought."

"I did not come here for my own pleasure," Festus Ankrah says, raising his left hand. "All I ask is that you tell me what my nephew said and I will be gone. His family is suffering. We are all suffering. We want to find him. Help us if you can. If not . . ."

"How?" the teacher says. "How should I help you?"

Festus Ankrah is standing before he knows why, his chair scraped back, his hands on the table. "Where is my nephew?" he says. His voice is raised, just short of a shout. He is aware of the door opening behind him, then closing quickly.

"Mr. Ankrah," the teacher replies calmly (but it is not the calm of self-possession; it is as much an instinct of defense as the other's rage), "please, remember it is you that has lost your nephew, not I."

And perhaps the teacher has started to say something else, but already Festus Ankrah is putting on his jacket. He feels the sweat rising to the surface of his body. He feels the panic pressing in around him, stifling him in his clothes. He feels his breath struggling in and out of him, his collar round his neck.

Now the teacher's voice is saying something to him—no, it is not the teacher's voice (Festus Ankrah is on the stairs now), it is the secretary following him with his briefcase, calling out his name.

And then he is outside again in the fresh air, his briefcase in his hand, standing on the gravel path leading to the main road, and he looks back: the school building, whitewashed, pristine, standing out against the hill.

He breathes deeply.

He stands and breathes and gathers himself.

A small child in a uniform, walking past, greets him, shoes polished like wet tar, head like an acorn.

"Wait," he says, before he can stop himself, and stifles his voice in a cough as the child hesitates—wait, he wants to say, wait, but forgets what he wants to say.

WHEN FESTUS ANKRAH returns to the hotel the proprietor is waiting for him. The guest book lies open on the desk. The proprietor makes a show of consulting it as Festus Ankrah enters the lobby, then addresses him without greeting.

"Do you really think you will find your nephew here?" he says coldly.

The hands of the clock behind him on the wall are broken, Festus Ankrah notices, the hour hand marooned between twelve and one.

"No," he replies, and neither approaches the proprietor, nor retreats, but stands in the doorway where the voice had stopped him, until the proprietor turns into his office without further comment.

Only when he's back in his room, standing beside his bed, does Festus Ankrah realize how unready he is to bring his nephew home. How a man cannot find what he does not know.

FESTUS ANKRAH spends most of the afternoon in his room. He is afraid to go out. What a scandal his presence must be here. His own surname has been no disguise. Everyone knows who he is. Everyone wishes him ill.

Hunger, at last, makes action necessary.

He enters the village, passes the roadside stalls made of palm branches, and the brick and tin metalwork shops surrounded by their scrap, and then he is in the main road.

All along the heat is on him. He feels it on his neck. It pins his damp shirt to his back. His eyes scan about him as he passes the taxi rank, finding out the water sellers who crouch in the shade of a stone wall, tying water into plastic bags.

They look back impassively as their fingers work the knots, hidden by the lip of the blue buckets from which they draw water.

Festus Ankrah slows his pace but he does not stop. He would rather go thirsty than have to ask for anything.

In a restaurant overlooking the empty tables of a market he eats chicken and watches the children fetch water in buckets from the hand pump at the market gate.

The evening has begun to draw in when he steps out of the restaurant. The air is cool, the colours deepening. When he sees the teacher standing on the other side of the road waiting for him he feels no surprise.

"And still you are here," the teacher says, smiling, when they are standing together.

The teacher's clothes are crisply ironed, and unwrinkled. He smells of soap, smells cleaned, prepared, everything about him fresh, a man for whom leisure is a thing to dress for, not a thing to be taken idly.

"Well, I have not yet left," Festus Ankrah replies.

"You mistake me. I am glad you have stayed."

Festus Ankrah clicks his teeth and looks down the street.

"There's an hour still until the light is gone," the teacher says. "I have ordered my car. Come. It will be good for both of us," then turns and begins to walk without waiting for Festus Ankrah.

The taxi is parked further up the road, in the shade of a ceiba tree. The engine startles into life, then purrs as they approach. Purple blossoms lie on its yellow bonnet. It has been waiting some time.

They climb into the car. The taxi driver looks over his shoulder at Festus Ankrah before they pull off slowly toward the gate. The teacher turns his head and stares through his reflection in the passenger window.

The houses, as they pass, hold the pale, uneven light of paraffin lamps. And then they are out of the town.

They pass along the road that links Akwapakrom with Aburi and beyond. Stretches of forest give way to the intermittent fields, steeples rising beyond them from the banana and palm and mango trees—stone churches built by the Anglicans, brick and tin churches of the Methodists, their windows empty, their roofs thin as gold leaf; and beyond, a hinterland of villages and hamlets, remote from modernity, from electricity and the telephone.

"Where are we going?" Festus Ankrah asks.

"To Daisy's," the teacher says, and when Festus Ankrah does not respond, "Nana Oforiwaa's rest house."

They travel on in silence.

"I guess it isn't hers anymore," the teacher says a few kilometers later, "though it hasn't yet become someone else's. Somebody bought it up but still it's shut. Sometimes tourists find their way up there, the ones with old guidebooks," and he laughs.

Short of Aburi, at the bottom of a dip in which a stream flows over the road, they turn off and climb slowly up the flank of a valley until they reach its crest and a row of buildings built in amongst the trees.

To one side of the road, rising between a few low clustered dwellings, stands a water tank on five steel legs, reinforced by a web of steel struts and bars, around which creepers have wound their way up to the cylinder, where small blue flowers, and the red of the rusted steel, show between the leaves.

To the other side, where the land begins to fall away sharply, is a two-story structure, its back to the road.

The car comes to a stop and they get out.

The teacher crosses the road toward the building, Festus Ankrah following closely behind him. A low wire fence separates the house from the road. A gate leads down two steep stairs directly to a doorway.

The teacher steps off the road, a level down to the path that circumnavigates the structure.

There are claw marks in the plaster where a bougainvillea has been cut back, though it covers half the wall, and at least two small windows. The place is still neat, though dereliction hangs about it.

The teacher pauses briefly before the door, then walks round the rest house.

Festus Ankrah follows him. The two men climb onto the verandah, from which the land falls away steeply, and below them stretches a wide valley, out towards the horizon, where the distance sews the fields to the sky.

A naked light bulb hangs like an exclamation mark from a wire swaying from the ceiling in the breeze.

"Someone should really polish this floor," the teacher says. Cracks have begun to appear like spider's webs in the concrete.

"This is where your nephew came every day. Right here where we're standing was a restaurant. Just behind you, your nephew and I and Celeste and Nana Oforiwaa used to take tea. Right here, in this space, where we are. It's nothing now, but once it was grand. There was a chef that Nana Oforiwaa brought in from the kitchens of the Hilton Hotel down in Accra. The menu was written in English and priced for tourists, except for one sentence in Twi: sixty per cent discount on request."

Festus Ankrah turns and looks down into the valley. Sunbirds dart through the branches of the giant trees at the end of the plot like ticks.

"This is a beautiful place," Festus Ankrah says. "It is a pity that the memory of my nephew is so unwelcome here."

"As you said, the people blame him," the teacher says, "but that is because they are afraid of what else to blame."

Festus Ankrah's silence is an invitation to continue.

The teacher says, "They are afraid to blame Nana Oforiwaa, although they know they should. People saw. They knew. How she was careless of her duties. Forgetful of her position. They want to blame her for her carelessness. But since they also love her, they can't, and so hate your nephew more."

The teacher stops. He examines his hands, the soft light flesh of his palms.

"And I too feel something of that," he says, his voice soft now, "even if I was something of a party to it. . . . Nana Oforiwaa, she was obsessed with those children. I see that now. She always wanted to be near them. She seemed so strong but really she needed other people."

"For what?" Festus Ankrah asks coldly.

"Why do we ever need other people?" the teacher says, but knows himself, as the words come out of him, that the question is far more easily evaded than answered, just as he is evading it now.

But what would he say if he had to say?

He tries to think what he thinks.

That he himself had wanted to confront Nana Oforiwaa. That he sensed in her a danger, he sensed in her a desire to own, a covetousness, though what she coveted he could not quite tell. That he wanted to stop her, but did not know what to stop her from.

"Why are we doing this?" he wanted to ask, though always he knew the response he'd receive: Why are we doing *what*?

And then he would not be able to answer, because there was no answer that did not incriminate him as well. After all, had it not all happened on his watch too? Was it not he who brought the boy to the rest house in the first place, and soon every day? It was under the supervision of both of them that the children left together, it was both their authority that the children were allowed to defy—the long disappearances, the immunity to school timetables and routines, the silent shaking off of discipline, the known immoralities.

"Your niece . . ." he gathered the strength to say one day, after they'd seen the children disappear together into the long grass near the southern fence of the rest house, where they would not be able to follow.

Nana Oforiwaa had cut him off: "And your student."

It had sounded more harsh than she'd intended. She attempted quickly to reassure him, taking his hand in hers, as she had months before on the evening on which they'd made their decision to leave the children to their affair, without so much as speaking a word.

"Life is so empty," she had said at last, as they'd stood in silence, the wind going through the grass, and then she'd turned away.

"But that is how we know when it is full," the teacher had replied.

"Yes," she said, "but I am not sure that for us it will ever be full again," and began the long slow walk back to the rest house where more than three years later the teacher now stands alone with the uncle of that boy.

"But come," the teacher says, turning to face Festus Ankrah, "now you have seen this place. It is the scene of many times that were happy in your nephew's life. Here, at least, your nephew *was* happy."

Festus Ankrah seems stuck for words.

"You say," he says at length.

"I do," the teacher says, and stepping now towards Festus Ankrah, "so let us try to leave as friends."

Festus Ankrah takes a step back himself.

The teacher says, "What is it?"

"The way you talk," Festus Ankrah says—hesitates—"what you say, but don't. It makes me fear that something very wrong has happened here."

The teacher says, "That is nonsense. Now you sound like the people we have talked about. The ones who blame your nephew," and Festus Ankrah, seeing the shadow of a smile pass across the teacher's face, knows he's been outsmarted.

Without another word he turns and makes his way towards the car.

The teacher watches him go, then walks to the edge of the lawn, now long and mixed with stray plants.

Hands in his pockets, shoulders squared, he looks over the valley, remembering how from up here he and Nana Oforiwaa had sometimes watched the storms approaching from a distance. First the smell, then the diagonal sheets of rain, then the darkness coming from all around.

Though on the day that Nana Oforiwaa died the sky had started clear. The sky had been beautiful, completely unaware of what it soon would become.

THURSDAY MORNING.

Eating a meal of bread and jam and coffee at the small table under the window, Festus Ankrah faces the prospect of defeat. Why is he here? Why has he stayed? His nephew is gone. Nobody here can help him find the boy. Would they, even if they could?

He thinks: *What do I know? What could I ever know? How much more than the daily acts of being me, not some other me; what more can I claim as my own?*

Nothing? Or something yet?

He waits for the answers to come.

Something in between.

To have seen a place, lived a little in a place, know the shape of the land and the smell of the air, to have the same things inside you as somebody else—is this not also knowledge? Is this not also sharing?

He thinks of what he can do. What clues has his nephew left him?

Then he remembers the Presbyterian church and the reading room next door—the only place he can recall his nephew mentioning specifically from the days they'd lived together. They used to meet there—his nephew and Celeste, where all the children of the school used to get away to meet, on the pretext of needing to consult a book that wasn't available in the school's library.

He sets out to find it, and later that afternoon does.

To an outsider there is nothing grand about the church. But he tries to imagine it as people would in whose lives it is part of the daily geography: the prefabricated concrete fence, gray with rain and moss, the neat enclosed yard, the tall blunt steeple nudging the sky, with its clock face like a child's wristwatch.

And then the rain strikes, and he realizes how caught up in his own thoughts he must have been not to see it coming.

At the first gust people scatter, heading for cover. People are shouting, calling each other toward shelter, laughing at their helplessness in the rain, at the rain itself, but no one calls to Festus Ankrah, and nor does he expect it.

Still, he too starts running in the direction of the plantation and the hill down which he'd come on his way earlier in the afternoon— not because it would make a difference to him now, but so the people do not see him walking and know why.

When he reaches the plantation he stops running. The sand has turned to mud, but the stones and gravel keep the path firm, and he makes his way slowly up the steep hill, the steam now rising from him, rivulets about his feet and the deafening sound all around as the rain pounds on the trees and bows the palms and gathers and flows down the fleshy stems from the reservoirs of the banana leaves.

He's heard it said, but now he knows for himself the suddenness of the weather in the hills. He'd seen the clouds come over, hard, blue-edged, then the sky turn to milk, though still he thought there'd be an hour or so in it. But with hardly a warning the storm had come in—just a single gust of wet choking air before it hit.

So now I know, he thinks—how easy it is for somebody to be caught in such a storm, to lose their footing on a muddy river bank, to fall down the side of a hill, to strike a rock with their head and drown.

By now the rain is streaming over him, warm to the skin as long as he moves. He can feel the suck and release of the soles of his feet against the leather of his shoes as his feet lift from the ground.

Steadily he makes his way on through the rain. The gradient of the hill is now in the muscles of his thighs, and the back of his throat is raw and tastes of copper, and he concentrates on maintaining the rhythm of his walking so as not to think of either.

At last he nears the bungalows that separate the plantation from the road. He can see it fifty paces above, with a fine mist of raindrops dancing on the macadam. When he gets there he will turn left, and by that route return back to the hotel. This is what he is thinking when a voice calls out to him.

"This way."

It is a woman's voice, an old voice.

He stops, and when he stops the rhythm of his walking is broken, and it feels as if he can go no further. He looks to where the voice has come from. He stands beside a balcony, closed on three sides with the fourth open to the alleyway. In the dim light cast by the fire lit in an old liter tin, he can see the shapes of people. He approaches, and as he does, his eyes adjust, and he sees that it is only one person—an old woman, sitting on a concrete bench built into the back wall.

"I am saying you should come this way from the rain."

He hesitates. He thinks: *I can be in my room in twenty minutes*—but already he is climbing up the stairs. As he does it occurs to him that he is not doing this for himself at all, but for the woman, whose voice seems to want his presence. He thinks how absurd it is—it is merely an offer of kindness, the tone of asking a formality—and how absurd he is. And how he really wanted to say no, but somehow feels a responsibility to a stranger who seeks to give him shelter.

As he approaches he sees that the woman is not alone. She is seated, and a child stands against her knees, and a dog the size of a sack of potatoes lies with its back to the burning tin, warming itself, asleep.

The woman nods at him.

The bench is L-shaped, and Festus Ankrah takes a seat facing the woman and the child. The woman, watching him sit, gestures to a piece of cloth on the balcony wall.

"Use that," she says. As Festus Ankrah turns to take the cloth, she nudges the fire in the tin closer with her foot so that he can share its warmth.

He dries as much of the water as he can from his skin and clothes and hair, looking up from time to time toward the woman. He wants to catch her eye so that she can see he is grateful, to acknowledge her kindness. But she has turned her body and is looking away, and seems to be caught up in her own thoughts.

He draws the cloth around himself. It is heavy, and under it he begins to feel dry, and he waits to feel the heat of the fire. The truth is it is good to be out of the rain.

Then the woman moves, and Festus Ankrah thinks she will turn to him, but she does not, and she begins addressing herself to the child. She whispers in his ear, and the child smiles, and she strokes his head, and looks out the side of the portico beyond Festus Ankrah.

The sound of the heavy rain carries on around them.

The dog, finding the heat gone, turns its head, moves closer to the fire, looks lazily for a moment at Festus Ankrah, then closes its eyes.

"Thank you for your kindness," Festus Ankrah says at last.

He sees the shape of the woman's face turning toward him.

"I am thanking you," he says, speaking a little slower.

"It is just kindness," the woman says.

"Nonetheless," he says.

"To keep a stranger dry in the rain is not difficult," she says.

It is a dry voice, drained of intonation, tired, Festus Ankrah thinks, with harshness near its surface.

The evening has begun to gather in now, and he tries to see his watch in the light of the flames. The light is too weak. He stretches his legs out and feels the warmth of the tin in his shins. He sits back and lets the heat rise into him.

He looks at the woman's face, mostly covered in shadow, though the light catches her eyes. He sees momentarily an absence in them that makes him uneasy. The gratitude he feels dissipates at the thought of being in the presence of somebody who might not be in full control of their faculties. He feels stupid for having responded to the asking in her voice. He wishes now that he'd kept on walking. Perhaps he will start again soon.

He has already considered the conversation with the woman over when she speaks again.

"Kindness becomes easier with age," she says, and it is as if by saying it the harshness goes out of her voice, and there is kindness in it.

Festus Ankrah turns toward her again.

"I have found it the opposite," he says cautiously, but the woman evidently has said her piece, and does not respond.

The child standing against the woman stirs. He cannot be much more than three or four. His arms are propped against the woman's legs. His face is quiet and it has an expression of drugged contentment. His eyebrows rise like two gentle hills, and the milk of his eyes is as white as linoleum.

Noticing that the child's attention is fixed on him, Festus Ankrah smiles. Caught in his observations, the child retreats into the woman's embrace. Her fingers move across his chest at the pressure of his movement as if they have a life, an intuition of their own, and Festus Ankrah looks away.

"You are not old," the woman says.

"These days I am very old," Festus Ankrah replies before he can reconsider the wisdom of exposing something true about himself in the company of a stranger, just because it is true.

"No, I have seen you in the town," the old woman says, and there is wiliness now in her voice, "I know who you are."

That the woman has knowledge of him surprises and unsettles Festus Ankrah.

The woman smiles. The child moves in her embrace and she leans forward. Festus Ankrah can see her clearly now, her head, smooth as a coffee bean, covered in a black scarf only a few shades darker than her skin. Her cheekbones stand out through the loose skin under her eye sockets like solid balls of meat, and her mouth is as wide as a scythe, and seems to cut her face in two.

"All I say is you are not old," she says.

When she talks it is as if her mouth peels back to let her teeth and gums speak. Her face moves in expressions of wonder and concentration, as if she were telling a story to a child, or confiding a wonderful secret. "As for me," she says—her hand falls onto her chest—"me, I know my full account, before my God I do. Everything now is in its place, everything now is over; the shape of everything—it has all happened—this tree is now forever, rain is now forever, ground is now forever," and she pats the stone bench with the flat of her palms. "Nothing now that happens gets added to the past. It makes a person free. Everything just . . ." and she brings her palms together, and opens her fingers like a flower, "—unfolds." Then she brings her fingers to her mouth, and her laughter is like the laughter of an embarrassed girl, coy and uncertain.

Then Festus Ankrah is no longer afraid. *This woman is mad,* he thinks to himself, she can do him no harm, and how little it would cost him to give her her moment, and not turn on her, as he has on others who have shown him less kindness.

"Do you know something?" he says. "Do you know something you want to tell to me?"

To be able to ask the question fills him with a sense of control and strength he has not expected.

"I know."

"What is it?" Festus Ankrah asks.

The old woman does not respond.

The child, seeming to sense the change in Festus Ankrah's tone, becomes restless, and turns towards the woman, who in a single quick movement, lifts him into her arms and lays him across her lap.

They sit a few moments in silence in the rain.

Then the old woman says, "When a child does what he is not supposed to do, he suffers what he is not supposed to suffer."

Festus Ankrah finds himself unable to respond, though he knows the proverb.

The woman looks at him, and for a moment there is knowingness in her eyes that unsettles him. Her mouth creases in a shrewd smile. Then the whole expression unknits.

"To look a person in the eye who does not know themselves," she says, "you leave your own image in them. And children do not know themselves. They are all the same child in that."

Then she looks down to the child in her arms, who has fallen asleep, and she places her hand over his eyes, and cannot be made to say another word.

IT IS NIGHT on the Akwapim Ridge. Night lies over the fields, holding them close. Night holds the towns and the churches and the steeples in its soft fist. The bells of the churches are muffled in darkness, the taxis huddle in their ranks like birds. In the houses and the shacks, in the villages and the boarding houses and seminaries and under the trees in the open, the people are asleep, the only light is the moon's exclaiming O, and the stars, like sand scattered on a dark mirror.

Waking the owner of the hotel gives Festus Ankrah some satisfaction. For more than a minute he stands on the step of his house, set a small distance from the hotel, pounding heavily on the door with his fist. A light comes on, the sound of footsteps approaching the door.

"What do you want?" the voice says.

"Open your door," Festus Ankrah replies.

The door opens. The hotel owner stands naked but for a towel around his waist. As the hotel owner strains to see, the creases of his squinting eyes knot the whole lower half of his face, drawing his top lip from his teeth like a snarl.

Festus Ankrah smells of wet clothes and fire smoke. The hotel owner stares at him, says nothing.

He is going, Festus Ankrah tells him. First thing in the morning. No breakfast, just the bill. And something inside him laughs like a child as he leaves the hotel owner standing on his step and walks back out into the night.

Back in his room he begins to pack his bags, and when he is finished starts to straighten up the room.

But once he has moved the beds and furniture back into place he finds he cannot stop. With water from the barrel in the bathroom, soap from his basin, he cleans the tables, the bedframe, the window sill where the mosquito coils have burnt into black ash. He gets down on his knees and sweeps dust with his facecloth, wrings it out and shines the floor.

It is ridiculous, he knows—the pleasure he takes from removing by himself the signs of his habitation in this place; but he takes it nonetheless.

And as he works into the still early hours of the morning, his mind begins for the first time since the discovery of his nephew's disappearance to turn to other things. Loose strings of memory, unrecalled for many years, and unrelated, fire behind his eyes—a conversation in the street, a young person who exists now only in his head, something said in an immigrant bar on another continent, in another life—so quickly, though, that all he is sure of is the act of memory itself, while the thing remembered is lost.

How fast it has all been, he thinks. The passing of all that time. The endlessness of experience, of things happening. Endless because it never stops, though it's over the moment it's happened, too fast to store, pitting the body, pitting the pits of the body. Like trying to catch the rain—that's what it is.

When he finishes cleaning the room he undresses and lies on the bed with his hands on his stomach. He feels the rhythm of his body moving in the palms of his hands.

For the first time in almost a month he feels the ability to endure what he cannot control.

The muscles know it first.

An easing in the neck's stiffness, in the weariness of the heavy frame. The ache of constant vigilance leaving its ghost in the joints. Nothing is true that the body does not feel, nothing is true that isn't verifiable in the flesh. So that when the knowledge comes the flesh is where the body knows.

And then he sleeps, and later wakes, and he senses without having to open his eyes, the square of dull light at the window.

He tastes a sourness in his mouth—cigarettes and food and not enough sleep.

He draws comfort from the physicality of his own body, these things that are truly his. The pain in his muscles and joints, the cramps of his digestive tract.

In the hotel lobby Festus Ankrah recognizes the boy behind the counter as the same who signed him in on the evening of his arrival. He does not wait for the boy to count the money he hands over in two envelopes. He slings his bag over his shoulder, and leaves the hotel for the last time.

The boy lifts his eyes to see him pass through the door, his lips moving silently as he counts the notes.

No car waits for Festus Ankrah to take him to the taxi station. He walks the shortcut through the grass to the edge of the town, avoiding the turn-off to the school. Is there something to regret in spending time in this place without having established the smallest connection of sympathy, of kindness? If so, he cannot find the place inside himself in which he feels it so.

Arriving at the station he walks past the taxi rank where cars for hire will take you single-drop down the escarpment to Accra. He heads for the tro-tros. The noise surrounds him—of baggage carriers, and hawkers, drivers and touts. He throws his bag to the baggage boy on the roof of the car, then takes his seat in the back of the tro-tro, and stares down the steel tube through the window. A child's shoe hangs from the mirror, flags and stickers are arranged on the dash. He waits for the car to fill.

A large woman with chickens in a reed bag squeezes herself into the seat in front of him, sweat lining the creases of her flesh. A man takes two sleeping children onto his lap. Three boys take the front bench, talking loudly. The driver saunters over to his cab and leans against his door, while his tout takes his place in the open sliding door, slaps the top of the tro-tro with his open palm, and shouts out in his clattering, treble voice, "Accra-cra-cra-cra-craaaaa!"

Then passengers waiting in an emptier car are hustled unwillingly into the worst remaining seats in the tro-tro. The fares are passed from seat to seat, overhead to the driver. Change passes back. Now the hawkers start hustling round the windows, passing up bread on dustbin lids for forty cedis, water in plastic bags, nuts in newspaper cones, plantain from the forest, oranges, eggs, ice cream, sodas. Prices begin to fall as the engine is fired and the tout jumps out of the car, slams the door shut and slaps it one more time with his hand.

Then the car begins to move over the stony yard of the taxi station. The head of Festus Ankrah, wedged in the far-right seat against the side, begins to rattle and jump against the window. But he feels nothing. Already he has been asleep for ten minutes, and will not wake up until the shuddering of the chassis finally stops in Tema station, and the driver leans over him, holding his bag, telling him this is no hotel, and to be now on his way.

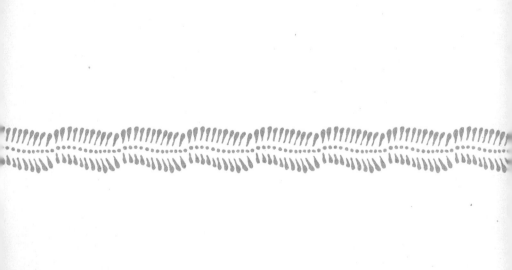

THE TEACHER'S WALK IN THE NIGHT

THE TEACHER, from the back of the taxi rank, observed Festus Ankrah climb into the tro-tro. As he made his way back to the school he heard the tro-tro sound its horn. He withdrew to the side of the road, and from inside a shed housing a small provisions store, saw the vehicle pass by on its way towards Peduase Lodge, and the winding path down to the plains that stretch all the way to Accra.

The teacher returned quickly to his quarters. He poured himself a glass of water, then went into his study and closed the door. He sat down at his desk, where less than three weeks before he'd been sitting after classes and had heard the voice of the boy downstairs for the first time in years, then the familiar sound of his whistling—a new tune, but the same tone, the same lips pursed around the same needle of air.

The teacher had looked up, then returned to his work, as he heard the sound of the boy mounting the stairs, then the footfalls reach the landing outside his room. The boy was at the door. The teacher had looked up a second time, then finished the sentence he'd been writing in the margin of the paper open before him, beside the pile of forty at his right hand, bound in faded pink ribbon, and eight at his left hand.

"Strong point," the teacher had written. "Compare Okonkwo with the bureaucrat in Ayi Kwei Armah." He had assigned the paper a grade, closed and placed it on the pile to his right, taken another from the pile on his left, set it squarely before him, sat back, and waited.

Then the door to his study had swung open and the boy stood on the landing, an expression of stupid satisfaction on his face, and challenge in the posture of his man's body, and the teacher had felt the dryness in his throat but had not swallowed, because he had not wanted the boy to know the dryness in his throat, and mistake the swallowing for fear.

As on that day, so on the day of Festus Ankrah's departure, the teacher stayed in his room. Towards evening the old woman who tended the house knocked at the door to announce that she was going home. There was no response. On the other side of the door the teacher sat at his desk, surrounded by his papers, though now he paid them no attention. He'd long since lost track of where he was, what he'd been reading. For a long time he'd been thinking. But now he just sat. The visit of Festus Ankrah had disturbed him more than he'd thought. Now the teacher felt the beginning of a fever. His skin was wet, his muscles alert. In the room he was sitting at his desk, but inside he was crouching, did not know whether to run or wait. Run or wait. Run.

Wait . . .

How the time had passed he could not say. But he knew—when the old woman knocked on the door, and a minute later let herself out—that he could not spend another moment there. That he too had to leave the house, had to walk, though where . . . but in a moment he knew.

Unsteadily he lifted himself from his chair, stepped round the table, descended the stairs and swung the wire door open. The sun had already slipped down the ridge, and rested beneath the horizon. It left a cool afterlight, that deepened colour and slowed motion, and even the shallowest objects were lengthened by their shadows. He felt the coolness of the hour against his flesh, the temperature of his body rise to meet it, dampness on the bare skin. The first signs of sickness announced themselves at the end of the nerves.

In front of him the forest rose up the side of the hill. Everything not leaf, vine or trunk was a contourless wall of darkness. Sounds came out of it: the ubiquitous undertone of crickets, a sharper trill, a sound of birds, three deep plumbing notes repeated, like a stone reaching water from the bottom of a well. A little further down the path round his yard the water tower rose three stories into the air, and the wind rustled in the reeds growing at its base as tall as a man, in the mulch of water-logged soil.

Then he passed round the side of a series of storage sheds and up onto the main plateau. The school buildings were spread out to one side: the administrative offices, a square of lawn, the whitewashed slatted cabinet of a weather station raised on tall legs. To the other side he could see the road that would take him down towards the town. Ten minutes' brisk walk would get him only to the gate. If he didn't hurry he'd get there after dark.

He walked faster. Breathing was like breathing through a wet rag. He felt the cold jewels begin to form on his forehead. He clenched his teeth against it. *Not yet,* he thought, and immediately the words fell into the rhythm of his strides, became part of his walking—*Not yet. Not yet.* A little further. A little further from the town. And then it was as if the part of his body with which he was concentrating had begun to think on its own. Not something foreign inside him, but a version of his own voice, which the sickness had drawn out, lifting the silence off it—exposing the nerves, all the channels in the brain ready to receive experience, only a little dusty, but not sealed, not grown over, not healed.

I am choosing to do this, he reminded himself—only it was the voice saying it: *I am choosing to do this. I am choosing.*

Though he knew in fact that all along he had never chosen. That already, in those first weeks at the rest house, all those years before, when it first started, already it had been happening a long time. Already it had a direction of its own, a steady pull, taking him along, taking them all along. Yet there must have been a moment, when the four of them sat together, and the boy looked at Nana Oforiwaa and the teacher looked at the boy, and then the boy looked at him, and they all knew what they knew. There must have been a time when someone first started it. A first tacit consent. A first *I-will-not-stop-you.* Before words became impossible, and nothing could be acknowledged, and anything could happen, and did, and the strength of that silence took hold, and still held, all those years later, when the boy returned and still he could not accuse the teacher.

Accuse the teacher of what? What was taken from the boy that he did not give himself? Are we not all responsible for our actions? Although it had not been necessary to use these words. The boy had not returned to the ridge for recrimination. Anger did not drive him. Not after the first show of confidence, which melted away in a moment at the teacher's first gesture of kindness.

It had been too easy for the teacher to absolve himself, at least while the boy was there. Although only at the end of the boy's visit did the teacher know what it was that he'd come for. What the boy needed was for the despair inside him to be released. Because that was what the boy was full of—not anger, but despair.

And he could have given it, the teacher knew, and thought to himself now as he walked. So easily he could have given what the boy wanted. Except when the moment came, he couldn't. When to himself he'd said it a thousand times before, the teacher could not say it to the boy, who—too weak, weakened by being so vulnerable to this man—could not himself ask the question straight out. And so in place of an apology, which the teacher had been ready to give, the boy asked for something else—an explanation. "Why," he asked, "did you not protect me?" "Protect you?" the teacher had replied. "Protect you from what?" invoking the things that could not be said, and so ending the boy's hopes, when what the teacher should have said—how he knows it now, and wants to shout it out—was that he did! *He did!* But in the end, too late.

Now the teacher quickened his pace. He came to the top of the path, to the gate, then turned right. A pineapple seller beside an electricity pole raised her hat to the teacher. He barely noticed, nodding just in time. A dog ran out across his path, and stopped in the road, yapping. Its jittering feet threw up a scuff of dust. Its gums were bared, its tail wagging. But he walked straight past the dog, and it scurried into the grass. The teacher strode on and the town fell away and then he was out of the town. The light was still deep but a little deeper, and the shadows a little longer, and the soft wind swished in the grass and lifted the branches on the palms with a crinkling, rattling sound.

The teacher's clothes fluttered around him, the wind picked up. The sky, a brief silver, began turning metal gray. The shadows began to draw in, closing vision down to a few barely distinguishable tones of blue and black. Soon the line between path and forest grew indistinct, and the teacher moved now by sense. The regular beat of his footfalls on the road, the sound of rubber against compacted earth assured him that he still had the path. He sensed the gradient through his tired ankles. Besides this, his shallow breathing, and his heart, beating its rhythm in his ears, against his forehead—not hard, not insistent, but *there*.

Then the forest started becoming the night. The small shavings of the moon's light lay on the path. Then the forest *was* the night, having dropped away either side into a ravine, and he felt the darkness, unencumbered by the wood and the flesh of vegetation, flowing across the path.

Now he'd arrived. He took a few paces onto the bridge. He stopped, let his senses sharpen. His breath slowed. He walked to the railing, let its weight support him. Somewhere in the darkness the sound of the river, in between the sound of the wind in the reeds. He leaned over, trying to see into the steep ravine. How weak the eyes in darkness, how useless. He could see nothing. Had it changed? In three years had it changed? His eyes were blind in the darkness. But his memory searched for the path leading down the side of the ravine, that traversed the slope almost horizontally, then turned, and passed beneath itself in the other direction barely two meters below its last pass, and two meters above its next. He remembered the wet grass growing over the track. The treacherous slipperiness of the stones. And somewhere below, after the precipitous winding, a leveling off, and a softness underfoot, made of the leaves' mulch and the sheets of fern.

That is where he'd stood all those years before. He did not have to go there now to know. And in his mind he saw the rain coming down in slanting sheets, and remembers being surprised to see a figure further down the path, stumbling through the reeds—a shape he knew well. As he approached, wondering what she was doing there, he saw her lose her footing and slip, and go down on her shoulder, her left leg under her body. For a moment her face was in the water, water was flowing in her hair, as he made his way towards her, water shearing down around him, water rushing in the river at his feet. He saw her try to get up on one arm, but either it slipped, or she wasn't strong enough. Then she saw him. "O—John," she said, waiting for him to come and help. She let herself relax, shifting her body round away from him to untwist her leg, which was facing down the slope. The teacher crouched beside her. She felt his presence, familiar and safe, and the current flowing round his haunches as he got down, before it flowed round her. She waited for his touch—an arm under hers. But when it came it was not what she expected. Just his palm on the back of her neck, holding her. "John?" she asked, but had only time to ask it once, as her head was turned, and her face was in the water again. She felt a leaf catch against her cheek, and though she tried to move she could not. Then his other hand was on hers, stroking her wrist, and all she heard was his voice, telling her that soon it would be over, soon things would be back again as they always were, before the boy and her niece, what they'd made her do. "Shhh," she heard him say, "shhhh, Nana," and then the sound of his voice became the sound of the water, flowing against her head, and the calm settled round, and the darkness drew in.

MAN TRAVELING

K WASI DANKWA, setting out on his journey, slips out before dawn, leaving the house, unnoticed. During the night it has rained, and water has gathered against the street curbs, reflecting the gray sky. A child is washing outside a shop. A woman is sweeping the ground in front of her stall. Another day is about to begin in Tudu and Ada-braka. Another day is gathering, preparing itself, but when it comes he'll be long gone.

With a false name he gets the last seat on the bus to Tamale. His family will expect him to head west. So he'll travel north, to Ouaga, and then on to Mali, and in Bamako pick up the train to Dakar.

In the bus he sits up front, wedged between excess baggage and bags of rice. But in front of him there is only the driver and the road, and as the bus travels it feels as if he alone is pushing through the scenery; that the tangled forests are wrapping round him, the dense green hills giving way, the gray clouds rising up from the forest.

The bus travels on towards Kumasi, muscling its way through the village traffic, past road works, accidents, the carcasses of old accidents. Where the cars and buses and trucks bunch up, people appear from the forest and stalls are set up beside the road. Yams fry in skillets over flaming branches hewn from the trees on the sidings. Kenke is wrapped up in leaves, and bowls of chilies balance on the young girls' heads.

But after Afrancho the road begins to clear. The clouds begin drawing back and folding up, becoming a thin layer miles up in the sky. The land flattens, the trees start dispersing and the horizon reveals itself—pale blue sky, anticipating the dust and heat further north.

He sleeps the night in Tamale, above a shop near the market. Up at dawn, he catches the first vehicle north. The clouds are down again, but the earth is flat and dotted densely with trees. None of this he has seen before. As he travels through the morning he feels the strangeness of the land begin to surround him.

Then he reaches the border, and the car pulls over, and the people unpack themselves slowly from the benches, then stand at the side of the road as the baggage boys crawl over the roof, untying the possessions strapped to the bus, and throwing them down.

He waits his turn watching, twenty paces off, a queue taking shape in front of a shed, while small birds colonize the trees beside them, chirping madly.

From the other side of the shed, people with stamped passports begin making their way across the hundred meters or so of no man's land to the next border post. Dangerous-looking boys mill about, accosting strangers, offering their help, grabbing hold of bags and suitcases, shouting and altercating.

Looking dead ahead, he tries to make himself unnoticeable. And it works. Nobody approaches him. His passport is stamped and he moves on by foot towards the other side, where he joins a group of women traveling with small children, busy in negotiation with a taxi driver.

He can see a small mosque behind a tree on the Burkinabe side. A couple of dilapidated stalls line the street. He notices the small traders cycling lazily by, passing through the borders unhindered.

Then a second taxi pulls up. The women split up with their children, and he travels on with one group. They drive to the second border post and get out. From here on he will be a foreigner, connected to nothing.

And that is how it is, later that afternoon, as the streets of Ouagadougou pass by, and he thinks of his father, and chooses not to stop.

Four days more to Bamako—through Sabou, Boromo, through Bobo Dioulasso, where mango trees line the streets and for a night he stops, and sleeps in a room made from a steel transport container, in the shade of some trees in a mission yard.

Then on through San and Ségou to Bamako—towns and villages that pass from the back of a car in a haze of red dust, and the heat rising from the road—different cars, station-side hotels, the tightly packed bodies of different strangers.

In Bamako he spends the night in a dormitory bed at the Carrefour des Jeunes. A luxury of clean sheets he allows himself before the final leg by train to Dakar.

This is the part he has heard of from before. Everything before Bamako is just the beginning.

HE GETS TO the station well before time. Already there is a crowd. He fights his way along the platform and onto the train, through the other passengers, well-wishers, through ambulating vendors, beggars, hustlers, touts, con artists, pickpockets, and into the seat of a third-class carriage. The appointed departure time approaches, then passes. The crowd continues to mill about. The carriages fill up. Baggage is stowed. People settle in for the journey. Then the sound of a whistle and the first jarring shunt on the old rusty line. The city begins unraveling around the train, and soon the train is out in the country, and the soft weaving light comes round, and spirits the landscape away. Everything is still to come: Kati, Diamou, Kayes, Kidira, Tambacounda, Kaffrine, Guinguinéo, Diourbel, Thiès, Dakar. Outside the window there is only his own reflection, and that of the lights in the ceiling and the crowded bodies sharing meals, talking, settling down for sleep, a single shifting surface of flesh, but for those who've arrived too late, and are standing still and will for much of the next two days. The train picks up speed. Its movement is endless. Its voice constant. Sometimes a squeal, sometimes a whistle as of escaping air, and a lower, briefer tick—like a match catching; and then its main voice—a high-pitched whirr, like the sound of metal shearing through bone, until the speed is so fast that it all mixes, like water rushing past incredibly fast—a single, even sound, to which all movement is an accompaniment. All through this time his thoughts have been narrowing. The world apart from movement, apart from sound, begins to recede, the world apart from what the eyes can see. He has a wall to lean against, and a window, scratched and scored by fingers, luggage, by washing rags wet with water full of dirt. The night draws on. People talk less, though many are not asleep who are silent, and he imagines that they, like him, are gathering strength— because only a few hours have passed and still two days lie ahead and already the body aches with discomfort and the anticipation of endless discomfort. People curl round their bags to sleep, though it's not only theft that they fear, but the closeness of strangers, the tangle of flesh, the arm that you see but don't feel as your own; the smell of food, the inconsolable babies, the short tempers, the animal warmth that covers them over already (though still the sun hasn't risen yet) and fills the carriage, and takes him to sleep, then out again. Dawn has broken. Soft light lies over the still carriage. The fresh smell of morning. A light chill on the skin. In his dream they were all stumbling from the carriages, thick-eyed, full of sleep. From the whole length of the train people were pouring. The arcs of the electric lights were full of insects darting, dust rising from the ground where they walked. Families, young men, traders, soldiers, businessmen, mothers with their babies bundled into them, children pulled along by the arm. The train was still warm with movement. The breathing of the engine throbbed through the wheels. He cast a look back as he joined the stumbling crowd. The train's weak lights glowed dully, and suddenly he was afraid to separate. Afraid of being left in the night. Except he realizes, as he wakes, that this was no dream. That the border was crossed, his papers were stamped. He feels his back pocket. They're there where he left them, his papers, and he let himself wake. The dark conch of a woman's ear drifts in and out of focus. Small bubbles gather at the corner of her mouth, multiply, pulse in the air of her breath. In the fold of her eye a crust of mucus the colour of mother-of-pearl. The train is stopped on the tracks. It purrs like a fridge. It seems so innocent—you'd never know its strength. But then it jerks. Eyes snap open inside the carriage. The expanse of flesh shudders. Somebody exclaims in indignation—ah! The train is hardly moving, but the purr deepens, a sound from the throat. Then the first tug of unevenness catches in the movement, like a stone against tin, though it's not just a sound, but something stronger that registers in the body. A small jolt, and then another, and another. In the walls against the seat, in the glass, in its frame, in the light fittings in the roof, all these parts of the body capable of sound. The wheels pick up a heavy double beat: da-DA, da-DA, and somewhere in the train another set answers, more softly, da-DA, faster and faster as the whole train starts picking up the music. The wheels, the walls, the windows, the track and the horn braying—a sound of warning; but not only that—of pure pleasure—on through the day, the first endless day, too endless to resist, as hard as he tries. But silence is patient, is always waiting at the end of each sentence, which falls into nothing, though throughout the day people try to talk. To pass information. To remain themselves. To be people coming from somewhere, going somewhere, to have stories. Someone has left a husband. Someone is fleeing war. Someone doesn't know a soul in the place where he's going. Someone wants to achieve something with his life, who has never been beyond the compound of his parents. Someone recounts the beauty of his woman (don't worry, a voice comes from the other side of the carriage, you'll find her again in Dakar, and other voices laugh). Some who have traveled before have advice, encouragement, and in softer voices, stories to tell. Of time in foreign countries. Time spent getting there. Time in jail. In the no man's land between borders, penniless, unable to go forward or back. Stories of traffickers, and scam artists, and the brotherhoods that make life possible in the towns they hope to reach. Some have come to trade, some to work, some come to steal, some just to see. From all the capital cities, all the large towns. Wherever people are hungry. Wherever the young are brave. For some, Dakar is the end of the journey, for others, a stop to somewhere else. By ship, by land, by air, but always north. Some, they know, will be thrown from cargo boats to the ocean. Some will die of thirst in the desert. Some will suffocate in the back of vans, be beaten to death in the mountains of Algeria, or die on their own of filth and desperation. Some will be stopped at the border, at the passport desk, on the quayside. Some will be caught, then return, and be caught, then return, as many times as it takes. Some will reach refugee camps, prisons. But many will make it through to the coasts of Spain, of Italy, France, Britain, through seaports and airports and on, to cook fast food, sell handbags, sweep streets, stack boxes, pick fruit, hawk watches, hats, perfume, in a thousand towns and cities—wherever a living can be made, wherever existence can be justified. But only so much can be said, before the journey takes them back again, and he loses himself, becomes part of the passage, his energy dissolving into it. The sun is everywhere. All that matters is the water he takes to survive. The heat is breaking him down. His clothes are warm and wet with him. Dirt covers him. Sweat comes out of every part of him. His body is giving up its water, giving him up and he can't stop it as the train carries on racing across the land. Or for no reason stops in the middle of nowhere—although everywhere now is the middle of nowhere. But still, people rise out of the land with their wares, shouting their wares, their food, their drink, their plastic hangers. Where do they come from? Where is the settlement he cannot see? The settlement of these people pressing against the glass, so many words flowing from them, so many words for just a few eggs, just a few packets of water. And then they disappear, one by one. He doesn't notice it until, somehow, they're gone, and the next night is already beginning to settle in, coming from the distant horizon, and here he is, still going nowhere. Passengers start leaving the train to stretch their legs, and look about them, to see what it's like to be nowhere, and he jumps down too, and when the need takes him, goes to the back of the train and empties his watery guts under the carriage, squatting as the sun finally dies into the sand. And then without warning the train starts to move. A mother screams, and a child cries steadily, and men shout. But the train does not stop for the separated family. Goods are thrown from a door. The woman and the children jump down. And then he sees the lost child standing at the tracks, paralyzed with the prospect of being left behind. But the train cannot stop. Doesn't know to stop. And it leaves them behind, a family lost along the way, in a strange place, with not so much as the language. And now he hates the train, until it starts lulling him again, with its rolling and jolting, with a soft rocking that comes up through the cushion of the seat, and he falls asleep. A second night. When he wakes again, he is covered in leaves and the fresh smell of sap. (They have ridden through some bushes at night, and the branches have whipped the train, and win dows have torn the ends of the branches. He remembers now the sound of it from his sleep, the scraping and ripping.) Gray light sits upon the land. A second morning. Birds are circling over a tree, where something must be dead. Mosquitoes drift in. Most people still sleep, the women like rolling hills, children bundled into the crooks of them. A few talk softly in a far corner. His shoulder is wedged against a bench. He feels a screw against his hip, that must have been there all these hours. He doesn't feel he can move his body, all the suppleness is out of it. His right arm, lying across his left, is covered in bites. Somebody turns a radio on, a handset they hold against their head, and there's a whisper of voices, a thread of sound coming out of the static that still reaches him, somewhere out here, between the world he's come from, and the one he's going to. A light wind brings the smell of fuel. Then the landscape of flesh around him begins to unfasten itself. The hills rise and unfold, and the children are lifted out of the valleys and folds of flesh, some oblivious, some still asleep, limp and pliable in mothers' arms, others howling. The train sounds its horn. The last hours are arriving. The movement starts again. Today, a grinding, circular motion, as if milling corn beneath the wheels, and something else new: in the clatter of the carriages before and behind, soft and steady like the sound of rain. Diourbel . . . Thiès. The towns start approaching. Rubbish is piled beside the track, hills of it, fluttering in the wind and full of stench—a thin, bitter smell. In places the earth is claiming it back, soil growing up into it, creepers clinging to it, trying to hold it down. But still it gets loose and catches in the thorn bushes, or is held down, and becomes part of the ground. Patterns appear through the bush. A fence swings down to accompany the track. Roads appear in the distance, maybe more than one, and begin to bend in towards the approaching town, pulled like gravity. Animals—a donkey, sheep, more than one sheep, a cow tethered to a tree. The town is still approaching, it must be drawing close. The thorn bushes start coming down to the track, lining it, then suddenly break away, and there are shacks, people sitting on their porches, watching. He sees a father lift his son in the air, and the boy shriek with happiness, but they fly by in an instant, and then a horse is drinking water that's collected in a tire, there are goal posts in a dry river bed, and small children in a yard, jumping and shouting and waving at the train, men carrying heavy sacks and a row of small naked boys, squatting in a yard and chatting away as they shit. How many hours to Dakar, he does not know, but the endless landscape is behind, there are baobabs now, and the land is lime-green with a thin covering of grass. People notice, sit up. There is shuffling in the benches. The sea appears—just for a moment, before the land rises above it again, and houses begin to intervene, but there it was: a sliver of blue—bluer than the sky—and rocks, and a road, along which there were buses driving, each behind the other, as in a child's cartoon. Now the houses are coming in thick. Markets. Roads. The land is overrun by the city. Already he's in the city. Only the station remains. People are gathering their goods, those who know the route, while those who know nothing observe and do likewise. Some have already found their way towards the exits. Young boys open the door and hang out, scooping the moving air with their arms. Now the train enters the station, which at first is no more than a ragged concrete platform. Then he sees the station building in front. The high roof, and the whole city gathered round. He can hear traffic, he hears music and shouting as the people stream from the doors. So many people—he can't believe that so many people have come this far. The porters hustle round. The conductors with their whistles and their uniforms flapping round their midriffs. All he has is a single kit bag as he moves quickly through the crowd, feeling the solid ground beneath his feet. The smell and the sound and movement of the city is everywhere, as he steps beneath the doors of the station into Place de la Gare, and Dakar opens up to take him in.

WITH SOME DIFFICULTY he finds the hotel, ten minutes' walk from the station, in a side street, above a shop. He climbs the stairs to a dimly lit landing. In the back, under the stairs, is a counter, a rack of keys, a light hanging on a wire, and a bell to ring, that brings an attendant out.

"I have a room," he says.

"What name?" the attendant asks.

He gives the name they've told him.

The attendant consults one of the scraps of paper on the countertop, then brings out a key from under the counter.

"*Deux jours en avance,*" the attendant says, and names an unexpectedly high rate. But he doesn't care. He pays the money, and he takes the key, and finds his room at the end of a windowless corridor on the third floor.

For a day he sleeps. He wakes and eats and washes himself with water from the sink, cleans his clothes with soap, and lays them on the floor where the sun comes through.

The afternoon passes. He has nothing to do. He stands at the second-floor hotel window, looking out at a strange city. He wonders which way to face. From where will the end of his waiting come?

Here he is no one. He thinks, *If I died on the street nobody would bury me.*

He imagines his mother standing on the stair leading down from the verandah. He imagines her returning into the house, getting on her knees by her bed.

He sits in his room and waits. He waits for a knock on the door. He goes down and asks whether anyone has come for him. He walks round the block so that he can ask again on his return. But it's always the same: *"Personne. Pas encore"*—he has only to pass through the lobby for the attendant, not looking up, to tell him.

He lies on the bed and smokes cigarette after cigarette as the light comes through the drawn curtains, growing blunt.

He traces the wiring all over the walls, and the scars where the old wiring used to be, like dried rivers.

The mosquito net above the bed is tied in a large knot, hanging from the roof from its hoop. The gathered gauze is looped into a bunch and fastened round itself, so that it looks like a head resting on a shoulder, held in an embrace.

Is it possible his heart will let him off? he wonders, but knows it will not.

He shuts his eyes. He thinks of Celeste—not as he left her, but much before that.

From the first time he saw her.

Turning him into a boy, and her into a schoolgirl, sitting on the edge of a tall chair, flipping her legs while she waited her turn in the Christ Call Ventures Telecentre.

Who was that? he asks himself. *Who was that* then?

The girl flipping her legs—what was it like *not* to know her?

And he remembers when she stood up from the chair, how he couldn't stop watching, and missed his turn in the queue. And later, after she'd made her call, how she walked out with a friend, and they were laughing at him, because they'd seen him looking. And how her body had folded in its laughter, and he saw her shoulder blades rise under the straps of her dress like wings, and how all her movements seemed to join so smoothly together, like a fine cursive hand, like water.

And then he slips over the border of sleep, and is no longer thinking of her at all, but of water itself. Of the sea. How for a moment he'd seen it from the train, after two days of desert, at the end of the journey. And he'd known he was almost done. It had lifted his heart and calmed him. It had made him forget.

Why do I love the sea? he wonders.

Why? For its completeness, for its adaptability, for being capable of filling any space.

Whenever he thinks of the sea, he feels homesick, though he doesn't know what for. For a place? For a time in his life? For a time when the sea belonged to him? And he imagines himself standing at the edge of the sea, and thinks that dying would mean no more than wading out into it forever and not coming back.

Each morning he is ready to leave. He goes through his papers, he packs, he washes—but nobody comes. He pays again for his room. A third night. And then a fourth.

Late in the evening he goes out to get supplies—cigarettes, sweets, and water. He gets back after midnight and climbs the stairs beside the concierge's desk, passing the restaurant on his way to his room. The flowery metal door to the bar is closed. A woman is sitting in the warm room with a glass of wine in front of her. The attendant sits at a table closer to the door.

Can he get a drink, he asks.

The attendant says that the bar is closed now.

"No," the woman says, "he can come in." She will give him a drink. She sounds drunk.

"Open the door," she says happily from her table, "pull it."

He tries to pull it but it won't open.

"No, it is closed," the attendant says.

He tries to push it and it gives a centimeter or so but no more. The woman gets up and comes to the door. She wears a black jacket and a dress that shines like metal.

She opens the door with a hard pull. Her eagerness startles him momentarily. A man comes out of a door marked "Private" a small distance down the corridor behind him. He turns back to look at the man. They look at each other. The man's face is saying nothing, not interfering.

"No," he then decides to say, "I see you are closed. I will come back tomorrow."

"Yes, we are closed," the attendant says.

"Never mind," says the woman, and she steps out of the bar. "Come and sit, I want to talk to you," she says.

Her hair is braided into slick ringlets.

"What is your name?" she asks. "I am Janet."

She is smiling and laughing as if she is shy and flustered and overwhelmed. They exchange such facts as where they are from.

"You are alone?" she asks.

He tells her that he is and she laughs.

"You don't want to have me?" she asks, as if he's already refused her.

"I cannot," he tells her.

"And tomorrow?" she asks.

"No," he says, laughing with embarrassment. "Janet, it cannot happen," and he pats her leg and gets up and goes to the stairs and starts climbing to his room.

When he turns back he can hear his heart beating in his ears. She has climbed two steps up from the landing, following him.

"Are you sure?" she asks.

He looks at her, and she holds his look, and then drops it and laughs shyly.

They don't talk again until they are in his room. He sits on the bed and opens his trousers and pushes her head onto him. She runs her mouth along the length of his penis.

Then he suddenly grows fearful that he doesn't want to do this anymore, but pushes the thought to the back of his mind. How could he say no now? He tells her to stop and to take her dress off and not to bother with anything else.

He stands behind her, reaches down, to his surprise finds her wet, and enters her. Later he comes out of her and he pushes her back down into an arch and enters her anus.

She says "no" softly, but does not try to move. He is holding her lightly. He can feel the resistance of her flesh, but he carries on, lifting his hands up her body and holding her buttocks and pushing her abdomen into the bed.

He starts noticing the tears and flakes in the plaster and buttons in the fake leather bed rest, like small coated chocolates, and then out of the window, the light flashing in the building two blocks away, and then it is all filtered away, and he comes inside of her, and feels his blood banging against his forehead like alcohol.

As he withdraws from her the condom comes off and is left inside her, unpeeling off him as if it were a stocking. The warm smell of her shit rushes up to him, and he begins to weep.

He climbs over her as soon as he can and curls into the corner where the bed meets the wall. She lies there, still, as if she is asleep.

Then he hears her begin to move. Nervously she asks if he is all right. He ignores her. A while later he hears her dressing.

"There is the money on the dresser," he tells her, and that she must take her price.

He hears her at the dresser and then he hears her close the door behind her, her first few steps, and then her laughter on the stairs.

He is filled with shame. And terror at the thought of her walking around, a packet of his semen buried deep in her body.

It takes a day before he can return to the hotel bar. He arrives early, and watches the Lebanese family that owns the hotel at their table closest to the television. They talk among themselves. The woman and her two sons do their accounts and update the menu prices with black and red pens on pink cards.

It gets dark and people come in, filling the room from the back. They call the waiters and the waiters bring them beers and they talk quietly among themselves.

One waiter stands behind the bar, laughing softly with a man in a shiny shirt. Another sits on the edge of a table, his face looking so weary. He is surveying the room, waiting like a man waits for boats to return from the sea, waiting and waiting.

He tries to catch the second waiter's eye. Can the waiter not see that he is just like him? But the waiter will not hold his stare.

Maybe the waiter knows about Janet. Does everyone know about her? But then why do they let her in?

He sees Janet in a corner with a glass of wine. She won't catch his eye either. He knows that to apologize to her would be absurd, yet that is what he wants to do.

He starts to take his coffee and sees Janet go away with the man in the shiny shirt. The bartenders begin returning glasses to the glass cabinet. The restaurant owner turns the television on and people watch the news.

Later Janet slips back into the restaurant and sits at a table with her back to him.

Should he talk to her? No, leave her.

He finishes his coffee and goes to see if anyone has come for him.

Personne. Pas encore.

He returns to his room.

He reaches into his trousers. Two eggs in a silk purse. He hears a cat, and a child screaming, happy, gleeful screaming, fearful screaming—he cannot tell—and the sound of a motor turning, dull and repetitive.

AND THEN the waiting ends. There is a knock on the door. The attendant is standing there. He tells him that somebody is there for him, he should go down. A man is waiting in the lobby, standing against the counter. He is wearing track-suit bottoms and a vest. His head is shaved. There is a scar across his forehead and a blankness in his expression, as if the man has not yet seen him, though he stands squarely before the man. Then the man extends his hand, which is rough, the grip firm when he takes it. The man guides him with his other hand to the door of the hotel, so that they are standing on the step looking towards the street.

"You are Eddie?" the man asks, in English, not releasing his hand.

"Yes," he says.

"From?"

"From Accra," he says. "I am Eddie from Accra."

He feels the man's grip relax. "Very fine," the man says. "I am Adams. I was sent for you." The man smiles now, there is warmth in his voice, as if they are old friends.

"OK," the man says, "so get your things."

When he returns with his bags there is a taxi parked in front of the hotel. The man called Adams sits in the passenger seat, looking towards the door. Adams gestures towards him. He climbs into the back seat and Adams talks to the driver. He catches the French word *aéroport*.

The car begins to move through the traffic. Adams and the driver stare silently ahead. There is no radio in the car. Blue and yellow buses pass by. They skirt the sea, and he realizes how close he has been all that time. The street lights don't work, and the road is filled with long shadows, as the shapes of people appear in the dusty headlights, and shopfronts flicker past in the light of kerosene lamps, or sticks of pale fluorescent light. Then the traffic thins, and the street lights stop, and they are out of the centre.

He says, "Adams . . ."

"Yes."

"We are going to the airport?"

"Somewhere near."

He waits for Adams to add more, but he doesn't.

"Ibrahim sent you?" he asks.

"I don't know," Adams says, then corrects himself to keep him quiet: "Something like that. Why not."

They travel on, and get caught in the traffic. A slum is on the side of the road. He watches boys playing football in the dusk light, on a sandy open field crisscrossed by tracks. There are two telephone poles in the middle of the pitch. The cars edge patiently past a cart attached to a donkey that won't move. Its owner stands above it, beating it.

Then they are past the slums, and the houses grow bigger. There is electric light coming from out of them, there are compounds under construction, and billboards beside the road.

Between a row of houses, he catches a glimpse of what must be the airport. He hears the sound of an idling jet engine. He turns and watches the airport disappear as they pass.

They move off the main road, and come to a row of shops next to a building site, walled by metal sheets. The car stops. Adams pays the driver and opens his door and takes his bag. He follows Adams down the road.

"I am sorry," Adams says, smiling. He is walking fast, slightly ahead of him. "It is better not to speak too much English in the taxi."

He tries to keep up with Adams.

"You are Senegalese?" he asks.

"No," Adams says.

They are in a good neighbourhood. Some houses have tile walls with doorbells, and gardens, and walls. There are very few people on the street. They turn left into an alley. He sees four blocks of houses stretching down the road, bathed in fluorescent light. The only sound is their feet moving over the sand road, and music from a radio, growing closer. They come to a door in the wall, beside a tree, on the left of the alley, on which the lettering on a mural reads "Coiffure Chez Émile," above a painting of a large electric razor painted in red and black.

A gauze curtain hangs over the door.

"We will talk," Adams says, and pulls the curtain aside and walks in, and he follows Adams into a barber shop, not much bigger than a cupboard.

There is a customer sitting in the barber's chair, waiting for a haircut. He has a piece of cloth around his neck, and is picking his teeth with a wood splinter. A second man sits on one of the chairs against the wall, stretching his legs across the floor. His shoes almost touch the wall opposite.

"This is Eddie," Adams says, and puts the bag down.

"*Salut, Eduard,*" the tall man on the chair says and stretches his hand out. He extends his, and the tall man slaps his palm.

"*Je suis Emmanuel,*" the tall man says.

The man called Emmanuel has a wide nose and the whites of his eyes are opaque, off-yellow. His skin is marked and has wide pores.

"Eddie speaks English," Adams says, and turns his attention to the client in the chair.

"Okaaay," Emmanuel says, his voice rising on the second syllable, "welcome. Take a seat."

He sits.

"Welcome to Se-ne-gal," Emmanuel says, "yes," and he laughs.

Adams cuts his client's hair. He tips the chair forward, and sets about his work. He shaves the head in zones, dividing the back into two hemispheres that he clears in turn, each from ear to nape. Then he moves to the top of the head, cutting from the forehead backwards, cleaning each section of exposed scalp with spirits, and a piece of foam cut from a block on top of the cupboard. When the head is complete he stands back, changes blades, and smooths the joins between the sections, pushes and brushes over the lumps and dents in his client's scalp, until the whole head is seamless and smooth.

He thinks of speaking to Emmanuel, who all the while is tapping his feet to the music, then thinks against it.

Adams finishes up. He applies powder to the man's head, takes off the cloth, and brushes him down.

"OK?" he asks.

The client turns his head and surveys the work.

"*C'est bien,*" the client says, stands, stretches his neck and shoulders, then fetches some bills from his pocket and pays. The customer slaps hands with Adams, then Emmanuel, and nods at him as he leaves.

"Whoow," Adams says, and he smiles, "this is a good day today. Everyone today wants barbing."

"Everyone wants barbing," Emmanuel repeats, and clicks his teeth.

"What time is it?" Adams asks.

Emmanuel stretches out his huge arm to find out. It is ten before eight. Emmanuel must be two meters tall at least, he estimates.

"So maybe you keep the shop now," Adams says to Emmanuel, "and me and this boy sit outside."

Adams takes two chairs from the shop and sets them out against the wall under the tree. It is fully night, and the voices from radios and televisions filter down from the houses, and a breeze blows over their feet and down the alley. He sees a car pass down the next road. If something terrible is going to happen to him, he thinks, this doesn't feel like the moment.

There have been a few problems with the arrangements, Adams tells him, but everything now is fine. He, Adams, will be passing him on to the next handler, who will take him through the airport, when his papers are ready, and their man inside is in place. In a few days' time, Adams says. That's how long it usually takes.

"Ibrahim, have you spoken to him?" he asks.

"I don't know who Ibrahim is," Adams says, smiling, "but somebody does if I've been told to keep you in my barbing shop a few nights."

And when Adams has finished laughing, they sit in silence.

"You know what they call this line of work?" Adams says, breaking the silence.

"What?" he asks.

"The flesh machine," Adams says.

He wonders if Adams hasn't had this conversation a hundred times out there on the street side.

"Well," he says.

"Well what?" Adams asks cheerfully, in a way that he senses is intended to bring him back to the normality of Adams's cigarettes and tired evenings.

"Well, either I'm screwed, or I'm not," he says.

"That's normal," Adams says. "E-ve-ry-tin' is normal," and that in a few days' time he'll get a call from somebody he doesn't know, to take him to the airport, and then he'll be on his way to—?

"I'll be on my way," he says.

Adams smiles. "That's quite right," he says.

Later in the evening Adams leads him round the corner to the main entrance of the house and they climb up to the second floor to take the evening meal. The steps have been recently cast and they make their way carefully past the kitchen on the top floor, where a woman is sitting on a bucket, pounding spices. A skinless pink chicken carcass hangs over the back of a chair.

The house is still under construction, Adams tells him. A family in France owns it. They only come in the summer.

"Oh," he says.

"I just watch it for them," Adams tells him, answering the question he hasn't asked.

"And they run this show?"

"I never ask who," Adams says.

Though the house has tile floors, the walls are still raw concrete. There is a landing on the second floor, the kitchen to one side, and to the other two rooms leading off an uncovered passageway. One of the rooms is closed. In the other there are chairs against the wall, and a window with wooden bars. They have electricity there, and a television, and in the corner there is a mattress and some crumpled sheets.

"Sit," Adams tells him, and he sits on the floor. For at least twenty minutes he waits in this room alone, watching the television, in the background the sound of cooking and low conversation.

Then Adams returns, followed by a young woman and a small girl, no more than five years old. The woman sets a cloth out over the floor. The girl throws herself onto the mattress and stretches on her stomach, wriggles round, and smiles at him.

Adams seats himself on a chair beside him and watches the television.

There is water on Adams's face. He notices the skin around his collarbones has begun to go soft and fold. He wonders if Adams isn't sick.

"Astou," Adams calls out to the girl, who wriggles with glee, and Adams smiles, and he knows what it is the girl is delighted by—the solidness of this man, his warmth and strength and handsomeness. He thinks, *She must be in love with him.*

The woman brings a bowl of yassa poulet and places it between them, and they eat it together, as she and Adams ask him about where he is from and what it is like in his hometown, and the girl called Astou jumps all over them, or plays by herself with a nail clipper, and for the first time in a while he does not feel unhappy.

There is kindness in their questions, solidarity. They too no longer own the lives they lead, he realizes.

He looks at the woman and the child. He looks at Adams, and he thinks that if there were more time, it would be good to understand this man better, to know something about him. How he makes a life for himself here, how he makes it beautiful for other people.

Later, after dinner, as everyone prepares to sleep, he climbs with a cup of tea and a cigarette to the top floor of the house, which is still just an open platform without walls yet, or a roof.

There is still the breeze. Lightning that isn't going to become rain stutters in the distance like a fluorescent bulb. Blades of light from passing cars sweep through the alleys beside a distant road, and from the dark houses comes the chanting of the dahiras, and it feels to him that everything in that darkness is a mystery, everything is an unknown place.

To have survived the heat, to have survived another day, feels like something.

Over the dark minaret of the mosques, between the half-built villas and the steel rising from the concrete, he can see the airport, white with light. He watches the movement on the runway, the thunder and scream of the big 747s, the airbuses headed for Europe.

He thinks to himself how close he now is. How soon the future is going to begin.

And then he goes down again into the house to prepare himself for sleep.

· · ·

THROUGH A WINDOW, a forest. Trees. Vines. A gray, stringy sky behind. Foliage moves in the wind that the eye can't see, but the smallest vibration, a shift in pressure, tenses in the glass that catches the light, which the eye *can* see.

The teacher is standing at the window.

His ear comes into view.

His neck.

A collar.

Gray in the hair.

In the glass the view begins to blur, refocus.

He's not looking at the view at all, but at his face's own reflection.

Studying shapes, lie of the flesh, as if for the first time.

Back further still.

The figure of the man at the window, in the foreground a desk, papers on top, neatly stacked, a glass, a pen, a package—paper wrapping, tied with string.

The teacher turns, looks towards the desk, and the package on it.

. . .

A woman's hands.
Black hands, fingers laced, full of lines.
Mrs. Dankwa's hands in prayer.
A bedspread underneath.
Nails neat, filed, square, white as gravestones.
Forehead descends, a crest of hair.
Momentarily, lips.
Lips upon the hands in prayer.
A middle-aged lady gets up heavily from the bed.
Through the open door, her husband watches over his paper from his chair.

. . .

An empty room.
Bed stripped.
Cupboards bare, door ajar. Mirror dull, mottled with rust. On the glass, corners of tape where a page once stuck, long torn away.
Circles on the floorboards where a cup once stood.
Dust on the sill.
Dust on the floor.
Dust on the flat fins of a ceiling fan.
A chair turned towards the bed.
Two wire hangers on the seat.
Down.
Through the floorboards.
Through the ceiling below.
Into the room downstairs.
Festus Ankrah at table. In his vest.
Radio beside.
A bowl.

Cereal finished.
Hand moving still from bowl to mouth.
Eating milk with a spoon.

. . .

Meat-threaded sticks, cooking on a grill.
Coal glowing red.
Light and heat between.
Smoke.
Fat popping like bubble wrap.
Tables on the street, benches.
Customers eating, drinking water from plastic cups.
A woman cleaving cabbage on a board.
A child collecting plates.
A man, watching from across the road, hair wet with light, gold around his wrists, waiting for a space to clear.
The woman cutting cabbage looks up. Sees him on the other side. Smiles secretly, looks down.
He smiles back.
An A-frame sign beside the grill.
"Ibrahim's Snack Shack."
In cursive hand beneath:
Where da black man is black.

. . .

Leaf spinning over itself.
Blowing across the ground.
Over grass.
Sand.
Edges scratch the dust.
For a moment catches, shelters in the crook of bark.

Root of a tree like knotted wool.

Jumps again.

Comes to rest against the smooth side of a carved stone.

A view down a hill.

Graves all the way.

Beyond, the view—valley stretching, all the way out to the milky sky.

GOOD BUSINESS

A PARCEL was delivered to Festus Ankrah's post office box at Luttcrott Circle. It waited for a while. Other letters piled up on top of it. When Festus Ankrah came to get his mail he saw the parcel but first went through the other envelopes. He opened a few while standing in front of the row of post office boxes, his eyelids dipped in shallow u's as he sifted through them.

Then he put the other envelopes under his arm and pulled the parcel out. He turned it over. He looked at the return address, the stamp. He put the parcel back and closed the post box door and went away.

The parcel waited a week. Two.

The door opened. Festus Ankrah's hand came in quickly, found the parcel, and took it out. The door closed.

Festus Ankrah got a taxi up Kojo Thompson and walked the rest of the way home.

At the dining room table he put down the parcel and went to the kitchen and got a knife to cut the string.

He unpeeled the brown paper.

There was a book, on it a note.

The note didn't have a greeting. It was written, "When your nephew visited he departed so quickly and left this behind. Perhaps it may help you. You will know best what to do. JB."

His mouth turned down. He put the note aside.

The book was upside down. Festus Ankrah turned it over to see its cover.

"What is this?" he said aloud.

The book was all in French.

Festus Ankrah flipped through the pages.

The book purred.

The pages turned halfway through, then stopped. There was a piece of paper, folded over, used as a bookmark.

Festus Ankrah took it out and unfolded and looked at it.

It was in handwriting, in blue pen—his nephew's writing. It was divided into seven columns. Festus Ankrah recognized it as a calendar of some kind: S, followed by M, followed by T, W,T again and F—the days of the week, but no dates.

In each column were different combinations of letters, many repeated: RK, KQ, ET, AF, and strings of numbers.

Festus Ankrah studied them. Then put the paper back in the book, got up and put the book on top of the cupboard.

It was Friday night. Outside the streets were starting to become lively.

Festus Ankrah took his coat and went out to work.

WHEN FESTUS ANKRAH went to visit his sister he thought it better not to call in advance.

It was Saturday afternoon.

When he arrived his brother-in-law, Simon Dankwa, was watching television. His brother-in-law had come back from Gaborone after his contract expired. Now he was retired. He'd been back half a year. His son had left while Mr. Dankwa was still away. Mr. Dankwa hadn't seen his son in three years and maybe now he never would.

Festus Ankrah let himself in by the front gate. Mr. Dankwa heard the sound of the gate opening from his front room. He got up and pulled back the lace curtain over the window and saw Festus Ankrah.

He came out onto the verandah in his socks.

Festus Ankrah latched the gate, then turned around. There were a few mangos in the grass, that had fallen from the tree growing over the gate. Festus Ankrah picked up two as he came up the path.

Mr. Dankwa shook his hand.

He said to Festus Ankrah what a nice surprise it was to see him, and that his sister wasn't in.

Festus Ankrah gave his brother-in-law the two mangos.

Mr. Dankwa thanked him.

"Can I still come in?" Festus Ankrah said.

Mr. Dankwa said that of course he could, that he was glad to see Festus Ankrah, and that he was welcome.

Mr. Dankwa turned and went back in carefully, making sure not to slip on the polished concrete in his socks. Festus Ankrah followed.

"Kwabena," Mr. Dankwa called out. A girl appeared at the door of the kitchen.

"This is Kwabena," Mr. Dankwa said. "Kwabena is working here now. She's from the church. Your sister is there now actually. Kwabena, this is Mr. Ankrah, my wife's brother."

The girl called Kwabena lowered her eyes. Festus Ankrah detected in her expression not only shyness, but suspicion.

"Kwabena, please bring Mr. Ankrah some soft drink and see what there is to eat. Biscuits, Festus? Biscuits. Please bring Mr. Ankrah some biscuits."

"Thank you," Festus Ankrah said.

Mr. Dankwa said, "So welcome. Sit down."

The two men sat down on the sofa in front of the television. It was tuned in to the American channel.

"Do you watch the television much?" Mr. Dankwa asked.

"Not much," Festus Ankrah replied.

"It is very interesting," Mr. Dankwa said. "In America all the cities are clean. It takes years to execute a criminal. Not like here. A few months back two criminals came running down from the main road to Nii Boi Drop. The people caught them, beat them, then held them down and banged six-inch nails into their heads. Then they let them go. They got up and ran a few steps and then they died."

Festus Ankrah noticed a mosquito coil burnt out on the floor at their feet, like a charred animal turned in on itself. His brother-in-law must be spending a lot of time in front of this television, he thought.

Mr. Dankwa said, "I've been watching the *Money Programme*. See—it's still on. I see these two people every day. I don't know them at all. Strangers from a strange place speaking about money I know nothing about. Do you have any stocks, Festus?"

Festus Ankrah laughed.

Mr. Dankwa continued. He said, "These two people—this lady and man, I watch them every day. Every day. What is this now? We know strangers better than our own family members."

"I don't know how much we really know them," Festus Ankrah said.

"We know them pretty well," Mr. Dankwa replied.

They were both watching the television now.

The male presenter was talking—talking and smiling and talking and smiling. The woman was nodding her head and smiling.

"It must hurt their lips to smile like that," Mr. Dankwa said.

Festus Ankrah said, "It's exercise. That's why their lips are so thin."

Mr. Dankwa smiled himself.

He said, "Let me tell you something very interesting I have observed. I've been watching three months. This man called Stuart Barney. Three months ago he was almost bald. Yes! His hairline had almost crept back behind his ears. It was hiding there. And now look at it—it's almost tickling his eyebrows. Just look at this man in the space of three months. Festus, these people are truly powerful. You, incidentally, are looking fine. How are you?"

"Fine," Festus Ankrah said.

The girl brought in a tray with soft drinks and biscuits and set it down before Festus Ankrah.

Mr. Dankwa opened the bottle of Coca-Cola and poured a glass for his brother-in-law, then watched him drink.

Mr. Dankwa said, "Your sister goes to church a lot."

Festus Ankrah told him that he knew.

"I mean she goes to church a lot more. Me, I go a lot less. Actually, I don't go at all."

"Did you attend church in Botswana?"

"Yes, but since my boy disappeared . . . I hear you went to Akwapim."

"Yes. In May."

"Mary told me. Did you find anything?"

"I met the head teacher of the school. Mr. Bediako."

"Did he tell you he and I were students together?"

"Yes."

"I wrote to him. I asked him to take Kwasi in. And he did. I said to him, 'Turn my son into a Ghanaian.' I regret this now. Bitterly. I do."

"We never know how things will end."

"Yes, we never know. Me, I wanted Kwasi to be a Ghanaian. A proud African. But I don't think he cared for any of that. And what was I trying to do anyway? Sending a boy halfway across the world to be what he already was."

Festus Ankrah knew not to speak. He passed his brother-in-law the soft drink bottle.

Mr. Dankwa poured himself a glass. He said, "Did you learn anything?"

"I don't know."

"You know or you don't know."

"I learned that the memory of your son is very unwelcome on the ridge."

"This I know without going there."

"Yes. It is felt that your son was a very disruptive influence."

"That is what shames us."

"People say it. But how? Your son, this quiet boy. It's hard enough for Kwasi even to cast his own shadow."

"Yes. He was very quiet. Sometimes I didn't even notice him. Most people never noticed Kwasi."

"But some did a lot."

Mr. Dankwa raised his eyebrows.

"The strong. The vain. Especially the vain. Such people—he drew them to him."

Mr. Dankwa looked away then, his expression beginning to set, closing down his face to conversation.

"Because he never says no, Simon, he never resists, and such willingness—it liberates people's inhibitions."

"What people, Festus?"

"You said it yourself—sending your child back to be an African. And me too. All of us."

Through all the time that Festus Ankrah was talking he had not been looking at his brother-in-law, but now he did.

"I do not mean to accuse you, Simon," Festus Ankrah said softly, responding to the pained expression on his brother-in-law's face.

"But you do."

"No."

"Yes, and in my own house," Mr. Dankwa said.

"No. You're the one I'm *not* accusing. You loved your son. Love him. Everyone else loved themselves. Especially that woman who drowned."

"Nana Oforiwaa."

"Nana Oforiwaa. Yes. He made her come apart at the seams. That woman. Shame. A lady of that age. And a boy of seventeen."

Mr. Dankwa did not respond.

"Simon, your son has never done anything without permission."

"Except leave."

"Yes, except leave. Exactly. But perhaps it is the best thing he could have done. Who knows who he'll be when he comes back."

"But Festus, to go away in such a way . . . He told nobody. This is not how a man should behave. Do you know that he came to visit his mother before he went—the day before. He could have said goodbye.

Instead, as always, they fought. Well, I have told you she is at church. But do you know what she does there? Every day she begs God to forgive her for all the things she said and will never be able to take back."

Mr. Dankwa looked at his brother-in-law and told him that he was sorry. For everything he had done, and for everything he did not do. He smiled sadly. He said that he thought his nephew would have listened to him if he had only tried to talk to him, but that he chose to believe that all Kwasi wanted out of life was to be as miserable and disaffected as himself.

Mr. Dankwa laughed at this.

They both laughed.

Mr. Dankwa said, "I think your sister should be coming back shortly."

"Then let me go," Festus Ankrah said.

"No, stay," Mr. Dankwa tried to convince him. "In ten minutes, after the news, they'll be interviewing the widow of the first man buried in space. Last week they sent some of his ashes up on a rocket."

"Why do they tell us such nonsense?"

"They don't realize we're not interested."

"But we are."

"Because we have no choice."

They were standing now at the door.

Festus Ankrah said, "Will you tell Mary that I stopped by?"

"I will," Mr. Dankwa said.

The men shook hands.

"What are you going to do, Festus?"

Festus Ankrah said, "I was thinking of taking a holiday. I haven't been traveling in a long time."

"Where will you go?"

"I don't know. I'll let you know."

"All right," his brother-in-law said.

Festus Ankrah was about to leave when he remembered he'd meant to ask a question of his brother-in-law.

He said, "Simon, I didn't know that Kwasi spoke French. Did you know that?"

"He started learning in Botswana. I didn't think there was any reason for him to learn Tswana. Why?"

"I found one of his books in the house in French. I can send it if you want."

"No, no, keep it there. We should keep all his things in one place for when he comes back."

The two men embraced on the steps of the house. Festus Ankrah walked down to the Fish Pond Drop to find a taxi.

Simon Dankwa went back into his house to watch television, where the interview was about to begin with the woman whose husband's ashes had just been sent into space in a metal container the size of a lipstick tube.

FESTUS ANKRAH walked along Tudu Street past a row of stationery shops and communications centres. Beside a flight of stairs, on the side of a three-story building, was a mural for a travel agency—a large aeroplane, banking, all rounded shapes and uneven lines, as if in the hand of a child: windows open like portholes, passengers leaning out, waving. Birds in close, like pilot fish. A flotilla of hot-air balloons observed from a distance. The colours, bright in the shadow cast by the adjacent building, were faded where the light struck directly.

Festus Ankrah knew immediately his nephew's work—thought he remembered him talking about it—the theme, the good site, but uneven light.

As he approached he recognized one of the figures in the window as a portrait of the stamp maker whose shop used to be beside his nephew's. He recognized a prominent opposition politician. A character from a television serial. He laughed to see, in the very last seat, a portrait of himself. He was smiling too. Fingers waving like a bunch of bananas.

There used to be a travel agency up these stairs, Festus Ankrah remembered. Now the second floor of the building was closed, the fluorescent light bulbs under the eaves removed. He could see the boarded windows. He climbed up the stairs. In the window was an old sign.

From his pocket he took out the piece of paper that he'd found in his nephew's book.

RK, KQ, ET, AF.

They were airline codes. Air Afrique. Kenyan. Ethiopian Airlines. Air France.

Where to and where from he could find out easily enough. He folded the paper and put it in his pocket, and headed back home.

Festus Ankrah got onto the floor and pulled out a suitcase from under the bed in what used to be the bedroom of his nephew and Celeste. Small silver insects fled for the skirting boards.

Run, my friends, run, he thought.

He lifted himself up slowly so that the tendons in the back of his knees didn't seize up. He removed a hanger from a chair and sat down. He clicked open the locks on the suitcase on his lap and opened it.

Inside there were papers. A few photographs. Some books. Whatever he'd found in the room after Celeste had left—though Celeste had been thorough. She'd filled the rubbish bin at the back of the house with everything else.

He found the notebook he was looking for. It had paint stains on the cover, a ring of paint from under a tin, like a welt over the cardboard cover.

Inside, the double-ruled pages were covered in Celeste's neat print, which Festus Ankrah knew well from his own business ledgers.

He scanned through the pages, which listed commissions by date, price and brief description.

He found the entry he was looking for, dated 7 March. *Global Travel Agency*—two months or so before his nephew's disappearance.

He saw that his nephew had been billing in foreign currency. A hundred dollars U.S. He turned over the page, added up the numbers to the last entry. The amount was considerable.

Though if his nephew had traveled by plane, he'd have needed papers, which takes money. And friends.

The money at least was no longer a mystery.

He flipped again through the pages. In the last few weeks business had been booming, until two days before the fire. Then nothing.

"Clever boy," Festus Ankrah said under his breath, "though not clever enough."

Festus Ankrah scanned again through the last three months of entries. Telecentres. Beauty salons. Restaurants. The inside of a bar, which Festus Ankrah happened to know from his younger days and wasn't aware still existed. The Lebanese Club around the corner—150 dollars U.S. for "mural of Scene With Cyprus trees and mountains based on a Postcard."

In the last few weeks the jobs had gotten larger, judging by the prices, except—Festus Ankrah noticed—for a few small jobs.

Eugenia Unisex Beauty International in Asylum Down—this a month before his nephew's disappearance.

Selma's Clothes Shop, Perfection Guaranteed—with an address in Nima.

Ibrahim's Snack Shack on Farrar Street.

This one was familiar to Festus Ankrah. He followed the ruled line to the left-hand margin of the page, where the owner was identified: Ibrahim Momo.

Outside the weather was looking threatening. Festus Ankrah got his umbrella and headed to Farrar Street.

He did not find Ibrahim Momo at the Snack Shack.

Two days later he did, at the beauty salon Ibrahim Momo owned on Afram Street. It was a tin shack, with windows cut out of the corrugated walls, strings of beads hanging over the doorway, and a fabulous sign along the top of the roof, by which Festus Ankrah knew he had the right place.

There were two work stations on either side of the room, at which attendants were braiding hair. Large women reclined in the easy chairs, heads in the laps of the attendants, necks bared.

Bob Marley was wailing on the radio about how he never shot the deputy.

Festus Ankrah came through the doorway, strings of beads parting on either side of him. He took in the sight in front of him. Everyone carried on about their business. After a while, one of the attendants, looking up casually, nodded towards a door leading out the back of the room.

Festus Ankrah went through.

He recognized Ibrahim Momo. Festus Ankrah smiled involuntarily. He'd seen him around the Snack Shack. It had never occurred to him that the place was his.

Ibrahim Momo was sitting at a desk, reading the paper. He looked up. He didn't seem surprised. He looked like somebody not easy to surprise.

"Good day," Ibrahim Momo said into the silence.

Festus Ankrah said, "Good day to you."

Ibrahim Momo smiled. In a voice that was not unfriendly he asked, "Do I know you?"

"No," Festus Ankrah said, "you know my nephew. He painted the sign out here on your shop."

"Ah. Yeeesss," Ibrahim Momo replied. "So. I am pleased den to meet wit you. I beg siddon."

The accent was unmistakable. The pidgin phrases stuck out from his English like sharp rocks in shallow water.

Festus Ankrah sat down.

Ibrahim Momo waved his hand, as if to say: You are welcome all the same.

Festus Ankrah said, "I am hoping you can tell me where he is."

"How I suppose know?" Ibrahim Momo replied.

Festus Ankrah said, "I have done my homework."

He noticed that Ibrahim Momo's fingernails, though not long, were manicured. He was very well turned out. Generous collar. Shirt all starched. Gold hanging down to the second buttonhole. He was dressed for the night in the middle of the day.

"I see," Ibrahim Momo said. "But dis is confidential. You understand. I no fit disappoint my clients."

"I understand," Festus Ankrah said.

He took out a twenty-dollar bill and put it on the table.

Ibrahim Momo's eyebrows turned down.

Festus Ankrah said, "I am not asking you to talk to me. But perhaps you can tell my friend there."

"Eeeeh. But I don't tink dat poor ting will ever talk to me o," Ibrahim Momo said.

Festus Ankrah put a second bill on the first—this time a hundred dollars.

Ibrahim Momo sighed. He pocketed the bills. He said, "I liked dat boy. You only had to ask."

"So now I'm asking. Where did he go?"

"Tsk tsk," Ibrahim Momo said, shaking his head. "Where he go? He go Dakar now."

"Why Dakar?"

"To get to Paris."

"How?"

"On his own. My people waitin' for him in Dakar. From then on I'd like to tell you but no know. He journeyed by aeroplane. He flew. Dat's all."

Festus Ankrah reached for his wallet.

"No," Ibrahim Momo said, raising his hand, "stop dat now. You tink I don't have enough of dat ting myself?" And before he could receive an answer, "I no know precisely who he went wit. Nobody knows anybody else. Dat's how it is."

"Do you know if he got to Paris?"

"I no sure."

"Could you find out if you wanted to?"

"E go hard."

"Could I find out if I wanted to?"

"Everyting is possible if a person tries well well."

"All right," Festus Ankrah said, making his mind up immediately, and he told Ibrahim Momo that he too now needed to go to Dakar and Paris. "Can you arrange this?"

"It wouldn't be my firs' time," Ibrahim Momo said, shrugging. But he could see immediately that Festus Ankrah was not a humorous man.

"When?" he asked.

"Whenever you can," Festus Ankrah said.

"All right. I will organize."

Festus Ankrah took a calling card from his jacket and put it down on the table. He said, "Contact me here when you have a proposal. My friends"—patting his jacket—"will take care of it."

"I'm tired of your friends," Ibrahim Momo replied—it seemed— sadly, and put the card into his desk drawer without looking at it. "You can tell dis boy of yours he can pay me wit paint when he come back. Business is good. Business going to be good a long time."

FESTUS ANKRAH received two personal calls in the weeks before he closed up his house and left town. Both visits took place early in the evening, just after supper. The first visit was only a few days after his trip to Afram Street. He had not expected Ibrahim Momo's people to call so soon, and so was caught by surprise when he saw through the mosquito mesh of the front door somebody he did not know standing on his balcony.

The man on whom Festus Ankrah opened the door was neatly dressed, in a checked shirt with a bow tie, and smelled of soap and looked like a seminary student.

Festus Ankrah invited him in.

He offered the man some Star beer, which he'd been drinking alone at his dining room table. The man said he didn't drink. They sat down together at the table.

Festus Ankrah took out a cigarette.

He gave the man some water and a straw.

Ibrahim Momo had done some research, the man said, the results of which he related to Festus Ankrah.

Festus Ankrah let the man finish. Then he said, "It's not very much." It was the name of a hotel in Dakar and a number of possible contacts.

No, it wasn't very much, the man agreed politely, but it was what it was, and did Festus Ankrah require any further services of Mr. Momo?

Festus Ankrah told the man that he did.

The man asked for two photos, Festus Ankrah's passport, and a thousand dollars.

Festus Ankrah told him the dollars would take a little time.

The man nodded. He said he would take the photos and the passport now. Festus Ankrah should have the money at delivery.

Festus Ankrah left the man in the dining room and went into his bedroom. He retrieved his passport from where he kept it, under a floorboard in the doorway between his bedroom and the hall, along with cash, some gems, a few photos and a small Russian-made pistol he'd once bought off an army captain in less stable times.

He and the man went round the corner to the pharmacy to get the pictures taken. The man waited on a bench on the balcony outside, in the orange light cast by the mosquito lamp above the pharmacy door.

Inside Festus Ankrah sat on a chair with a broken back, against a sheet hung up against the back wall.

The flash of the camera left two white squares over his sight.

He and the man stood outside on the verandah while the pictures were developed. Across the bar was a hotel. There were some guests gathered around a table on a tiled patio, whose voices drifted over. They seemed to be talking about, at the same time, a female judge who had been murdered some years before and the cost of a guided tour to the forts along Cape Coast.

Festus Ankrah and the man listened without comment.

The pharmacist came out, shaking the photographic paper to make the colour set. There were six identical photos on the paper, three by two, like a slab of chocolate. The pharmacist handed the photos to Festus Ankrah.

"Give them to him," Festus Ankrah said to the pharmacist, gesturing to the man with his head.

The pharmacist gave the man Festus Ankrah's photos and went back into his shop. Festus Ankrah and the man shook hands on the street. The man told Festus Ankrah he would be contacted in time. Then the two went their separate ways.

The next day Festus Ankrah sold a small piece of property of his in Nima, and called in a few outstanding debts. It was a lot more cash than he needed for the passport, and the month or so of travel that he reckoned would be necessary, but he was too old to travel as rough as he had as a younger man. Nor was he sure he could predict anymore what the price of information would be once he reached Europe.

At the same time he began to put his affairs in order for a protracted absence. He organized for a friend to run his business, another to move into his house at a day's notice.

Then he waited.

The second visit, also unannounced, was at more or less the same time in the evening as the first, two weeks later—not an unreasonable length of time in which to obtain the necessary papers, Festus Ankrah judged.

It was a different man this time, which Festus Ankrah saw immediately from the shape through the mesh when the knock came. Festus Ankrah opened the door to a tall elderly man with spectacles and a small bag in his hand.

"Good evening, Mr. Ankrah," the man said before Festus Ankrah could address him.

"Good evening," Festus Ankrah said, then turned into the room, adding over his shoulder, "Please sit"—he gestured towards the table—"I will be a moment."

When Festus Ankrah came down from his room with the envelope of cash, the man was seated at the table, his hands folded neatly over themselves on the tabletop.

He had a dignified face. Not a face for this business.

Festus Ankrah sat down opposite the old man and pushed the envelope across the table. The man calmly picked up the envelope, lifted the unsealed flap, and looked inside.

Festus Ankrah said, "Fifty times twenty U.S. dollar bills. Count it."

The man's top lip slipped beneath the bottom, the corner of his mouth turned down.

"Hmm," he said, impressed.

Then he smiled.

He said, "If I were really smart I would take this money and never come back."

He slid the envelope back across the table to Festus Ankrah.

He said, "Regrettably, I think this is for somebody else."

Festus Ankrah leaned over the table, retrieved his envelope and pocketed it in a single motion. He smiled back. Who then did he have the pleasure of addressing at his dining room table?

The elderly man said, "My name is Dr. Kwaku Wilkins-Adofo."

Festus Ankrah waited. He did not know the name.

"I am a friend of John Bediako," the doctor said.

Festus Ankrah raised his eyebrows in enquiry, although already he had begun to suspect, from the elegance of the Twi that the visitor spoke, and the man's old-fashioned dignity.

"I am glad to have caught you before your travels," the doctor said.

Festus Ankrah said, "What makes you think I am going some-where?" realizing as he did that he sounded like a caught-out school-child.

The doctor smiled in a way that Festus Ankrah believed was intended to put him at ease. No doubt it had many before him.

He said, "Mr. Bediako told me."

"What makes him think it?"

"Aren't you?"

"Yes, I am," Festus Ankrah said.

"It is not a mystery," the doctor said. "Mr. Bediako expected you would. In addition, the father of an ex-student of Mr. Bediako, Simon Dankwa, with whom Mr. Bediako has recently been in contact, con-firmed it to Mr. Bediako."

"So what does my old friend the teacher want?" Festus Ankrah asked.

The doctor stopped smiling. In reality it pained him to smile. He had not been in the mood to smile since his old friend had called him to a dinner that past weekend, and told him what he was now about to tell Mr. Ankrah.

The doctor said, "He wants me to tell you a story."

"Another story," Festus Ankrah said wearily, determined to show as little interest as possible. "Why?"

"Because he knows what you'll do with it."

Festus Ankrah shrugged. He said, "What is this story?"

"Mr. Bediako wants me to tell you how Nana Oforiwaa died."

"Everyone knows this already," Festus Ankrah said.

"No," the doctor said gravely.

And when Festus Ankrah did not respond, and the doctor knew he had Festus Ankrah's attention, he said, "Everyone remembers the heat, and then the rain," and with these words began to recount the story of the last day of Nana Oforiwaa's life, just as he'd started it so many years ago on that starry night on the grounds of the Methodist church, when he stood before the people gathered there, and told it as then the story was known.

PARIS

IT WAS EARLY in summer when Kwasi Dankwa arrived in Paris. His trip had been long and tiring, and at times dangerous, and he was grateful to be put in touch with a countryman of his, with whom he shared a room above a covered arcade near the Boulevard de Strasbourg.

His countryman's name was Denis Owusu. Within a month Denis was able to organize him papers, and then a job, washing dishes in the underground kitchen of the Restaurant Paros, just south of the river, near the Cathedral. He worked five days a week in that kitchen, and two night shifts that ended at three in the morning. On a hard day he'd sometimes spend over fifteen hours standing at the sinks, which were down a series of narrow stairs at the back of the restaurant, his hands in hot water and the sound of frying oil at his back.

A set of windows at the top of the wall above the basins was the only opening through which fresh air could enter. Particles of grease tanned the glass a light brown, and the angle of the sill limited his view to a strip no higher than a few centimeters, through which he could see the ankles of passing pedestrians.

Out front, the boss, a small man named Nikos, would shave *sand-wich grec* from a pillar of meat turning on the spit. Nikos brought a cowbell from Greece and hung it from the beams above the restaurant door. It made a hollow tonking sound when he struck it, which he did when nobody was looking his way or reading his menus, and he'd grin at the curious faces turned towards him and sharpen the blade of his long knife against his file with special vigour.

Nikos didn't like Arabs. He didn't like any immigrants, but he trusted Africans. At least he trusted them enough to employ them in his restaurant, although only *sans papiers*—since it made them easier to get rid of if trouble came up.

The evenings he had off he spent mainly in the streets of the quarter where he lived, and which left a very strong impression on him: the decrepit passages colonized by cheap restaurants, the Indian music clicking like rickety trains, the brass and tin candelabras and the drapes crawling with tattered, twisted patterns of snakes and amoebas.

Taking a drink at a terrace on the street he would watch the world passing by: a man with trays of sweets laid out like bright baubles and seeds; a man in a track suit, folding his baguette in half; a *clochard* sitting on the pavement cleaning his toes; a girl in a shawl running across the street shouting; a smiling bald white man with his half-caste child; a black woman with a mass of blonde locks, jumpy as Marilyn Monroe.

He would see the off-duty concierge walking by, shouting *"Bonsoir tout le monde"* on his way to his house, his blue coat brilliant with golden snakes, and shot through with a row of shining buttons. The brothers on the step in front of the steel wall-length shutters would slap hands. People would wave at the *clochard,* drinking on a step, and the *clochard* would tinkle his fingers in greeting.

Everything seemed to him to be thrown together: bars on a bay window, a warehouse of plastic rolls appearing through an open lobby; house, factory, house, house, warehouse; a fish shop with its slippery chunks of stinking meat and the wet sticky ribbons of squid's legs; a sign, a lamp, a neon light, and the hairdressing shops all the way down from Château d'Eau, with their shelves of wigs, black, red, yellow, and their window fronts packed with people being styled and shorn, the floors swept round the clock, of ringlets and splinters of hair, while the hum of electric shears seeped onto the street like the sound of unsafe electricity.

This, for five months, was his home. The company that Denis kept became his company. A large loose group of them inhabited the *quartier,* all of them West and North Africans, all of them *clandestin.* Their precarious circumstances quickly bound people together. It was a close community, but also it allowed for anonymity. Nobody knew who he was—his family, his district, his country, his home language. He could be who he wanted to be.

The freedom made him dizzy. He went to a different part of the city every Sunday and walked. He went to the districts—as he named them in his head—of clocks, of churches and palaces, the district of cemeteries, the district of film houses, clothes, street markets, inside-out buildings. He deciphered the maze of the metro, spending hours traveling round and round, surfacing here and there—sometimes randomly—to see what awaited above.

It was true he put himself at risk this way. On Denis's advice he tried halfheartedly, and more out of deference to Denis than out of any real concern of his own, to pass as a tourist. He bought a sweater emblazoned with the letters of an American university, and a camera that he draped round his neck, and he made sure to stop frequently in public squares to consult a large guidebook with an ostentatious cover, as the busy crowds passed around him, even when he knew where he was. But in truth he had no fear. Without knowing why, he felt invincible and immune to chance, and proud—of having followed this journey to its end, of having taken the risks necessary to have what he now did, of his independence, his daring—even his cruelty.

Mostly he succeeded in not thinking about the past, and what he'd done to free himself from his old life. But in quieter moments he would sense the old currents still inside him, beneath the surface of his thoughts. And when he was tired, or resting, he would feel their pull again, and his thoughts drawing back to his flight, and all the actions that preceded that action; and if he was at work and it was the end of the day, he would often get away to a particular church on the edge of the tourist district, that was dark and damp like a cave, with a small mouth facing away from the sun. It had a pillar in the nave, against which he would sit, on which the flutes curved round in a spiral and then spread out into the vaulted roof like a stretching canopy. Often he sat there looking up at the ceiling, and he felt that he was inside the great chest of a whale, surrounded by its ribs. When he stared long enough, and grew dizzy, the roof would begin to breathe, and sometimes in this state he'd fall asleep and wake in the morning as the windows were catching alight with wheels of fire, and he'd be able to walk out of that place and continue almost as if nothing had happened.

Closest to him, among the group inhabiting the *quartier*, was a tall Guinean, who they sometimes called Monsieur l'Ingénieur, though in Paris he was no longer an engineer, but checked people through at Monoprix, and repaired and sold old electronic equipment on the side. He first met Mamadou—the engineer's true name—on a Sunday evening in the back of a small café a number of them frequented, on the side street off the main boulevard. It was called Le Refuge de l'Ouest, and didn't attract much attention from anyone who didn't know it. He had been about to sit at a table outside, when he saw the group crowding a table near the rotisserie, playing woaley. The noise of their laughter and conversation drowned out the pinball machines that lined the wall. He decided to sit inside instead.

Walking past their table, he noticed the unusual design of the set on which they were playing. The pips were carved from a polished hardwood. The board was surrounded by an inlay of small stones wound into curling S-vines that double-backed on themselves to form a series of loops, and caught in the light when the table was jolted. He later discovered from Mamadou that the set—which they would play on many times together—had been presented to him by the friends with whom he now sat, in honour of his escape the previous day from deportation.

Given the circumstances under which they all lived in Paris, trouble of this sort could appear at any time. On this occasion, Mamadou told him months later, his wife, Juliette, had sent him down from the apartment to buy bread. As he turned from the door to cross the road he ran into a pair of gendarmes exiting the general store. They saw each other at the same time. Lowering his eyes and not altering his pace, Mamadou made his way directly to the *télécabine* on the corner, from which he phoned up to the flat to inform Juliette that he'd never stopped loving her from the moment he first set eyes on her in the shoe shop in Barbès where her cousin had been a sales assistant. He told her to hug the children and to wait to hear from him—as they had agreed she would do in such a situation. As he put down the telephone, the glass door of the *télécabine* was opened from outside and he was asked for his papers. He only laughed.

News went round fast. Soon the house was crowded with friends. A day passed with no word. The next morning Juliette phoned some French colleagues from work, who went down to the detention centre to find out how the situation stood. Mamadou's case had already gone before the tribunal. He preferred to defend himself than be defended by the advocate assigned to him, who had mentioned as they entered the tribunal that an aeroplane was already waiting on the tarmac in Roissy. His plea was rejected after a quarter of an hour. Every day Juliette phoned the centre to speak to him, dreading the news that a place had been found on an aeroplane bound for Guinea, and he was now somewhere over the Sahara desert, handcuffed to an official, with chemicals injected into his body to keep him quiet.

But Mamadou had one last card to play. He had not had his passport on him when he was arrested and he refused to give the address of the house. The Guinean embassy would do no more than provide the French authorities with a stamped piece of paper confirming that Mamadou had lost his passport. In the end it proved impossible to move Mamadou without his identity documents, since it was impossible to move anyone without an identity.

They had no choice but to release him from the airport detention centre. Without a centime, he made his way home on foot. Making sure he'd not been followed, he arrived home at midnight. Juliette opened the door and screamed with shock and happiness. The neighbourhood wives slipped out the back.

Twelve hours later Mamadou was in the café among his friends again, not two blocks from where he'd been arrested, and this was when he first saw Mamadou.

Surrounded by the noise of their company, Mamadou and his opponent—another of their friends at that time, an Algerian called Fawad—sat silent with concentration. Of Fawad, he noticed only his cheeks, which fell inwards into his face like the shadow of a hill. Mamadou, the African, with his strong coastal features, his high forehead and hair growing densely into a thick foam on his head, looked at Fawad from under his raised eyebrows. From time to time his top lip curled under the bottom in anticipation. His eyes smiled, even his skin, with its thick pores like small mouths, seemed to smile. He could not see the game, but he heard the tapping of the pips against the board and the fall of the die, and then the cheers of the small group, which accompanied the game to its end.

Mamadou won, and a drink was bought for him, and as he turned to receive it, Mamadou saw him sitting on his own and invited him to join their group. "An English is among us," Mamadou said as he made room for another chair, having noticed his accent. "Now let us see if you can play." He won the game against Mamadou in under five minutes. He noticed some of the observers smile, and Fawad wink knowingly. Whether Mamadou had let him win or he beat Mamadou fair and square, he did not ask and never knew.

Much of his time over the next few months he spent with Mamadou and Juliette, and their two small children. Their apartment was not too far away, and it was easy for him to stop over in the evening. If it was time to eat, Juliette and Mamadou would always invite him to stay. He would help them put the children to bed and then they would stay up eating and talking, and sometimes have a little too much to drink. Juliette would inevitably go to bed, and after clearing the table, Mamadou would take one of the video machines or radios or blenders from the pile in the corner, open it up and work on it with his tools while the two of them talked on into the early hours.

Mamadou and Juliette were among the few families in their group.

They had met in Paris. Juliette was Cameroonian—from a very good family in Douala, of civil servants, doctors and accountants, she was always pleased to remind Mamadou, whose family were migrant farmers making do in the shanties of Conakry. They talked of leaving, but as Juliette would say, Paris was the only place they had in common, and she didn't see herself living in a tin shack with fifteen other people spending her days washing the clothes of Mamadou's extended family. Mamadou suffered with good humour his wife's condescension from the lofty heights of her good family in Douala, though he had privately hinted that Juliette was from a clan that had fallen out of political favour and lived less securely than Juliette would admit.

And so Mamadou and Juliette were an exception. The risk of deportation generally discouraged people from starting families. "But I cannot help whom I love, and where," Mamadou would say laughing, and if Juliette was in the room he'd wrap one of his enormous arms around her, from which she'd invariably try to disentangle herself, teasing him that he should not remind her of her weaknesses, in case she repented of her past mistakes.

For this he admired them. He admired Mamadou and Juliette for the gentle, kind world they had created together. Those three rooms on the second floor of their building—with one window, little light, and rickety plumbing, but filled with humanity and generosity— seemed to him a rebuke of everything that made their presence there illegal.

It was not something they talked about often. When they did, Juliette would only shrug. What could they do? Mamadou would say that he knew people who had stayed twenty years *sans papiers*. He'd been there four already. Juliette, it was true, might sometimes have a bitter word to say, especially since Mamadou's failed deportation, but Mamadou would not. It was not that he did not recognize what Juliette did. But as he also once said, one night at the Refuge, when conversation had turned to heavier matters: All happiness is precarious, and that if one day a person finds themself sitting in darkness, would they not prefer to have enjoyed the daylight when they could, than to have spent their time fearing the night?

It was a short time after this conversation that, on his way one night to Mamadou and Juliette's, he met a young Congolese woman called Bernadette, who wore square black glasses and sang Jacques Brel songs about sad cities and was a cheese seller's assistant in St. Germain. She'd been sitting with a girlfriend at a terrace bar, drinking glasses of cold red wine, and smoking long thin cigarettes she didn't know how to inhale properly. He'd been walking past, thinking his own thoughts, when she'd called out to him—half in challenge, half in fun, "Hey you, why do you always walk this way and you never say hello? Where are you from?"

A few hours later she had ended up accompanying him to Mamadou and Juliette's. The four of them had stayed up until three in the morning and afterwards, walking Bernadette partway to the stop to take the night bus home, he kissed her close to the Tour Saint Jacques.

From the time that they became a couple he would often sleep at her place, which was all the way over in the 16th arrondissement, in a *chambre de bonne* on Avenue Victor Hugo. It was a district he loved. The straightest trees he had ever seen lined the road outside the building in which Bernadette lodged. The road itself was made of small stones set in flowing patterns as if an immense curtain had been laid out along the ground. In winter, he would linger on the mesh grills on the pavement through which the warm rushing air from the underground trains escaped, letting it billow up his shirt to warm his chest and back.

Bernadette, unlike most people he knew, was legally resident in France. She was one of the many children of a wealthy mine engineer in Katanga who, once bored with his girlfriends, had had them, and any associated offspring, shipped to France with papers procured through his contacts in the French government. He would be over to join them very shortly, her father would tell them.

"Hundreds of women are waiting still," Bernadette would tell people, laughing.

She remembered her father vaguely—a fat man, with plump hands and wet lips, who wore safari suits and a leopard-skin fez, in imitation of his distant relative (so he claimed) Mobutu Sese Seko—a sight so

ridiculous to see, Bernadette would say, laughing, that he would not
have survived a moment had he made good on his promises to come
to France, to join his wives and his abandoned progeny, there among
the nobility of the "Société des Ambianceurs et Persons Élégants"—
the extravagant *sapeur* dandies of the Zairian community in France.

Not that Bernadette was much impressed with this nobility either.

To her, a man who wore three-thousand-franc sunglasses at night
but slept in a box in an alleyway was an embarrassment of a man.

"Even if the box smelled of Yves Saint Laurent," she would say.

"While you," she would tell him, "my funny-accented Anglophone,
will do quite fine. I prefer that you spend your days washing plates.
Look at these hands"—and she'd take his raw, calloused hands in hers—
"what *sapeur* would take around a pair of these?"

Of his past she noticed that he talked little. She told him she didn't
need to know, unless he thought there was something she should. He
told her he'd say if there was, but he didn't.

Of Celeste, he said nothing directly, but for one occasion, when one
morning in the early hours, he'd woken up suddenly from a dream of
his last night in Accra, of Celeste asleep as he'd left her on the morning of his departure—how she'd stirred at the sound of his movement
as he got up, reached out unconsciously with her hand over the ghost
of his shape in the bedding, then fallen back asleep, confident that
what was gone one moment would be back the next.

Bernadette lay beside him sleeping. He had listened to the sound
of her breathing for more than a minute before gently shaking her
awake. Her voice was soft and heavy with the weight of sleep, but her
mind was awake.

"Tell me," she said gently.

"There was a girl," he said. *Il y'avait une fille.*

"*Bien sûr,*" she said, "*mais elle était toujours là.*"

And at that moment he felt unable to talk and a very deep sudden
sadness rose up and dissolved the possibility of his having to say anything else.

After a while he noticed that she had fallen asleep again, but he
could not feel angry that she had not remained awake when he cried.

Nor did he want to be able to make the claim on her that anger would imply.

The next morning when they made love she cried, and he cried afterwards too, though not out of love, but out of gratitude.

Whenever he left Bernadette's *chambre* he would take his time getting home. A little way down the street from her rooms was a flower shop, the inside of which reminded him of the abandoned houses he knew from his own country, in which the trees and bushes would grow up the walls and through the windows and roof. Inside this shop it was as if a garden of flowers had risen up against the city—against all the gentility and civilization. It teemed over the furniture, overran the molded fixtures of the front room, and colonized the good furniture and the piano and the side tables.

There were flowers of all kinds in pots around the shop—on the black piano with the candlestick holders set into it, on an old cabinet, on marble and wooden tables: lilies and roses, irises, tulips and many others he did not know the names of. In one corner were statues of semi-dressed white women, their skin smooth as milk, in another were large pots the colour of dried clay, and the floor was made of thousands of small white stones as in the bathrooms of the Romans who inhabited Italy many years ago.

He visited the shop irregularly, and at one point—when he noticed that he was not unwelcome there—more frequently. The owner of the shop was a French woman. But from the manner in which she dealt with customers, and also the way she seemed absorbed by tending to the plants and flowers in her shop, he could tell that neither had she been born here, nor was she entirely comfortable among those she served.

He learned later that she'd come from the south of the country, from a small town in the Alpes-Maritimes, where her people had lived and farmed vegetables but also, from time to time, flowers for the local market. After a series of family misfortunes that she was reluctant to discuss, she made her way to the capital, as a young woman, and set up shop, with the help of relatives. This must have been some twenty years before he met her.

It was she who first alerted him to the museums of Paris, where she told him the great art treasures of the world were stored. And so, for the price of a few meals at a time, he went to see the paintings and the sculptures in these museums, and he spent many hours in front of the art stored there. He learned much through Madame la Fleuriste and the books that she lent him, as well as those one can read on the shelves of the bookshops on the street or in museum bookshops, once one has bought a ticket, besides what he observed with his own eyes—which was a great deal.

He saw Milon de Crotone—the man who got his head caught in a tree and was eaten by a lion, that sunk valleys into his leg with its claws and tore with its teeth into his buttocks, about to eat him from his anus upwards, entering into the guts in the soft cave of the stomach, as a lion eats an animal. He saw Valentine Balliani lying in her grave, leafing through a book while her puppies jumped on her dress. He saw sleeping knights praying to God and peeping out of their helmets at the heavens, as out of portholes. He saw the carpets and the jugs and the painted tiles of the Arabs, and the bulls of Mesopotamia and the flying horses with their men's heads, their hair curled up like centipedes, and the men carrying chariots on their heads, and their prisoners bound to poles by their hands. He saw paper-thin Egyptian fish, little pieces of slate swimming across the walls, and shelves of those people's jars and bottles and shallow dishes. He saw the inside of a church at night in Holland in the seventeenth century, where the poor sit on the stairs and become the colour of shadows. He saw their gods playing in their lakes and their landscapes made of hills and stringy trees. He saw the people in their villages dancing madly in circles, eating and drinking and falling to the ground, and suckling their babies while the dogs sniffed at their baskets and plates. He saw angels sliding down rays of light. He saw the studious astronomers in their quiet rooms, the light dropping in like a sheet and at the same time like a river, the table covered with papers and a flowing curtain. He saw the glass windows in a Dutch house, and the wooden doors and the white plaster walls, and the light spilling around like soft fires, and in the corner, the children entering and leaving through it.

He saw Italy with its temples and castles rising up from the sea, with its beaches on which hawkers sat with their donkeys and their wares, and the servants waited around the boats. He saw men with the feet of goats jumping out of the reeds and catching the flimsy girls. He saw a city on water where the sea was as smooth as marble and was cut up by veins under its skin. He saw the naked ladies of northern Italy, the white bulls and the saints being whipped, the monks flying supernaturally through the air, the angels surfing down from heaven, the spiky red devils, the heads of saints grown round with gold, and the air that is so clear you can see every thread on the robe of a pope, and every grain in a plank of wood. He saw Saint Pierre with a machete in his head, and his forehead leaking blood. He saw a woman standing at a balcony with an umbrella, staring past him, and poets sitting around a table set with flowers. He saw apples and cake set out for a picnic in the forest attended by men in clothes and women without clothes. He saw a small soldier playing the flute, and babies and angels tumbling down the doors of hell. He walked among centuries of statues, pure and white, with their eyes blind as eggshells. Occasionally he found images of himself, or from his world: at one time the statue of a Mauritian girl, caught smiling, half-flattered, half-shy, her eyes dropped, both her nipples plucked through her dress, the one an onyx bauble, the other still clothed, and wearing in her hair a beautiful flower that opened like a water jug, sticky with pollen. He saw himself in the same century, his face swimming out of a pink dress as he looked quietly upon the form of his mistress, the whore; and again, a slave holding up a quarter of the world.

Outside, though, when he walked nearby through the streets by the river, past the shops full of artifacts from Africa, he was everywhere. The breasts of the women spirits were cones; the eyes and noses were scars carved into the face; their mouths were holes punched in and out of the flesh; and their hair was a flurry of scratches stabbing the wood. Never had he seen these things in such number until he saw them displayed in the shops of Rue de Seine—dolls for fertility and war and placation and honour to the spirits of villages long since cut down for the making of the great road, or emptied for the slave galleys.

But the feelings of dejection and estrangement with which he came away from the museum in the old d'Orsay railway station—a world away from the enthusiasm with which he had arrived in the city—were also coloured by events that had just then begun unfolding across the river on Boulevard de Strasbourg, where by now he had been living for four months. The first of two police raids in the district during that time took place in the early hours one Sunday morning in November. He had slept the night before at Bernadette's, and had gone directly from there to work the next morning, and so when he reached Boulevard de Strasbourg late on Sunday afternoon everything was already over.

Around fifteen people had been taken. The searches had gone door to door. There must have been informers, Denis told him, as he moved around the floor, packing his things. Though their room had been raided, Denis had climbed through the trapdoor in the roof and escaped detection. Denis suspected the landlords they rented from. "Ici c'est chaud," he said. Later in the day Denis left, for Barbès, he said, where he had friends he could stay with. Denis advised him to do the same.

He went down to see who was around, but the Refuge de l'Ouest was closed, one glass door crossed with masking tape where he could see the frame had been kicked. He stood there for a moment. "Ils sont partis," Jean-Louis, the grocer from the general store across the road, called out from behind his back. He turned around. Jean-Louis stood squarely in his door, leaning against the frame. Then he turned and walked back into his shop.

At first it was difficult to know who had been taken and who was hiding, since those who escaped returned only in the next few days to collect their belongings and move on. Fawad, he knew, was among the unlucky. So were the Ivorian brothers, Sulaiman and Ali, who frequently joined them on their evening games in the Refuge. Monsieur Richard, who owned the café, and was naturalized, returned on the Tuesday. He'd been arrested, and could tell them the names of a few more, including the four to whom he had rented. Of their immediate group, only Denis, Mamadou and his family, and he had escaped. He moved his things to Bernadette's. Mamadou decided to stay where he was. Mamadou had been in Paris much longer than most of them and had seen these raids before. And then there were Juliette and the children to take into account, who he did not want to move if it wasn't necessary. In any event, he estimated, the trouble was past (and to make sure, Mamadou had paid his landlord their next month's rent in advance).

In the days immediately after the raids he would call Mamadou and Juliette every night, or drop by. Life resumed its more familiar rhythms. They all began to relax. But when, a fortnight later, the phone went unanswered at Mamadou's, he cancelled his night shift and made his way across the river, fearing the worst. Mamadou and Juliette lived a short distance from Denis and his old lodgings, near the Metro Temple. He let himself into their building. The stairs had no light, and he climbed to the third floor in darkness. When he got to their landing he knocked on the door, though he knew it needed no more than a push to swing open. The lock had been broken for a while—at least his three previous visits—and the door was held in place by a piece of wood jammed from the inside between the latch and the frame. Mamadou had shown him how he'd cobbled it together a few weeks before, with an elaborate explanation of how it should work, although primarily for the benefit of Juliette, who stood in the middle of the room, her hands at her side, her usually wide smile folded into a thin line across her face in an expression of exaggerated disapproval. This was part of the game they played for ignoring poverty. Instead of turning away, and allowing herself to feel despair, she pretended to await appeasement. Mamadou pretended there was something to be done. "Look," Mamadou was saying to him, "look how well this piece of wood is working," and he shook the door in its frame, though not hard enough to dislodge the jam. Then Mamadou had him return out onto the landing to try to open the door from the outside (which earned Mamadou further scolding from Juliette, for sending their guest away the moment he arrived, and without food).

Now, a week later, he pushed the door open. The wood jam wasn't in place. But then Mamadou, it occurred to him, might not have been the last to close the door. The room inside was dark. He didn't need light to know his way around: the couch draped with a blanket; two chairs, the straw base of one lifting like the prongs of a fork (which was his when he and Mamadou stayed up late and the rest of the family went to bed); the television and video machine indistinguishable from the broken appliances Mamadou repaired to supplement his income, balanced in a stack in the corner of the room. The light from the landing cut a slice out of the floor. A plate of half-eaten food was on the table beside a pile of magazines. The sofa was pulled out at an angle from the table, the blanket twisted, it seemed, by movements of haste. The air was heavy with the smell of living—of soap, food, the weight of breath that fills an unventilated space. He let the door close behind him and turned on the light, and in the moment that the room sprang into existence was struck by the feeling that what until then he had regarded as the present had just become the past. He stood still for a few moments, then turned towards the doorframe that led to the bedroom. Mamadou had often talked of buying wood for a door, so that the presence of visitors staying up into the early hours of the morning would not disturb his wife and children. There had once been a piece of cloth hanging over the entrance, but that was now gone. As he turned he heard a whisper of movement—more a disturbance in the inner ear than a sound—and the cupboard door inside the bedroom slowly swung open to reveal Juliette, a stained bib tucked into her boubou, and a child holding on to each of her legs.

Mamadou, she told him a few minutes later—after he had sat her down and she'd dried her eyes, and the worst was confirmed—had managed to bundle her and the children into the cupboard before the police had come to the room. She had heard the scuffle, and the sound of blows, as Mamadou had charged them, trying to drive them into the corridor. Then shouting, the sounds of effort. Then silence. She hadn't known what to do. She was afraid to answer the phone. She was afraid to leave the house in daylight.

That night he helped Juliette and the children move into her sister's house in the north of the city. The next morning he started searching for Mamadou. But even with the help of their French friends they could find no trace of Mamadou—not in the police stations, nor in the detention centres, nor in the hospitals. There was little they could do but wait. He visited every day after work. Juliette was in a very bad way. It was difficult to see her so weak. She barely communicated. When she did talk, it was in whispers. He would sit with her and try to discuss issues, and comfort her, but she would keep her eyes lowered, and nod, and only reply with a yes or a no. One evening they found the children feeding themselves from their plate that had been brought in at lunchtime, while Juliette lay on the bed, a bundle facing into the corner. They grew afraid of how much longer this could continue, and talked of what they could do. But finally they had news—from a countryman of Mamadou with family in Conakry. Mamadou had been repatriated. A short time after that came the telephone call they were expecting, and they went into the next room to let Juliette talk to Mamadou in private, though the wall was thin and they could hear her crying. But when the call was over, and they came back in, Juliette appeared cheerful and full of purpose, though her cheeks glowed with tears. Mamadou, she told them, had plans to return—he was gathering together funds. No more than a few months, he promised—they would go to Marseilles, where Mamadou had family. Mamadou's family was already waiting for her. They asked her to stay a little longer, to rest, at least until Mamadou was safely back in France, since they knew how difficult and uncertain the journey was, even with means. But Juliette would hear nothing of it. They tried to reason with her. By the weekend, however, everything she and Mamadou had accumulated over four years had been sold off, and they waved goodbye at the Gare de Lyon, then stood and watched as the train threaded its way out into the dirty gray afternoon.

He returned to Bernadette's place that evening, drained and tired, and ready to put the events of the last month behind him. But the next morning he could not bring himself to leave the bed. He lay rigid with fear. Juliette's departure with the children had initially left him relieved—relieved that he'd no longer have to watch her helplessness and self-pity, from which deep inside he recoiled. But now that they were gone he realized that the helplessness and self-pity, and the feelings of violated dignity from which they arose, were his own. He was in turns angry and terrified. He could not bring himself to open the door and step out into a world in which the accident of being born in one place, not another, or possessing one piece of paper and not another, could turn your fellow human beings against you, and you into a hunted animal, on which all kinds of legitimate violence could be inflicted. Having never given much thought to that violence, he was now terrified of it. He cowered during the day, and at night, sleeping thinly, he dreamed a series of repetitive nightmares. One was of standing in his room while all around him men with iron mallets pounded his belongings into powder. Another was of being dragged down dimly lit passages that somehow reminded him of the Paros kitchens, with only the light of the streets shining through before closing time.

A few weeks later, after an argument with Bernadette that arose from her frustration with his sudden mental fragility, he packed his bag and left. She let him go. He took the stairs down from her *chambre de bonne* in the attic. Taking the elevator, she beat him down to the ground floor, and was waiting for him when he came through the stairwell; and in the lobby of the building, with its echoing hallways that amplified every last sound up into the salons of all the apartments above, she began screaming at him.

How could he leave as calmly as he was? His friends were gone, but still there was her. Did she count for nothing?

He told her to stop her hysterics. He told her that she didn't need him and that she knew it herself.

"You know?" she screamed. "I think that you're right. Who do you think you are? You can't hurt me."

He slept that night under the Pont d'Iéna. The next night he found a room near Pigalle. He paid dearly for the room, but he had it to himself, and he locked himself in there, with a chair jamming the door handle shut. He left only to get himself food. Towards the end of a wretched fortnight he began to gain control of his thoughts, and rein in the bouts of paranoia, which left him curled up in the corner of the room. His time in Paris would soon be coming to an end, he reasoned. Did he want it to end like this, cowering in a room, defeated? And so after many attempts at building up his confidence, and a few false starts, he set out into the city, to regain his place in it. He stepped out onto the road, and the sky was as he remembered it, and the walls of windows and doors and balconies were as he remembered them, though they seemed bleached somewhat of their colour, like the aftermath of a great headache.

He returned to Strasbourg, where everything looked the same, only the people he had known and loved—he realized it now—loved—were gone, replaced by new faces, new immigrants, new lives—just as good, only not those that had been part of his life.

He stepped into a music shop he had once known. Inside it was still stacked up its walls with records and tapes and CDs and videos. Those surfaces that weren't displaying wares were plastered with posters advertising concerts at Bercy and the latest albums recorded by Central Africans in Parisian recording studios. The giants of Francophone African music looked down from the walls, in impossibly shining clothes, decked in impossibly large jewels, surrounded by women whose hips exploded with impossible fertility from their thin waists. On the back wall a wide-screen television played to an audience that stood in the centre of the shop floor, as the large speakers placed all around the ceiling fed the jingling soundtrack into the shop.

A man and his three friends were arguing loudly with the owner behind the counter about a cheque. Their language flew out of them like streams of erratic bats. The men standing beneath the television were shouting back to them to be quiet so that they could watch the video.

"And whose shop is this?" the owner shouted back. "You who buy nothing and only come here like a cinema." But the spectators knew he didn't mean this, and they laughed and told him then they wouldn't come, and then who would buy his merchandise, and was there not another shop next door (which there was), and the shopowner knew the spectators did not mean it either.

He stepped back onto the street. He walked to Bernadette's house, and stood at the door and thought of ringing the buzzer, but didn't. Instead he went into the flower shop and Madame was there, and she laughed to see him after so long—she thought he'd disappeared (he had); and as she searched for a spare flower for him he looked down once again at the pattern of the whirling stones, and felt himself grow calm.

It didn't last long. After ten days into a new job in Les Halles, he found himself slipping into a new and different depression. Now even his fear, he realized, had left him. He no longer saw it hanging back at a corner, caught by a red traffic light on the other side of a boulevard. Even its company he began to miss. He felt totally abandoned. He grew restless. And then he grew reckless. He took himself to places where he knew himself likely to be picked up. He put himself in the way of danger. He hurried with his eyes down past gendarmes in the marketplace. He stood against walls in the metro, staring vacantly. He observed the commotion caused as a large African woman with three children was picked up without a ticket. "Shame," a passerby was saying to a policeman. "Can you not see how you have made her upset before her children?" But nobody came for him. He went up to a gendarme and stood before him. The Frenchman looked at him impassively, and his eyes widened with bored enquiry. Eventually he had to ask him the time.

The experience with the policeman stayed with him for a long while. He had given up his fear, but found himself more alone now than he'd ever been when he lived like a madman in his room, watching the days move across the walls. *Then* he had believed at least that those whom he feared, the fear of whom was his occupation, were likewise occupied with him. But he'd realized, looking into the face of the bored gendarme, that they were as little interested in him as they were in tying their bootlaces in the morning. He realized that he had in fact been comforted in his darkest hours by the thought of these men and women poring through papers, tracking down payment slips, utility bills, trying to seek him out, working meticulously towards him in his room. He'd been comforted by the idea that legions of them were anxious for his capture, were sleeping neither night nor day as they hunted him. He believed he was hiding. He believed he was avoiding capture, avoiding his enemies, who were growing frantic with his elusiveness, with his uncanny ability to remain invisible to them. And part of him, he knew, was willing them to get closer and closer; and when they'd find him his heart would go crazy with fear and joy, and he would embrace them, and they'd be glowing with conquest, and the exuberance of their long chase. And so it came as a great shock to him that he mattered so little to them. That if they picked him up it would be by chance. And that what had happened to them—to Mamadou, Juliette, to the whole community in Strasbourg—was no more than an accident.

In this new state of despair he grew aimless, and his aimlessness made him vulnerable. He was sitting one day at a quiet table in a cheap café in the 20th arrondissement when the waiter—who had served him many times without so much as a nod of recognition—made a joke of bringing a bottle of water without a glass, which he then proceeded to produce from behind his back, as if it were a gift offered to a child. And his heart opened to this man, with gratitude. But later that night he knocked him cold with his elbow when the waiter tried to feel his private parts as he sat in the waiter's little studio overlooking the rails in the valley of tracks where the trains from Gare du Nord carve their way out of the city. He left the man lying with his face hanging over the arm of his sofa, and the television dancing against the back of the wall, and he closed the door and went down eight flights of stairs and stood on the road, full of shame and anger and remorse. He reflected how deadening it felt to have nobody to sit opposite him and laugh with and share some food with, to take his hand, and to let him sleep beside them and watch them, and to give him a little of their life. His heart sat with deadness inside him. His living kept nothing alive. Days would go by where he could not throw his thinking into anything. He felt as if he were smoke, leaking out of himself.

He began to travel the metro endlessly, without a destination in mind. He did it for days, not knowing why at first, only later realizing it was simply to see the faces of people. To see that life was going on, and could go on, without him.

It was on one such day of travelling that, randomly exiting the metro at Filles du Calvaire, he mounted the stairs and surfaced into a chilly, overcast January morning. As he reached the corner of Rue Oberkampf he saw on the other side of the road an African woman with a blanket over her shoulders, followed by her three children in their lovely clothes—two girls, and trailing at the back, a small boy.

The braids of the girls were jumping off their faces, coloured beads at their ends. The little boy was wearing a necklace made of elastic threaded with small candies. His nose was running, and his cheeks glistened with mucus, and he was talking excitedly as he tried to keep up. As he watched the family walk by, it felt as if a piece of gauze were lifting from his vision. The world around him seemed to spring into focus. He was filled suddenly by an overwhelming feeling of pride in their happiness, that stayed with him as he followed them through the streets, until their journey took him into a road full of cut-price *agences de voyages*. He now let himself fall behind, so that within a few paces they had rounded a corner and were out of sight. Then he stopped.

In the window of the shop in front of which he now stood there was an advertisement displaying the prices of tickets to the various destinations of interest to the immigrant communities that inhabited the quarter. He scanned down the list. As he did his eye passed over the listing for Dakar.

He remembered the house in which he'd stayed—the man called Adams, the woman, the girl called Astou.

He thought about the journey preceding that.

The prostitute near the station.

The train.

The cars and buses.

He scanned down the list of cities in the window until he came to Accra.

He hesitated for a moment, then he turned around, and climbed back down into the metro, and made his way over to the 16th arrondissement.

THE BOATS AT TESHIE

MARY DANKWA received three envelopes from her brother bearing Senegalese postage stamps. Each contained a postcard, the text on which was continued over a number of handwritten pages torn from a notebook. Although they arrived at the same time, they were dated over a period of half a month.

The postcard in the earliest-dated of the envelopes bore the image of a soldier in ceremonial dress standing outside the wrought-iron gate of the Presidential Palace in Dakar. Behind him, through the gate, the pillars, stairs and walls of the palace itself were blurred. The soldier wore a thin, recently pressed, blood-red tunic, the wedge shapes of the iron still visible in the folds of the material. It had black epaulettes and a black collar with a gold buckle, and gold buttons down the front. The fit was slightly awkward, giving the soldier the appearance of a well-conceived but slightly ill-executed puppet. A large-caliber automatic assault rifle was slung diagonally across his chest. The barrel was ribbed like a husk of corn. The gun gleamed like polish. The soldier wore a red cloth cap, with a gold insignia, attached to his head by a black strap around his neck in the style of a train conductor of old. His head was slightly cocked to one side. The light made an S shape across the contours of his face. His mouth was closed. His eyes wide open, the whites like yellowed marble. The eyes themselves expressionless, as a soldier's should be, but for the musculature around them, Mary Dankwa couldn't help thinking, as if about to collapse like burnt plastic and reveal everything of the real person.

Mary Dankwa turned the postcard over.

In his message to her, Festus Ankrah explained that the Presidential Palace, figured in the blurred background of the postcard she held in her hands, was a few blocks from the Place de l'Indépendance—the Senegalese equivalent of their Black Star Square—and that a few blocks to the other side of the square, or *place,* as it is called in French, was the hotel where her son had stayed on his arrival in Dakar, which serves as a kind of clearinghouse. From here, he told her, Kwasi had moved into the care of other smugglers, about whom Festus Ankrah was trying to find out more. He would write again when he had news.

The second postcard, dated ten days later and relating to his sister the information that he had discovered, had on the front the image of a building at dusk. The building was made of thick, solidly built walls, plastered and painted an earthy pink, worn milky and smudged along its balustrades, balconies and pillars, as if by the touch of human hands over many, many years. The building was divided into two levels. At the bottom, two sets of stairs with waist-high walls rose from a courtyard to a second story, in gentle symmetrical ellipses. The stairs were uneven and chipped. The second story comprised a gallery, with five pillars, obscured in darkness, behind which rooms led off further into the building. The gallery afforded an unobstructed view of the courtyard below, which was deserted but for a small child carrying a lantern, pausing, looking over his shoulder at the camera. Between the rising sides of the staircases was an arch that led to a passageway. From there, a long tunnel led under the building to its exit onto the sea, from which—through a distant doorless frame—a rectangle of light from the setting sun burst into the centre of the picture.

Isle de Gorée, the postcard said on the front.

On the back of the postcard, Festus Ankrah had written to his sister that from the Place de l'Indépendance clearinghouse, Kwasi had moved to a group operating close to the airport. He intended to visit there soon when he knew more. But already he knew that after a few days Kwasi had gone to Paris by aeroplane—not directly, but thankfully nor by boat or overland. As soon as Festus Ankrah could contact the people who had procured Kwasi's ticket, and establish who facilitated his arrival and settlement in Paris, he himself would follow.

The third and last postcard, dated only a few days after the second, and about a month before the day that Mrs. Dankwa held it in her own hands, bore the picture of a flotilla of long canoes—hundreds of them it seemed, tied up together in harbour so tightly that they resembled the scales of a fish; different colours, bleached almost to gray by years in the sea and dulled further by the evening light, seamlessly packed and overlapping, and covering the surface of the water at least twenty metres out from the shore, to where some sea birds were wheeling overhead in the low sun, indicating where pieces of fish gut and offal were to be had. On a distant boat two people, a few pixels in silhouette, appeared to be discussing the contents of a yellow bucket between them.

In his message Festus Ankrah told his sister that the postcard she held in her hand was of a fish market, Soumbedioune, and did it not make her think of the beach at Teshie, from which their father and the other fishermen had set out on their boats when they were children?

He told her that he had found the house from which Kwasi had flown to Europe, that he had enough information to continue his search, and that he himself would be in France in the next few days. He told her that her son was somewhere in Paris, although he would not be able to find him directly, but would have to seek out others in that country first.

Mary Dankwa put the three postcards down.

Yes, the third did remind her of the beach at Teshie, as long ago as it was.

Their father, in his youth, had been the leader of one of the fishing crews that worked a watsa dugout on the sea near Accra—one with beautiful designs all along the topside planking: pictograms of swords and stools, writing she could not understand, and right at the front, the drawing of a man with enormous private parts.

This was in the days before motor engines. When they powered their boats by muscle alone. How everyone admired them. These huge, strong men, pride of the district, eight, ten of them, paddles carving the water as they headed the canoes out through the waves.

Admired them. But feared for them too.

"Where do they go to when we cannot see them anymore?" Mary would ask her mother, where they stood on the shore watching the boats recede.

"Out to where the sea is *sooo* deep," their mother would say.

"How deep?" Festus would ask—a little boy, beside himself with wonder.

"So deep," their mother once said, "that anything lost will never come back."

"But why do they get lost?" Festus asked, "Why don't they come back?"

"Because they die," Mary had said sharply, "they drown." Just because her small brother might have been fooled, she wasn't. She knew the measure of things, her mother's uneasiness, her father's restlessness when the season was slack and he had to stay home.

"No," their mother said gently, "they don't. They sink to the bottom of the sea, and continue to live, except that their memories of us are lost."

Mary noticed her brother's mouth open as he listened, his eyes still trained on the distance.

Their mother said, "That is why we must send them out to sea with memories of us that are so strong that they may never forget."

"And so that we can find them afterwards and bring them back!" Festus said, with a tone of triumph.

"Yes," their mother had said, "that is correct."

"You?" Mary said contemptuously to her brother. "You can't even find the path to our compound." And to finish off the conversation, "You are only six."

"Yes," their mother had said. "But he is only six now," drawing her reluctant son into the folds of her skirt, her hand falling round his head.

Mary Dankwa, more than half a century later, frowned at the memory. Taking a last look at the postcards on the table, she began walking slowly to the bedroom, to the mat in front of the bed where she prayed.

But then she didn't.

Instead she went out onto the verandah, and lowered herself into a wicker chair and closed her eyes, and started to call into her mind images of her son—every one that would come, starting from the moment of his backwards birth.

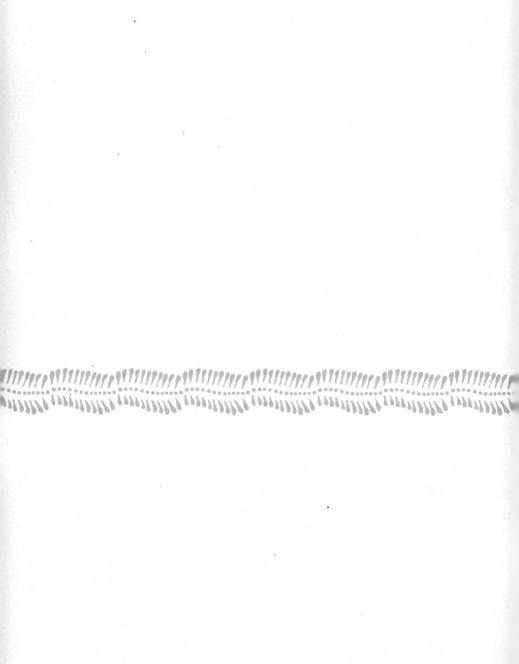

LE REFUGE CLANDESTIN

WAITING OUTSIDE Bernadette's apartment building on Avenue Victor Hugo, Kwasi Dankwa stood back against the wall where he could least be seen. The sodium lamps dropped pools of light onto the pavement.

At last the door opened from the inside and a woman and her child, bundled up in wool against the cold, came out.

He slipped behind them as they left and caught the door before it closed. He let himself into the lobby, with its marble floors and walls, its potted plants and its mirror, which a month before had reverberated with the sound of his and Bernadette's final argument.

He got into the elevator and pressed for the sixth floor.

The doors closed over the lobby, and he watched the six floors gliding past through the lattice grill, and it felt like time passing and passing, each stage a life, there, then gone.

On the sixth floor he got out and walked to the stairwell and climbed the last flight of the service steps up into the attic.

A thin corridor ran the entire perimeter of the building, off which the converted servant quarters now housed the au pairs and lodgers and servants who lived in the eaves above the apartments.

Bernadette opened the door on the second knock.

At first she said nothing.

Then she saw the small canvas bag at his feet.

"No, Kwasi," she said, her eyes narrowing, her bottom lip rising, as if in indignity at an undeserved and suddenly realized unkindness. "Why should I? Tell me why I should."

Her voice had risen, and he could hear in it her incredulity and simultaneously her hurt.

He said softly, "Give me a week. I'll tell you then."

She sighed and leaned against the doorframe.

He didn't look good at all to her. He wasn't eating properly. Probably he was living on sunflower seeds and bread, she thought, which is what he snacked on.

And he hadn't cut his hair, for what that was worth, which made his head look round. The light shone off the oiliness in his skin. There was only one bulb in the corridor and half of his face was in shadow. He looked like the moon.

Already, she could feel her anger subsiding. She could see how this was going to turn out if she didn't stop it now.

How could she trust him, she wondered, as they stood there in silence—this man, half in the light and half in the dark.

He lifted his eyes towards her.

He'd caught her in the middle of cooking. The kitchen was two portable electric hobs under the window. The room was filling up with the smell of frying.

Over her shoulder he could see that the windows were closed. The glass was mottled with steam. He knew that if she didn't open the windows the smell would get into her clothes and airing them out from the pole he'd once rigged up out of the window would probably not do the trick by morning.

He shifted on his feet, raised his eyebrows questioningly.

On the other side of the windows he could hear the pigeons padding around in the eaves where they nested. He could hear the ruffling of their wings. The purr of their communication.

Without realizing it, Bernadette was still holding the wooden spoon with which she'd been stirring the chilies and tomatoes. A slow stream of hot red sauce was inching its way down the handle towards her fingers.

He watched it but didn't say anything.

Still she hadn't responded.

The truth was she never thought she'd see him again. She was used to people coming and going. She was used to not relying on other people. Certainly not men.

So what had there been to feel so cheated by? What had he promised? Nothing. Nor had she wanted any promises out of him.

She stood aside to let him walk past her into the room. As she started to move he grabbed the spoon by the handle just above her hand.

The sauce flowed over his knuckles.

He winced but didn't say anything.

She saw what had happened. She let go of the spoon and he put it down.

"That must hurt," she said calmly.

"It does," he said.

"Thank you," she said with a little less disinterest—now she was trying to wipe the hot sauce from his hand with the cloth she'd held in her other.

He let her dab away and then tried to take her hand.

She felt anger flaring again. She was thinking about the scene down in the lobby from his departure, the humiliation it had caused her. How could she have done that? She still couldn't look some of the tenants in the eye. It was his fault. To have made her do that? That wasn't her.

She pulled away.

But this wasn't her either. She didn't want to feel angry and proud. She said over her shoulder, "It had better be a very good story."

She opened the window, and tried to wave the steam out of the room with her hands. He laughed from behind her, and she laughed too.

Then she turned around and leaned back on the counter on her hands.

"Are you all right, Kwasi? Are you hurt? Nobody's seen you at all. Where have you been living?"

"Under a roof," he said.

"Oh," she said, the sides of her mouth turning downward in non-committal interest.

She asked if he'd been alone.

He told her that he had.

She nodded.

Then he leaned down and picked up the bag he'd brought with him, which was at his feet. She thought it was clothes inside, but it wasn't. He opened the bag and it was flowers he'd picked up from Madame la Fleuriste.

"I brought these," he said.

What does this man think? she thought. But still she let herself smile and came over to him and took the flowers, smelled them, even as she hated the stupidity of being flattered by flowers.

But so what? She was.

"So is this sorry?" she asked.

"Yes," he told her.

"Idiot," she said, and she put down the flowers and let him hold her.

Then she asked him if he was hungry.

He was. So she added some more tomatoes to her sauce and made a double portion of rice. He got out the knives and forks and the water and salt and they ate the meal together.

He did the washing up and then they sat down together on her sofa that opened up into her bed, and for twenty minutes, speaking softly, not looking at her, he told her where he'd been in the last four weeks, of some of the things that had happened, and what he had done and what he had felt, and something of what he made of it, to the extent that he could make anything of it at all.

When he'd finished speaking they sat in silence.

Then he looked at her and asked her if she thought he was crazy.

She wanted to tell him that she didn't care if he was, but she didn't. She didn't say anything.

He said that maybe he should ask her rather if she could live with it.

"I can," she said, "until I can't."

But then she corrected herself because it wasn't quite what she wanted to say.

"Yes," she said.

He put his hand on her hand.

He said, "Thank you."

She said, "At least for tonight."

"Oh," he said, "so now you want me to stay the night."

She said, "You don't?"

"I wouldn't want you to think I'm easy," he said.

She smiled back. "OK," she said, letting go of him and getting up, "then I'll try not to," and she went over to the basin and pushed the pots aside and got out her soaps and her toothbrush and the creams for her face to get ready for bed.

It was the end of February. The month had but a few days to run. Over three trips he moved his clothes and his few possessions from Pigalle to Bernadette's rooms. On the last of the trips he stopped by his old apartment in Strasbourg to see if perhaps Denis had come back, or in any event learn news of the others.

Denis was gone. They were all gone. Nobody knew where he was. Six people from Vietnam were now living in his old rooms. They let him poke around for a few moments. There were still some of the pieces of furniture he and Denis had purchased, or found, or fixed—a large chest of drawers they'd once seen on a pavement in Barbès, and somehow managed to wedge in the back of Fawad the Algerian's station wagon. An old record player that Mamadou had given him. There was a framed painting he'd picked up in his first month in Paris from a *bouquiniste* on Île de la Cité—a van Gogh–inspired scene of Saint Michel, all garishly yellow and blue—still hanging, though on a different wall, and behind which he and Denis would keep the monthly rent.

He turned the painting round. There it was, three months later.

The franc notes folded up like a cigar, pinned behind a nail that held the plywood in its frame, which he took. It was all the cash he had.

Down on the street he recognized a few faces. He recognized the *clochard,* a knitted cap pulled tightly over his head like a tea cozy, as he slept under a stair. He recognized the tall Liberian waiter at Café Deux Garçons, who had a cut down the side of his cheek, scarred up like sofa upholstery; and two of the waiters in the Indian restaurant. He recognized in the small bar filled with mirrors, birdcages, and orchids, the woman tending the bar who was really a man.

But he knew better than to linger as the people of the *quartier* came in for the early evening, and instead went round the corner to where the Refuge de l'Ouest had been. It was still closed. What had he really expected? There were posters over the windows now. The glass at the top of the doorframe was marbled over with dust. At the bottom there was still the crack where the boot of a gendarme had kicked it, patched with heavy masking tape.

He stopped at the North African restaurant two shops down, where sometimes in the old days they would get something to eat after Monsieur Richard got tired of them and closed up the Refuge for the night.

The Arab restaurant was a long thin room stretching back from the street, where they had a few tables with plastic covers, and plastic chairs, and a television over a counter playing Arabic music, and a small Moroccan woman underneath playing patience, and a half-lit hovel of a kitchen behind, from which her husband, who lived in a haze of smoke and walked with a limp, would bring food to the four or five customers who'd been coming there every night for twenty-five years, and appeared to be the only justification there was for continuing to keep the place open.

The old man gave him a grunt of acknowledgement when he came in. *"Quelle jolie surprise,"* he croaked in a broken, smoke-scored voice, *"quelle jolie surprise,"* and had him sit down and brought him some mint tea unasked.

"Amis sont partis," the old man said, standing in front of the table with a bowl of sugar cubes, *"partis. Tant pis. Humph . . ."* and he shrugged.

He drank his tea slowly. The old woman, playing cards at the other end of the room at her counter, raised her eyebrows in friendship, then began cursing the hand of cards spread out before her.

The old man came back with another cup of tea and a piece of paper with a telephone number on it.

"*Fawad,*" he said. "*C'est Fawad.*"

Fawad's telephone number.

After his tea he shook the old man's hand. He waved at the woman playing cards. She raised her eyebrows, shrugged, sucked a lungful of tar from the cigarette hanging off her lip, and began dealing cards.

He put his bag on his shoulder, went round the corner, avoiding Rue Oberkampf, and descended into the metro.

The tunnels were full of the sounds of somebody playing drums. Some hawkers were selling sunglasses and scarves. It smelled of nuts down beneath the ground.

It took thirty-five minutes to get to the 16th arrondissement. When he resurfaced above ground it was getting to be evening. There was a fine mist of drizzle in the air. Behind him, over the river, the lights of the city were coming on. The gold dome of the Invalides shone like a child's painted sun.

He made his way towards Avenue Victor Hugo. Across the road from Bernadette's, the lights of the flower shop shone out into the early evening, intensified by the mirrors and the marble and the glass of the chandeliers. The door was half-opened. It was strange to see the place open at this hour. He stopped and poked his head in. There were large plastic sacks of dirt in a stack just inside the doorway.

"*Salut,* Madame, it's Edward," he shouted in.

There was no response.

He put his bag down and walked into the interior of the shop. The buckets in which the flowers for passing trade were kept on the pavement were lined up against the back walls. The floor around them was wet, where Madame must have dragged them in and spilled the water. On the long counter where she usually cut and wrapped the special orders, rows of pots were spread out, with seedlings recently planted.

He called out Madame's name again.

There was no response.

The cash register, he noticed, was turned off.

The statues of the naked white goddesses watched him serenely as he walked around.

The profusion of plants, which screened off whole sections, the clutter of noble furniture, and the sound of dripping water from two fountains made the room seem much bigger than it was. But it took little time for him to realize that he was alone.

He made his way around the displays, poking his head into the side rooms and vestibules, round the divisions made by shelves full of trays of seedlings.

At last he went to the back of the shop, where it curled round the inner courtyard and lengthened into a thin corridor without any windows. There was a kettle and sink. The temperature seemed to drop. The walls, he noticed, were thick and rough, and ended in a series of shelves stacked with packets and implements and rolls of wire and string. And he noticed, where before he'd assumed there to be only shelves, that one whole wall was in fact the back of a door, that was slightly ajar. As he approached he could see a dim light rising from beneath, up a series of steep steps that wound immediately downwards in a tight spiral.

He opened the door further and shouted down, "Hello?"

"Hello," came back the voice of Madame.

He waited, and then walked down the stairs.

Beneath the floor, where he descended, there opened up a large cellar, at least two or three feet under the ground. It was illuminated along the ceiling by rows of fluorescent lights, joined by metal pipes that housed the electric cables. The cellar must have stretched the whole length of the shop underneath. The walls were made of arched bricks. The floor was set with paving stones. The whole space was washed white and was completely empty but for a large stack of plastic bags—the same as upstairs—stacked five high against the back wall, which Madame was heroically trying to move to the stairs.

"Welcome to my cavern," Madame said, leaving the plastic bags and standing up and brushing her hands down her skirts.

"Do you need some help?" he asked.

"In effect, yes," Madame said.

As he helped her haul a couple of bags of compost she explained that she'd never use the cellar at all if she weren't so cramped upstairs, but what was she to do?

He told her he had no idea this space existed.

Few people did, she said, and that now he knew her *grand secret*.

The room, in fact, was the original cellar, she told him, and had been reinforced as an air-raid shelter during the war. She had once found a few old coins and some spoons and what looked like the wheel from a model car in various nooks and crannies. It was, he had no doubt noticed, completely impractical, and why the workmen who delivered the sacks of compost had decided to stack them right at the back was a complete mystery to her, but here she was, a little old lady (she was hardly that, he protested), with nobody to help her, and how glad she was that he'd happened to come along, and perhaps, in fact, he could come more often, she suggested after they'd been talking a while—to help her out, perhaps three times a week, paid of course, unless possibly he was working somewhere else—how presumptuous it was for her to assume . . . ?

But no, he told her, it was not presumptuous at all. He told her that he had been going through a difficult time, but that now he was optimistic that things would turn for the better, and from the way he smiled—sheepishly—she felt comfortable asking if his optimism had anything to do with the flowers he had bought from her the week before. He confessed that it did, that in fact he was living nearby with the recipient of those flowers—Bernadette, he told her ("Ah, what a lovely name, for a lovely lady no doubt," she said)—and that he would be glad not to have to travel into the city to work. She realized, he assumed, that he had no papers ("Papers, what are papers? Paf!" she said). How much less likely to be picked up if he stayed in the *quartier,* where the police were so few. She couldn't agree more, she said. The state was a brute. She apologized for the madness of her countrymen. Were we not all human beings under the same sun—or moon, as the case now happened to be?

And so he had good news when he got back to Bernadette's a little later, after she herself had returned from the cheese shop in Saint Germain: flowers, every night after work, of which the bunch of azaleas bursting from the water jug on top of the television would be the first of many.

"This is going to be very nice," she said, and went over to rearrange the stems.

So she was pleased?

She was.

And he said that he too was pleased—to have a job already, without even having to look, and so close by. Best of all he wouldn't need to travel at all.

She looked up at that and he knew she was disappointed and he shrugged.

She turned back to arranging the flowers.

She said that it was all right.

No, he told her, it wasn't all right. He told her that he knew the burden that his caution placed upon them. That it made no sense. He'd lived with the possibility of being picked up all his time in Paris, even before he met her, and all his life before that with the tyranny of chance.

She said, "I told you it was all right."

But he told her again it wasn't. He told her, "It's easy to be indifferent when you have nothing to lose," and how in the last few months before his episode he'd been more free than at any other time. Whatever he had, he'd chosen himself. That perhaps was why he'd been afraid to choose her.

She moved away from the flowers.

"So now do you choose?" she asked cautiously.

"Yes," he said.

"So then I choose you back," she said.

They were now standing at the window against the kitchen fixtures, and he reached out and took her hand. She gave him a tired, happy smile.

Then he told her he'd stopped by his old house. That Denis was gone. He'd almost forgotten the rent money, which he wriggled to get out of his pocket of his jeans.

"A gift from the past," he said.

He told her that the Refuge was still closed. Nobody was left, though the old man from the Moroccan restaurant had given him a number for Fawad.

She asked him if he was going to phone.

He said that he didn't know. What for? To try to put that world back together? The Refuge was gone. That life was gone.

She said, "But it's only gone because it's gone. Make it again. Isn't that what Mamadou did, the first time? He came straight back."

"Why? It will only get broken again."

"And then somebody else will make it again. And on and on, and in that way it will never stop, it will go on forever."

He folded the piece of paper into a neat square and put it under the telephone.

"Let's see tomorrow," he said non committally, though inside he felt lucky to be falling in love with such a wise person.

His employment with Madame la Fleuriste was nothing like the hard work which he was used to. Every now and then there were early mornings, meeting the delivery trucks from the flower depot at around six a.m., before the *quartier* woke up and cars came out and the traffic turned the roads to glue. Sometimes there was heavy lifting—bags of compost as on the first day; pallets of seedlings from the truck; plastic pots stacked like ice cream cones; terracotta moulds packed with newspapers and balanced between multiple layers of plywood, like baking bread. Sometimes, when business was brisk he'd help out thinning leaves, cutting stems, pre-cutting ribbons, plastic and paper wrap. Other times he'd go round with Madame la Fleuriste on the three or four large deliveries she did every week, from the back of the old van she had parked in the back—of metre-high floral constructions in faux-stone urns, which he carried for her into the drawing rooms and lobbies of the neighbourhood's great residences.

But a lot of the time there were long periods where not much was to be done. Madame would work away at a small order, or prepare bouquets for supply to the local fruit shops and chemists, and they'd listen to the radio and talk, while he paged through the magazines and papers she bought each morning, and sometimes help her with the less complicated tasks.

She already knew of his interest in painting—from their brief interactions in the previous year, in the days when he stopped by on his way to Bernadette's and so intrigued her with his remarks on what he'd recently seen in the museums or bookshops she had told him of. She was not surprised to learn, when the topic of conversation shifted to his home, of his previous employment in Accra as a signwriter, which is what led her, after a few weeks, to suggest that he undertake a small commission for her, right here in her shop—a tropical scene, she suggested, on the three walls of one of the side rooms. What she had in mind was a forest, something to go along with the plants she stored there—verdant, brimming, dangerous, secretive, like the forests of Rousseau's tiger paintings, she said—had he not seen one in any of the museums? (Yes he had.)

For a week then, instead of helping with the flowers, he painted— a forest as she'd asked for, covering the walls, as high as the sky-coloured ceiling, and in which, if you looked closely, there were camouflaged birds, their feathers the colour of leaves, monkeys the colour of bark, butterfly wings in the shadows, eyes in the under-growth like speckled pebbles.

"This is too beautiful," Madame la Fleuriste said when she saw it complete. She stood in front of it and laughed out loud.

"But no tiger?" she asked.

"No tigers in Paris," he said.

She walked around looking at the details.

"Too beautiful," she said. "There must be more," but not—she said—for the shop. She said, "This is not for the world," and would he consider doing the next painting not in the shop, but downstairs— in the cellar, he could paint what he wanted, they would clear it out, clean it, it would all be undertaken just as he directed.

"But why down there?" he asked.

"Let it be something that needs to be found," Madame said.

"Or not found, but hidden," she later suggested when he started planning the commission and it occurred to her that the cellar, insulated by three feet of stone from the ears of the world, would be a perfect venue for a reincarnated Refuge de l'Ouest (of which he had told her much over the previous weeks), where its old patrons, dispersed around the city, could meet from time to time, hidden beneath the flagstones of Paris's wealthiest *quartier.*

And so in the space of a few months Le Refuge Clandestin was established in the cellars beneath the florist. The walls of the narrow staircase leading down from the rear corridor of the shop were painted to resemble the flow of water falling down a chute. The water was painted in strands, like a twisted plait, of which the topmost extended up into the corridor above, where it resembled a scrape mark against the white paint, and gave no hint what lay below.

In the staircase itself, tumbling into the cellar, the water was interspersed with images of flowers that stuck to the strands like burrs, and larger images of the paraphernalia of the shop—the marble figure of a naked lady, stately and oblivious to her descent into the underground cavern, a piano, its keyboard unraveling like a scarf, upended tables, a radio, magazines, birdcages and books, and right at the bottom, a bathtub containing a figure, calmly waving, unambiguously that of Madame la Fleuriste.

The staircase now ended in a small specially constructed space, separated from the rest of the cellar with a thin drywall, and which contained the ordinary contents of the shop's stores, stacked tightly up to the ceiling. The only signs of anything out of the ordinary were the small angels he painted, surrounding the room at the junction between the walls and ceiling, figured identically to those in the paintings of the medieval galleries of the Louvre, but for their mischievously grinning West and North African faces.

In the Refuge itself, which you entered through the false back of a cupboard behind a pile of compost bags, the fluorescent lights from the ceiling were taken out, and replaced by many small standing and table lamps, which they bought one afternoon in the secondhand shops in Saint-Denis. Each cast a thin low-wattage pool of light, no two the same, so that when the Refuge was full the room was illuminated in shifting patterns, as the light flowed between the movement of the people, and as a result of which the images on the walls and ceiling shifted in and out of visibility, and appeared to be moving themselves.

The Refuge Clandestin was simply furnished with what could be easily obtained. Aside from the lights, it had three tables with chairs, a small sofa with a Moroccan-style leather table, two large beanbags, and at the back, a counter made of crates and an old door, from which food and drink were served, and where they stored the music that was always playing when every fortnight or so, always on a Saturday, the room was in use.

Over the course of a few weeks the survivors of the original Oberkampf community were able to reestablish contact. Fawad the Algerian was the first, who was in touch with Fawad the Moroccan, who had heard that two of the Senegalese contingent had found a situation in the 11th, who in turn had kept their links with Janetta, who being Beninoise was able eventually to contact a few of the West African contingent.

Nobody knew of the new Refuge other than those who were invited, and those who came as their guests. Given the small size of the Refuge, and the need for discretion, numbers were kept low and people signed up for alternate weekends. Simple plans were established to allow the participants to enter the premises, through the florist shop, without attracting attention. In some cases they borrowed Madame's small truck, and so passed for a crew from the depot making a late afternoon delivery. Others came dressed up as foreign dignitaries, others as tradesmen, one or two as customers. Madame would always keep the shop open until the last of the guests were in, at around six in the evening, and then would close up and come down to the Refuge herself.

The new Refuge was still under construction when the meetings began. At first, the walls and ceiling of the room were covered by only a light gray wash, to form the undercoat for the depiction of a cavern, in which he intended to paint a number of vignettes, only the first of which he had completed by the time of the first meeting. Close to the door, it was a scene depicting his train journey across the Sahel, the one end of the train in Bamako, the other edging into the cathedral of Dakar station, and in between the desert, the baobab trees, circling birds, the border post, the family left behind, the hawkers, the small towns. It was Fawad the Algerian who had asked him to explain the picture, and who afterwards suggested he complete the wall with depictions of all the journeys to Paris of the people gathered at the Refuge; and this was how—over a number of months—the walls and ceiling of that room came to be populated with fantastical vignettes of the stories of each of those gathered there: of farms, villages, towns, cities across Africa, of car journeys, desert walks, container ships, overpacked dinghies, mountain hikes, beach landings, sojourns in hospitals, detention centres, safe houses.

The Refuge Clandestin was completed three months after Madame la Fleuriste first thought of transforming her cellar. Sometimes he would go down to work when business in the flower shop was slow, but most of the painting was done in the evenings after work, and on the weekends, when Bernadette could join him. Then they would take down the radio and open the air vents at the back, and the stair-well at the front, which brought a cool breeze flowing through the cellar, and she would keep him company— reading, or studying for her English for Foreigners course, or taking care of letters or bills, her papers spread out around her where she sat cross-legged on the floor.

The patrons of the Refuge would collectively decide whose story would next be figured on the cellar wall, but they left it to the sign-writer to interpret in images the stories that they painted in words. Sometimes people might drop by to see the progress of the work, but it was only Bernadette who would be there from start to finish.

She loved to watch him paint, to see these pictures come out of this man who in his own life was so slow to show himself, and so awk-ward. Painting spared him speech. Whereas he stumbled with words, he could express himself articulately through a vocabulary of images she learned to interpret as the scenes slowly worked their way from the entrance to the Refuge, towards the vents at the back.

"Why are there no people in this town you have drawn?" she would ask. "What does the smile on this lady's face mean?" "Why is the bed floating on the sea?" "What are the crying people crying about?" And in his telling her she would know: the loneliness of empty space, the pocketed hands of loss; the meaning of clothes billowing on a washing line; women floating up into the trees; the gutted meat; the orange on an out-held hand; the slimmed eyes of desire that the clenched muscles of the mouth turn to cruelty, then shame.

Into the stories of their friends he implanted his own. Bernadette learned to look for the characters hidden in a crowd, in the corner of a scene, who seemed just slightly out of place, or whose faces were rendered more real by an unexpected detail or gesture, and so hinted at a meaning beyond the paintings themselves. These were the aspects that she asked about. The lady with the outstretched arms, Bible in her hand. The man in the desert on the balcony of his house. The small man with his books. One man driving a taxi—his eyes, she noticed, closed. Another man, fat as a tub, walking, it seemed, through blossoms. And the two women who appeared more than once across different vignettes: in one domestic scene, setting a table together, the younger's hand caught in midair by the elder's; in another, as the heads of snakes intertwined; in another still, figured through the window of a building in the background—the younger, standing at a mirror, recognizable from the back by her braids, the elder in her reflection; and in their last appearance, as the cellar was close to completion, at the corner of an image: standing on the top of a misty hill, surrounded by trees, plants, birds, and animals, painted initially in sharp relief, but in the last moment of their creation, late on a Saturday afternoon that he and Bernadette had spent quietly together, obscured in a fine patina so as to be recognizable only in their shape.

It was the sharp smell of the paint thinner that had made Bernadette look up from the magazine she'd been reading, sitting against the wall behind him, as he completed the image. He was standing in front of the mural in process, on a paint-stained sheet with which he protected the floor, his tins around his feet, his thumb hooked in the streaked back pocket of his jeans. In his other hand he held a piece of cloth which—getting up to see what he was doing—she saw he was dabbing on the image of the two women.

Standing a step behind him she observed the previously sharp image begin to dissolve under the application of the paint thinner, the outlines undoing themselves as the two figures retreated behind a gauze of mist until they were hardly discernable.

She put her hand on his elbow to let him know she was there.

Feeling her presence beside him, he stopped.

"What is it?" he said.

"This," she said, but did not say what, instead reaching out with her hand, tracing in the air above the space into which the figures had melted.

He reached out himself, put his paint-covered hand over hers, and before she could guess his intention, gently forced her fingers onto the surface of the paint.

She turned her eyes from his hand over hers, to look at him.

She had expected there to be a playfulness in his expression, but there was not.

She let out a small laugh.

When he did not respond she pulled her hand from under his.

Quicker than the time she'd have needed to stop him, he grabbed her hand again, and this time smiling, slowly turned it over in his, to reveal the flecks of paint on her fingertips.

"Tsk," she said with half-feigned irritation, and wiped her fingers on his trousers.

He bent forward to look at the detail of the wall. She bent forward too.

"What?" she said.

"Your fingerprints," he replied, and stepped back, leaving her standing alone in front of the now complete mural.

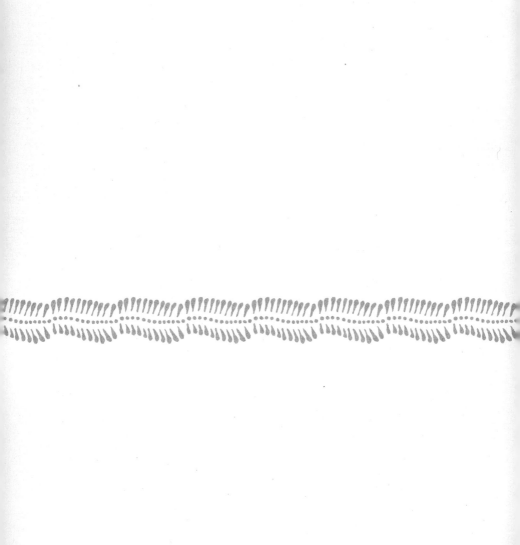

BERNADETTE

Bernadette, after work, sits at the wood table in the apartment.

It's early evening. She's drinking milk from a carton. The windows are open, through which she's looking to the other side of the courtyard, to an identical set of windows, in which a woman is preparing food, and in the window adjacent a man is ironing a shirt.

The soles of her feet are tired. She has them up on the cushion of the chair opposite, straight out. Her spine is right up against the seat back. She's shaped like a hex key.

A gecko scurries over the tiles. Above the eaves the television aerials are like the skeletons of winter trees.

Bernadette observes the scene calmly.

A radio plays old-fashioned songs from somewhere downstairs.

The texture of the whole milk in her mouth makes her think of the small blue cloth she cleans her glasses with.

Every now and then the elevator engine growls as the tenants return from work.

The apartment is tidy at this time of day. The bed is folded away.

The clothes are in the boxes on top of the cupboard and under the sink.

She's waiting for Kwasi to call to say he is coming back. Then she'll start supper, cutting the courgettes she's bought earlier in the day from the vegetable shop two doors down from the cheese shop where she works, and which are in a brown paper parcel on the chair beside her.

Kwasi will be back within a quarter of an hour of his call.

Before dinner he'll leave to take a shower in the bathroom two doors down the corridor. When he returns they'll have the food she's cooked. Then she'll watch the television while he washes up. Afterwards he'll join her. Maybe they'll make love. Or maybe they'll go to sleep without making love.

A normal evening. Like a hundred or so evenings past.

Enough to keep a person happy for a lifetime.

But when the telephone rings it isn't Kwasi's voice at all, though a familiar one nonetheless.

Denis Owusu.

"Back from the dead," she says, and how long has it been?

"Too, too long," Denis says, laughing on the other end.

And where is he now?

In Lille, it turns out, to which he'd moved not long after the raid of the previous autumn, and where he's now working in a small auto mechanic's shop.

"I'm flourishing here," he tells her, "flourishing," and that she and Kwasi should come to visit sometime soon—as of course they will, Bernadette tells him; and after the invitation is returned and accepted, and they exchange news and memories of times past, Bernadette tells Denis that Kwasi will be back later and asks whether she should pass on a message, and could she take Denis's number.

But Denis says no—he will be going out shortly. He's called because somebody's contacted him asking after Kwasi. He thought Kwasi should know.

"What somebody?" Bernadette asks. She puts down the carton.

"One of Kwasi's people," Denis tells her, and that he's just arrived.

"Arrived where?"

"Here, in Lille. He's staying in a room in the city."

"How did he come to you?"

Bernadette hears Denis exhale in a short sharp breath.

"How?" she repeats.

"The same way Kwasi did when he came."

"How was that?"

"Ask Kwasi," Denis says.

"You tell me, Denis," Bernadette says.

"I cannot, Bernadette," Denis says.

For a moment there is silence.

Bernadette knows. Denis is thinking that if Kwasi hasn't told her it isn't safe that he tell her. She understands, but it makes her feel hurt not to be trusted.

And why hasn't Kwasi told her? Because she hasn't asked, she knows, that is all.

But why does she always have to ask? Why can't Kwasi just tell her things without her having to ask?

Not that she doesn't know more or less anyway—that Denis is in a smuggling ring, was Kwasi's contact when first Kwasi arrived in France.

"So what does this man want, who's calling after Kwasi?" Bernadette asks.

"To find him," Denis tells her. "I have only spoken to the man once—on the telephone. I told him I didn't know where Kwasi is. He asked me to find out. I said I would try."

Bernadette looks out the window. The sun is below the roofline. The woman who's been preparing a meal is sitting with a child, eating at her table. The man in the next apartment is finished ironing his shirt and sits in a chair against a wall, covered in the uneven light of a television.

Bernadette's thoughts begin to drift.

She thinks to herself that if Denis had not called she would right now be chopping courgettes. She can see herself in her own mind. That person cutting courgettes, just on the other side of this conversation.

"So what to do?" Denis asks her.

She thinks about it for a moment, then tells him that she'll speak to Kwasi, and could Denis tell this new arrival that he is still looking for Kwasi.

Denis says that he can.

She thanks him.

He tells her there's nothing to thank him for. He says that he'll wait for their call.

Bernadette puts down the phone.

It's now night. The soft shadows cast by the outside light lie across the furniture. She gets up and turns the light on. The room goes white.

Probably Kwasi has tried to ring, it occurs to Bernadette, standing at the light switch beside the door.

And if he has?

Then nothing. Either he will be back in a few moments, or he's going to be late.

Except now that time isn't going to go on forever it does matter.

She picks up the telephone and dials the shop.

Madame answers. Kwasi is still there, Madame tells Bernadette, they are working late. Does Bernadette want to speak to Kwasi?

No, no, Bernadette doesn't need to. Madame need only tell Kwasi that she called. She'll be expecting him late.

Madame tells her all right.

But it isn't all right.

Bernadette puts the courgettes away. She puts away the carton of milk. She can taste it somewhere in her throat. She's drunk too fast. It wants to come out. She tastes acid.

She gets her keys, and closes the door behind her, and descends the flights of stairs to reach the back entrance.

She steps out onto the road that leads off Avenue Victor Hugo. A thin two-story home has survived the grand apartment blocks, hemmed in between the tall façades. It has a crude stone wall to protect it from the street, grown with ivy. She comes out onto the avenue. The tires of the cars over the cobblestones sound like bubble wrap.

All the shops are closing for the night. Across the road the patisserie is still open. She goes in. The cakes and confectionery under the glass counter shine like polished stone. She buys three, and a baguette.

Next door in the *alimentaire* she picks up a bottle of wine and some tomatoes on the vine and some fruit and some Président cheese, all wrapped up in gold foil like a moon lander. From behind her, as she walks down the pavement towards the florist she hears the owner bring down the chain-mail grill.

She makes her way down the road. The headlights of the cars come past, yellow like the bottom of beer glasses.

The door of the florist is closed, the front foyer dark, although she can see the lights are on in the back of the shop. She raps on the door twice.

Madame comes walking out of the light in a white apron. She's carrying a reel of ribbon in one hand and a scissors in the other. She opens the door with a key hung on a hook inside of the frame.

Her apron is stained with green smudges. She smells of sap and perfume.

There are strands of hair coming loose around her face, going off in strange angles like tall yellow grass that's been walked through.

She greets Bernadette, her face that was pinched with curiosity as she approached the door, now uncrumpling in welcome.

She sees the bags of food and the cakes wrapped in their white paper. "Food, wine, tonight we make a party," she half says, half shouts back into the bowels of the shop, where Kwasi must be.

"It's just to feed the workers," Bernadette says.

She follows Madame into the room where Madame and Kwasi have been at work, at the large table they've pulled into the middle of the room, with thick wooden legs and a marble top that's an uneven milky gray colour. There are flowers everywhere, strewn over the work surfaces, in buckets on the floor, and vases all around the room in which they've putting together what seems like twenty, maybe thirty identical arrangements.

Kwasi is busy cutting stems of lemon leaf, which he's tried to pile up beside him but which are spilling out over the table. He hasn't heard Madame call out, and so is surprised himself to see Bernadette. He bends down as she comes around to kiss him hello, his hands around her waist, still holding lemon leaves, as she gets up on her tip-toes to reach his face.

She laughs with the effort.

She tells him she thought he might be hungry.

He asks her what she's brought.

"What I could find," Bernadette says.

Madame is delighted. "Excellent, excellent," Madame says upon removing each item from the plastic bag, clearing space for each among the flowers. Her face is flushed. Mottled spots show through the pale skin under the powder.

She comes to the wine, then goes off to get glasses.

Bernadette is now walking round the room, looking at the half-finished arrangements. She can see this is going to take all night.

She says, "This is a lot of flowers."

Kwasi watches her.

She admires some of the finished arrangements.

She says, "Is it for a wedding or a funeral?"

"A wedding," Kwasi says.

Bernadette nods.

He says, "Somebody is getting married."

Bernadette wrinkles her face.

Kwasi laughs.

Madame comes in.

"Somebody is getting married," Bernadette says.

Kwasi laughs at the private joke—a short exclamation from the bottom of the lungs. He catches Bernadette's eye.

He's cutting lemon leaves again.

Madame has picked up the wine bottle and has it between her legs and is trying to get the cork out with a rusty corkscrew.

Bernadette asks if she can help.

Madame tells her she's got it.

"With the work," Bernadette says.

The cork comes out with a jolt. Madame spills wine over her apron.

She laughs. "First you can help us eat," she says. She pours out three glasses in coffee mugs. "And drink," she adds.

Kwasi puts down his plants and comes over. Madame gets out the bread and starts cutting the tomatoes with the open blade of a pair of shears.

She hands round pieces of bread and tomato and cheese to Kwasi and Bernadette.

Then they have the fruit and afterwards the cakes. Madame grinds coffee beans from a jar with the hand grinder she keeps in the kitchen, and boils up some coffee.

When she comes back Bernadette is trimming palm fronds and freesias.

Madame puts on the radio. They work through uninterrupted classics of the sixties, a call-in dedication show, adverts, the eleven p.m. news, more uninterrupted classics.

They work until just short of two a.m. When they are finished there are thirty-three identical arrangements in glass vases set in rows on the floor, like ranks of pawns.

The flowers have to go at seven in the morning. Three men will come with a delivery van. The wedding is in a private house in Neuilly. Madame will not get much more than a few hours' sleep, she says, but it's fine. It was fun. Wasn't it fun?

It was fun, Bernadette tells her. She squeezes Madame's hand.

"It was," she says.

Madame looks exhausted. The skin under her eyes is loose like an empty water pouch.

They gather up the cut stems and the discarded flowers, the stray leaves and ribbon threads in sheets of newspaper.

Madame tells them they should sleep there tonight if they'd like, in light of the lateness of the hour.

Bernadette doesn't say anything. She waits for Kwasi.

"No," he says, "it's good. But thanks. It's a short walk home."

"Very well," Madame says.

Kwasi and Bernadette head out into the night.

It's chilly now. There are no cars on the street. The shadows of branches sway in the light cast by the shopfronts and the street lights.

They hold hands.

Bernadette asks him if he's all right.

He says that he is. He feels fine.

"Why did you come?" he asks a block later.

She says, "I missed you."

He squeezes her hand, and laughs the short laugh he did earlier in the shop.

He doesn't press her any further.

She says, "I love you, Kwasi."

These are not words they have ever used before, but they don't feel foreign or difficult at all.

He says, "I know it."

They both stare ahead, neither looking at the other.

He says, "I love you, too."

They carry on in silence, like they're taking their time getting used to the feel of it.

The door to the apartment building is now only a few steps away.

She says, "Kwasi?"

He says yes.

She says, "I can't help wanting to ask you."

"What?"

She says, "If I ask you to ask me to marry you, will you?"

It's only the sound of their feet walking and the wind in the branches.

"Why?" he says

"Because sometimes you just have to say things to make them exist."

They stop.

She comes up against him, her head on his chest.

He says, "Everything?"

She says, "Not everything. But this thing."

She looks down the road, towards the glow of the city. A lone car swings round the distant circle, then accelerates away. A small

mechanical pavement sweeper is making its way up the street, grinding along like a slow olive-green bug.

"All right," he says.

She feels his arms strengthen around her.

"Then do it," she says.

He says, "Bernadette Mary Luyundula, will you marry me?"

He can feel the fuzziness of her hair on his chin.

A small sound comes out of her, half-breath, like an exclamation of
approval. She says, "I tell you I love you and five seconds later you ask
me to marry you?"

She can't see his face, but she knows the expression on it without
having to.

"Such a tricky girl," he says, his voice smiling.

She pulls a little out of his embrace and looks at him. She says,
"Fine, but never forget it was you who asked."

"You haven't answered," he says.

"Sure, I'll marry you," she says.

"Then I won't forget it," he says.

Now she gets on her tiptoes and she kisses him, and they stand in
the entrance like that, until the mechanical street sweeper has almost
passed them. A middle-aged guy with a tired expression on his face
sits at its wheel, slouched. It must be a dull job.

"Good evening," the man says as he passes them.

"Good evening," they respond.

Then Kwasi opens the door to the apartment building with his
key, and lets Bernadette in. He steps through the doorway himself,
looks briefly over the empty street, then lets the door close shut
behind him.

When they wake up the next morning it is late. The sheets are all
undone because they didn't make up the sofa bed properly and before
they fell asleep they made love and whenever they make love the
sheets come undone, especially the ones that are too small for the
futon. Bernadette, who has woken up on the coarse material of
the bare mattress, pushes the heavy body of Kwasi over until he

moves up and she can slip in beside him onto the sheet. They lie in the corner of the bed, against the wall, not asleep, but for a long time not talking.

Why is he so quiet?

Just because he's waking up.

He hasn't changed his mind about what he asked the night before?

He tells her that he hasn't, and kisses her and then they make love again, and she does know that he hasn't changed his mind.

Afterwards he gets up to fix them coffee and something to eat. She watches him as he walks around naked, going from the fridge to the hob where he boils the water, forages in the cupboards for bread and cans, and in the drawers for a can opener.

She thinks suddenly how funny it is to watch this naked man walking around, strong and big, with his penis which is still not down yet bumping into the counter as he works on the coffee jar. She wants to laugh at how totally naked he is, with happiness, but also at the extraordinariness of it—such a large human being, covered in muscles, strong in the way that men are built strong, but in fact he's just a grown-up version of the small naked child you see running around with unconscious happiness, whether it's in a slum in Accra or the Jardin du Luxembourg.

Then she does laugh.

What's so funny?

She only tells him it's because his penis is bumping into things.

He looks down at it, then comes back to bed with the meal.

They eat a stale croissant and some crackers and yoghurt with coffee.

He tells her that the only thing he regrets about last night's conversation is that he didn't ask first.

Was he going to ask anyway?

Maybe not then, but eventually it would have come to that, he tells her; at least he was already in the state of mind that gets a person to that point.

She considers his words.

"But you did ask me first," she tells him, and has he forgotten already what she said? Does she have to remind him again?

No, she doesn't, he says, letting her have her way.

That evening, down in the Refuge, the Saturday gathering turns into a party to celebrate their engagement. Telephone calls are made to invite more people than can usually be accommodated in a sitting.

The guests bring pots of food wrapped up in paper bags. The Christians among them bring more alcohol. They bring cakes and fruit. They bring additional tapes of music to be played.

Madame brings down from the shop an extra flower arrangement that they'd made by mistake the night before, but which she only discovered when the delivery van arrived in the morning.

"If it's good enough for the weddings of Neuilly it's good enough for us," she declares, placing it in the middle of the table at which Bernadette and Kwasi are sitting, surrounded by their friends of the Refuge community.

Everyone applauds.

The party continues into the night. The time at which people must leave to catch the last metro approaches, then passes. Nobody notices. People should stay as long as they like, Madame declares eventually. She will close the shop on Sunday and people can sleep on the floor all day.

The celebrations continue until just before sunup, when the *quartier* begins to rise and greater care is needed. Madame closes the shutters over the windows upstairs, and tablecloths are removed from the tables and bundled up to make pillows and the guests drift up into the shop to find places to sleep on chairs or benches or on the mosaic floor among the buckets of flowers, the flower pots, the statues, and the fountains.

Although they can easily walk back to their apartment, Bernadette and Kwasi decide to stay with the guests. They occupy a deep wicker bench on which customers often sit and wait while orders are made up, which with two large Indonesian-print cushions makes a comfortable bed. They drift in and out of sleep, talk, exchange and laugh at stupid comments that in the moment seem hilarious, sleep again.

A little after midday Kwasi wakes up. Bernadette's head is on his chest. He props up his own head on his forearm by holding the side strut of the bench behind his neck. From downstairs he can hear the sound of people clearing up, low conversation, laughter. From outside comes the sound of streets—Sunday traffic, footfalls, the sound of dogs, car horns, passing pavement conversations, music from the bistro three doors down.

With his head slightly raised he has a view of the foyer entrance of the shop. The light comes in through the shutters, casting white bars over the floor.

He is reminded suddenly of his train journey from Bamako, now so long ago—almost a year. Couples are asleep in bundles, individuals curled up on their own covered in jackets or tablecloths. It seems that nobody has left yet.

But sometime they will leave. Today, in a few hours. And later? Forever. Time, the police, will scatter them all.

He thinks, *Where will this all end?*

A small happy life, here one day, and then gone in a flurry, with nothing left but furniture to pawn?

Can anyone tell him different?

Mamadou? What would Mamadou say now? Something about fearing the dark? No, he'd have nothing to say. His voice is already scattered.

And Bernadette? That marrying her will get him papers?

He pulls his hand from behind his neck and lays his head down on the bench and looks up at the ceiling.

He sees above him the identical depictions of Botticelli's Zephyr and Aura that Madame had him paint in the corners, blowing into the room, with their gold-pierced ears, their cornrows and braids.

The sight of those defiant figures suddenly fills him with shame at his easy acquiescence.

These are not new questions he is asking. He has asked them all his life.

Does he still have nothing to say after leaving his life behind and traveling such a distance?

He hears his own voice in his head asking the questions—the same voice from his last weeks in Tudu, that spoke to him in his painting shed, and accompanied him to Farrar Street and told him how everyone you meet on your way is an angel, and which he now knows to be true: Big Henry, Adams, Mamadou, Bernadette.

At that moment he feels Bernadette stirring against him.

"What's going on up there?" she says. She is awake, must have been a while, and is watching him looking at the roof.

He begins to explain to her the figures on the ceiling.

Upstairs, she means, and she taps him on his forehead with her finger.

"Nothing," he says after a while, "just listening."

"To what?"

To what? To the voices in his head.

"Oh," she says. "Any particularly witty conversation? Anybody say anything interesting?"

"One person," he says.

And what does he say?

He tells him, this person, that you never really have anything except if you choose it yourself.

"Yes," she says quietly.

"And not just once. You have to carry on choosing every day."

Yes.

And that if nothing can be taken away from you it doesn't mean you're free.

No.

It just means you have nothing.

Yes.

"I should meet him, this wise person," she says.

"You have," he says.

She has? "When?" she asks.

He smiles.

She knows she shouldn't have to ask anymore.

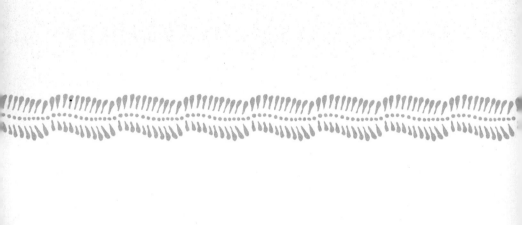

THE MUSEUM OF MANKIND

IT HAS JUST gone summer. A shipment of the last of the season's
tulips has just come in. Madame has buckets of them spread out over
the counter.

One variety among them she has never seen before, that must have
got into her order by mistake. They still have their leaves, like thick
blades of grass, from which the stems curve upwards into deep purple
petals, not rounded but ragged and pointy and lined with an almost
fluorescent yellow trim, just slightly parting around their stamens in
a way that makes Madame want to giggle, and as she does she looks
up from the table and out of the shop window.

A man is standing on the pavement opposite, a piece of notepaper
in one hand, a plastic bag in the other. She thinks little of him, but for
the fact that he must be foreign, which she tells immediately from his
clothes—an old checked jacket cut like her father used to wear, with
wide lapels, and too hot for the season.

Then the bell above the door is disturbed into music. A client
comes in, who is about to make an order, but then notices the purple

tulips on the table among the more common blooms. Conversation is diverted from the order.

The man, from outside the shop, sees the florist pick up a purple flower by the stem between two fingers, as if it were some strange creature. He sees her laughing silently from behind the glass with her customer, a distinguished woman with dark green clothes and gray hair pinned up in a bun like a small conch on the back of her head.

"I can sell them to you for a good price," Madame is saying to her customer inside the shop.

"I could not," the customer replies archly, "not with teenage daughters in the house."

The man, from outside the shop, watches the florist and her client transact their business. Then the client leaves. There appears to be nobody else in the shop. Possibly he has the wrong address. He looks at the paper in his hand, looks at the number above the door. No, it is correct. He puts the paper into his pocket and waits.

Inside the shop Madame shuffles through some order forms. Then she gets on the telephone. She begins to sort through the forms, lifting her shoulder and craning her neck to wedge the headset against her ear, so as to free her hands. Out of the corner of her eye she notices that the man across the road has not moved. He has put down his plastic bag and is leaning against the wall. He has a large umbrella of the kind that golf players use. She might normally assume him to be one of the old diplomats from the African embassies, with their impeccable French and their old-world ways, who sometimes walk through the *quartier* during lunch and might stop in on a Friday afternoon to purchase a bouquet for a wife or a mistress, except it is not lunchtime, and such men do not carry plastic bags or stand on street corners.

From across the road the man sees the woman begin talking on the phone. Suddenly she starts sorting through papers on her desk in a great hurry. Some of the papers fall on the ground. She puts down the phone to pick them up. She knocks the phone which pushes some flowers off the other side of the table and overturns a glass of water. She rushes round the table to pick up the flowers, then picks up the papers, some of which are now wet, sorts through them, seems to find the one she wants, and then picks up the phone again. The man smiles to see the small comedy playing out across the street.

After a while the florist appears to finish her business on the telephone. She puts down the phone. She seems overwhelmed. She shakes water off her hands. She calls out over her shoulder. She is looking for something on which to wipe her hands. Nobody comes. She disappears into the shop.

Kwasi, in one of the back rooms, has not heard her, since he is listening to music with earphones as he sorts through some of the other deliveries of the morning. Madame picks up a cloth and begins wiping her hands. Kwasi takes off his earphones. Madame tells him she has something interesting to show him.

They return to the front of the shop.

Madame asks him if he's ever seen such things before, again beginning to giggle.

He tells her, "Never, at least not in the flower world."

"I cannot sell such flowers in this *quartier*," Madame says. "Why don't you take them home tonight. I'm sure you two will enjoy them shamelessly."

He tells her she's blushing.

Madame knows it.

Kwasi gathers the purple flowers up in a sheet of newspaper, and heads back into the shop to finish off his work.

Madame, looking up, sees the man from outside striding off now down the road in the direction of Rue Saint Didier.

On regular weekdays when deliveries aren't coming in, Bernadette and Kwasi leave the apartment at the same time, at a little after eight in the morning, so that Bernadette can walk with Kwasi to work. Madame, who has been getting up at five a.m. for twenty-five years, is already in the shop, spraying water onto the leaves of the fleshy plants. Although opening time isn't until nine she has the music on already. She will already have taken the sheets off the two birdcages, so that the songbirds are hopping against their bars and chirping, and turned on the water pump so that the fountain in the middle of the central shop floor makes its water noises. The shutters may still be closed, but the slats are angled to let the sunlight in that slices through the fine mist from her spray bottle as she moves from plant to plant. Usually during the day she plays recordings from the half-price Mozart, Vivaldi and Handel box sets, but in the mornings, on her own, she plays the music of her own heart—which in recent weeks has been the piano works of Claude Debussy, and which, as she walks around her shop, makes her feel at the same time happy and wistful.

Some time before eight thirty there will be a knock on the window. She'll put down her spray bottle and go to the door, and there will be Kwasi and Bernadette in the doorway, and she'll have to squint her eyes to protect them from the daylight streaming in.

Then Madame will go into the back to get coffee ready, for which Bernadette will join them if it's closer to eight than eight thirty. Kwasi will start filling buckets of water and unbundle the flowers they expect to sell during the day. Bernadette will have pulled out the high chair behind the cash register, and when Madame joins them with a tray of coffee and a plate of croissants a conversation will already be going and there'll be hardly a moment to breathe between words, right up until Bernadette leaves some time before nine.

Bernadette's route to the Trocadero metro stop will take her down Rue des Belles Feuilles, where she will pass the Monoprix store in which Mamadou used to work, and in which she still knows some of the cashiers, although she's had little reason to stop in since Mamadou left, and hardly ever did when he worked there, as it's only since she started accompanying Kwasi to the flower shop that this particular route to the metro has become the shortest option—or so Kwasi tells her; she still believes it would be quicker to return up Avenue Victor Hugo, pass the apartment and continue up the avenue to catch the metro at Metro Kleber.

She's the one who actually does the walking, she tells Kwasi, but Kwasi is insistent.

"It's a waste of time to double back," he tells her.

She says, "Not if it's quicker."

He says, "I think it's quicker to keep on walking."

She says, "It only seems that way."

"If it seems that way then it is," he says.

She smiles.

Though she still thinks he's wrong she walks his route. She makes a point to him that she does it because she loves him, not because she thinks he's right.

He laughs and tells her she's a very stubborn girl, but he forgives her.

She scoffs with incredulity.

She thinks he probably knows he's wrong. She thinks that it's most likely a point of principle. Not turning back. Though it's never just one thing. Ever. He likes the idea of her walking past the place where Mamadou worked, she thinks—to keep up some of the associations of the past, even if he doesn't do it himself.

"You're definitely an acquired taste," she tells him, reflecting one afternoon on all the crazy games he makes her play.

"You talk too much about life," he tells her.

"You think too much about it," she says back.

That makes *him* smile.

Well, he's my acquired taste, she is thinking as she turns off the avenue and into Rue des Belles Feuilles.

As she walks over the cross streets the sunlight comes out from in between the buildings and warms her face.

The shopkeepers have come out onto their pavements with brooms and buckets and are cleaning away the dust and debris of the week. Water is flowing down the sides of the road, channeled into the drains by rolls of green matting, taking it away into the pipes beneath the city.

She passes a chemist's with its green fluorescent sign, the pattern of the light expanding and contracting like a concertina.

She passes the pavement terrace of a restaurant, lined with a herbaceous border made of plastic saplings in concrete bases with wood chips for soil. From inside comes the sound of a pinball machine, just burst into jingles, its paddles flapping and lights flashing, a teenager in jeans and a vest, back to the window, leaning over it menacingly.

Just before she gets to the end of the road she passes by the entrance of the one-star Hotel Anton, which now that summer is in has its side windows open. Taking breakfast in the small tiled dining area to the side of the reception (with its faux-impressionist sketches of Paris monuments, and its lace-covered table bearing fruit, cereal in plastic jars, a milk jug and a stack of yoghurt pots) is the large tired-looking man who appears to have been staying there now for more than a week, who takes his breakfast always at the same time, and who looks up from his newspaper just as she passes, and smiles at her kindly—a face that for no immediately apparent reason seems both knowing and familiar.

Until the reason comes to her early the next morning while she's getting dressed, and without explaining anything to Kwasi she rushes over to the Hotel Anton, and there waits for three hours until ten a.m. for the man to take his breakfast; except this morning the man does not appear in the dining room, and still she is waiting as the waiters start clearing the plates away and the tables are washed down, and it is then that she goes into the hotel to ask.

The hotel manager is friendly.

A very nice gentleman, she remembers in response to Bernadette's enquiries, who she believes has been visiting relatives in the *quartier,* although she can't be sure since her English is not so good. How long has he stayed? Almost three weeks, she tells Bernadette, although now she believes he's gone home, or at least checked out.

"Which was when?" Bernadette asks.

"Only today," says the hotel manager.

Bernadette returns immediately to the apartment. Kwasi has gone to work. He has left footprints of water next to the sink, where he'll have washed himself with a sponge and a towel because the shower down the corridor was occupied. She's about to get down on the floor and mop up the water with the damp towel hanging over the back of a chair, but then doesn't. She goes to the phone and calls Denis's number in Lille. Denis picks up. She hears the sounds of the garage in the background. Denis is his usual friendly self. Nothing in his voice indicates that more than a month has passed without a call from

Bernadette. He tells her that the man who came looking for Kwasi eventually left. That he stayed maybe ten days or so, each day of which he returned to the garage at closing time in the evening to learn if Denis had news for him, and each day of which Denis continued to tell him that his efforts to locate Kwasi had failed.

For her silence she tells Denis that she is sorry. She admits to him that she has not passed to Kwasi the message of the visitor's arrival. She knows she should have, but that she was afraid. It was a mistake, though one she will have to make amends for in her own way, and can she count on Denis not to preempt her. She can, Denis tells her, and that as far as he is concerned this is a matter between her and Kwasi. She thanks him for his loyalty. His loyalty she can take for granted, Denis tells her, but that others may not have been so loyal—that the visitor was determined, and that he had money. This does not surprise Bernadette, but she does not mention this to Denis, asking only whether the man in question was a large man or a short one.

A large one, Denis tells her.

After she has put down the telephone she walks over to the flower shop. She briefly greets Madame, who is with a client and only has time to raise her eyebrows in acknowledgement. Without looking for Kwasi she goes directly to the back of the shop, gets the key from its hiding place in the cupboard where the mugs are kept, and lets herself into the Refuge.

The light coming in from the shop is enough to see a little way in, beyond which the images on the walls recede into darkness, though she doesn't need the light; she knows each panel so well by now.

The image she is looking for is close to the door, before which she now stands—a big yellow taxi, the driver leaning back in the seat, body expanding around the seat belt, large forearm resting on the window frame, head cocked—Festus Ankrah, oversized, square-jawed and implacable.

A shadow falls across the floor and the wall, obscuring Festus Ankrah's face. Bernadette looks up. Madame is standing at the bottom of the stairs.

"What is going on today?" Madame asks, sounding flustered.

"It's hard to explain," Bernadette says.

"It is," Madame says, sitting down now on the bottom stair. She's wearing a large, loose-fitting floral dress resembling in shape a collapsed parachute. Its folds stretch over her knees, making a hammock in which she rests her hands.

She sighs.

"Kwasi suddenly leaves with a strange man . . . You arrive suddenly . . ."

She sounds perplexed.

"What strange man?" Bernadette asks.

The strange man that came in an hour ago or so, Madame explains, although perhaps not so strange, since Madame has seen him a few times in the *quartier* over the last few weeks, but this for the first time in her shop. He came in, and smiled at her—they both recognized each other—but said nothing, and just nodded when Madame asked if she could help him. And so Madame left him to browse, and in fact almost forgot about him until Kwasi came into the front foyer, at which point things took a turn for the bizarre, to say the least, Madame explains breathlessly now, because obviously Kwasi and the man knew each other. The man called Kwasi by his name, and started speaking to him in an African language Madame could not understand.

"Twi," Bernadette tells her.

"Yes, Twi," Madame says, "perhaps this is what it was"—at least it sounded to her like the kind of language that might be called Twi, she says, laughing nervously. In any event, she says, for a moment Kwasi was speechless when the man spoke to him, but then he started talking back to the man, and clearly Kwasi was not happy, Madame could tell. Madame has never seen Kwasi in such an agitated state before, frankly. But the man spoke quietly, he calmed Kwasi down. He seemed kind and patient to Madame, who had taken a few steps back towards the hallway but all the while was watching these exchanges she did not understand. At some point Kwasi turned from the man to Madame, and tried to explain something to her, but he was so agitated that he was still speaking Twi to Madame, who obviously did not understand, though she could work out the gist, and began walking forward to introduce herself to the man, but before she could take more than a few steps towards them Kwasi told her, this time in French, that he would have to take the morning off and then he and the man simply left, walked out, and does Bernadette have any idea of what all this was about?

"Some," Bernadette replies. "Which way did they go?"

"Left, down Victor Hugo," Madame says, and is about to say some thing else, but Bernadette is already past her and running towards the door.

Two men sit on a green wooden bench in a small gravel-covered square overlooking the Museum of Mankind.

A few feet off pigeons jockey for pieces of bread thrown to them by a child directed by its mother. The pigeons, growing bold, approach too close to the child, who steps back in alarm. The mother stamps on the gravel with one foot and the birds retreat. The child laughs. The mother takes the bread from her child, flings it over the pigeons, picks up her child and leaves. The birds pounce on the bread.

To somebody walking past the two men would appear to be strangers sharing a bench.

Neither of them have spoken since they arrived at this spot five minutes before. Nor the ten or so minutes it took for them to reach the square, the younger of the two leading all the way, not looking back once, the older following a few steps behind.

The younger man is breathing as if he had just run a race. The older is waiting for the younger's breathing to slow down before he talks, but it is the younger man who speaks first.

"How did you find me?" he says.

"I followed the signs," the older man says to his nephew.

The younger man is silent.

The older man says, "A person only has to learn what they're look-ing for."

Silence still.

"You left directions. It started with John Bediako. Once I got to Ibrahim it was easy. Ibrahim was very sympathetic."

"You mean you paid him."

"No more than you," the older man says, not allowing the interjection to interrupt his explanation, as he relates to his nephew how he traveled to Dakar, found the hotel in the Place de l'Indépendance, the people in the barber shop; how they eventually sent him to Lille, to his tight-mouthed friend Denis, where the trail seemed about to end, and would have, had he not found an associate of Denis more disposed to financial reward.

"This was almost two weeks ago," the older man says. "I have been staying here in the neighbourhood ever since."

"Spying on me," the younger man says bluntly.

"Taking a holiday," the older man says, "visiting relatives."

"Am I meant to thank you?" the younger man says.

The older man doesn't respond, as he has not responded to any of his nephew's outbursts.

He says, "You have a beautiful girlfriend."

"You don't know anything about her," his nephew says.

"I know what I see," the older man says.

"We're going to get married," the younger man says softly, looking into his hands, the belligerence suddenly out of his voice, the words spoken with a soft childish intimacy that so takes his uncle by surprise that for a moment he cannot talk.

"I am very happy for you," he manages to say.

The two men continue to sit in silence, observing the square.

"I can see that your seeing me hurts you," the older man says at length.

His nephew ignores the observation. They have not been looking at each other. But now the younger man deliberately looks away.

He says, "What are you doing here?"

"I should ask you the same thing," the older man replies, trying to make a joke.

The younger man says, "I ran away, and this is where I ended up."

"So you have," says the older man.

Two shop assistants on their lunch break come into the square. They pick a bench furthest from the two men talking, lay down a newspaper on the seat, take out their sandwiches and begin to talk.

The men watch them, though neither of them is much interested.

The older man says, "To see you here, living like this, it makes me proud. If I'm allowed to be proud."

"As you like," the younger man says, the hostility returning, that his uncle knows was never gone, and will not completely be gone, at least during this day's conversation.

"Kwasi, I know why you left," the older man says.

"You cannot possibly know why I left."

"I know enough."

"What do you know?" the younger man says.

And so the older man tells him. He tells his nephew that he went to Akwapim. That he knows what happened there. That he knows about Nana Oforiwaa and John Bediako. He knows that his nephew came back to Accra and burned his shop.

"What do you know about Nana Oforiwaa?" the younger man says scornfully.

"Do I have to say it?" the older man replies.

The younger man looks at the older.

"No, uncle," he says softly.

"I went back," the older man says. "I was there."

The younger man folds his arms over his chest. He sniffs. He is waiting until he can trust in the steadiness of his voice.

His uncle does him the kindness of not noticing, looks ahead himself, quietly, waiting.

Then the younger man says, "If you've come all this way to tell me how ashamed I should be and what you all think of me, then you've wasted your time. I already know."

"No," the older man says, "I haven't come to tell you that. And I don't think it either."

"Then why have you come?" the younger man says.

"Many reasons," says the older.

The younger man waits.

The older man looks down at his shoes, brown and scuffed on the toes. He bought them new shortly before he began his journey. He looks away now to the centre of the square, where the statue of a general on a horse stands on top of a high concrete plinth. The horse, and the general atop it, stride out towards the traffic, great and immortal.

The older man feels suddenly tired, and small, and unequal to the responsibility he has come all this way to acquit.

Then he says, not looking at the younger man, "Shortly before I began my journey here I learned that Nana Oforiwaa didn't die by accident. John Bediako killed her. Drowned her. In the middle of the storm when nobody could see. That is what made him mad."

Nothing.

"He wanted me to tell this to you."

At first the younger man appears not to have heard. Suddenly he starts laughing. "I don't believe it," he says, though the laughter is far from a happy sound, and the older man recognizes it for what it is—a sound at the edge of hysteria.

"I think it's true," the older man says softly.

"Did he tell you this himself?" the younger man asks, his voice rising, as if in accusation.

"No," the older man says, and explains the circumstances by which he came by this knowledge.

"So why do you believe it?" the younger man says sharply.

"He has no reason to lie," the older man says calmly. "Also, I am the easiest person to tell the truth. Who would believe me anyway if I repeated it? Not even you . . ." and he laughs dryly before adding, "And because of how carefully he worked things out. How he made sure of me—that I really wanted to find you, that he could trust me, that I had the means to get here. No, he went to far too much trouble for this not to be true. I was in his power from the moment I arrived on the ridge."

The younger man says nothing. He is rocking softly backwards and forwards. For a while a small humming noise has been coming from his mouth.

Then it stops.

He says, "Why would he have done such a thing?"

"For the same reason I am here."

"What is that?" the younger man says.

"To free you. To let you go."

The younger man laughs. He says, "Free? Look how free I am. None of you exist."

"But here I am," the older man says.

"And tomorrow you'll be gone again," the younger man tells him.

"As it happens I will. But it won't stop the past from having happened," the older man says. "It takes a lot of imagination to become somebody different. You are full of imagination. But ultimately you will run out of it. Then all you'll have left is what you started with."

"What is that?" the younger man asks.

"You come from somewhere. You are the child of parents," the older man says, and that having total freedom is not the opposite of having no freedom, and that everyone is dependent and that in the end, in the very very end, everything is connected.

"I come from somewhere," the younger man says, "but I can choose where I go."

The older man says, "You can, Kwasi, until you can't."

Then he adds, "It's unfair, but you don't get to choose everything."

"Right now I can," the younger man replies.

"I know," the older man says, "I know how that feels. But don't enjoy the feeling so long that you can't come back when you need to."

"Come back where? So many bad things have happened at home," the younger man says.

"But are they unbearable, Kwasi?" the older man asks. "Can you really not bear them?"

"I have borne them," the younger man says.

"I know," says the older man.

Then nobody says anything. There is just the sound of the traffic behind them, and the noise of the eastern part of the city coming up the embankment.

Then the older man says, "Also, I have come to ask you for forgiveness."

"For what?" his nephew asks him, surprised.

He says, "I am asking your forgiveness for what happened to you."

When the younger man hears this he begins to cry.

His uncle puts his arm over his shoulder.

He says, "Somebody said to me that even when children defy us they still want our approval. What is my approval worth? But I can give you my blessing," and he tells his nephew that he does have his blessing, wherever he goes.

Then his nephew says to him how ashamed he is, and how he is sorry for what he has done to him, and to Celeste and to his parents; that it's unforgivable, and that he knows it.

"But it's forgiven," the older man says.

"All right," his nephew says at length.

He regains his composure, and after a short while sits up.

The two shop assistants, who have observed this scene, are getting up quickly. They bundle their sandwich wraps together and stride out of the square.

"*Pédés,*" one says under her breath, as they pass the two men on their bench.

"*Putains!*" the younger man shouts after them as they walk towards the pavement.

"They called us queers. I called them whores," he tells his uncle.

"A curse on the whole world," his uncle says, smiling.

They fall into silence.

"Are my parents well?" the younger man asks.

His uncle tells him that they are, although they will be better when he tells them of this visit, and better still when the younger man contacts them himself.

The younger man nods, but doesn't say anything.

"So what now?" the younger man says after a few moments.

The older man says, "My suitcases are already in storage at the airport. I will fly tonight."

The younger man doesn't respond.

He is thinking about the journey his uncle has taken to get here. How difficult it must have been to find him. He is thinking that so many of the people he has met to get here, his uncle has met, and so many of the places he has visited, his uncle has visited too.

"You don't want to stay a while?" he asks the older man.

"I've already stayed a while," the older man says. "I had a wonderful time."

"I understand," the younger man says, and he does.

"Thank you, uncle," the younger man says softly.

"Thank *you*," the older man says.

Then the two men get up.

"Don't stay away too long," the older man says, brushing imaginary dirt off his trousers.

The younger man watches his uncle prepare to leave. The older man puts on his jacket, which his nephew knows will be too hot. His nephew notices the old clothes. He notices the five-dollar rubber Casio watch that his uncle takes out of his pocket to consult, since a watch can be too easily damaged on the end of a hand. He smells the aftershave that he knows his uncle purchases at Makola market, and that he has not smelled in a long time.

The older man picks up the plastic bag in which he has been carrying his wallet, diary, passport, baggage tag, ticket.

"Goodbye, Kwasi," he says.

The older man embraces the younger man. For a long time they stand like this in the middle of the empty square.

Then the older man lets the younger man go, and without looking back walks out of the square, catching sight as he does of the woman on the other side of the road, who he is sure will recognize him from the Hotel Anton, and to whom he nods and smiles thinly and who nods and smiles thinly back.